Just a C.... .....y

"I love my cowboys and there are none better than Carolyn Brown's."

—*Fresh Fiction*

"Brown provides an up close and personal look at the rodeo arena, with exciting action scenes written in her vivid, you-feel-like-you're-right-there style."

—*USA Today Happy Ever After*

"Another great read by Carolyn Brown… these two are steaming hot whether they are fighting or giving in."

—*Night Owl Reviews* Reviewer Top Pick, 4.5 Stars

"Brown's writing holds you spellbound as you slip into the world of tantalizing cowboys and love of family, with a lot of fun added in for good measure."

—*Thoughts in Progress*

"I know when I read a book by Carolyn Brown, I'm in for a treat."

—*Long and Short Reviews*

"I can't turn down Carolyn Brown's cowboys. They're as addictive as Janet Evanovich's Ranger."

—*Drey's Library*

"A witty, adrenaline-packed contemporary romance that I read in one sitting, unable to put it down."

—*Romance Junkies*

Also by Carolyn Brown

Women's Fiction

How to Marry a Cowboy

Carolyn Brown

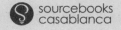

sourcebooks
casablanca

Published by Sourcebooks Casablanca, an imprint of Sourcebooks, Inc.
P.O. Box 4410, Naperville, Illinois 60567-4410
(630) 961-3900
Fax: (630) 961-2168
www.sourcebooks.com

Printed and bound in Canada
MBP 10 9 8 7 6 5 4 3 2 1

This book is dedicated to all of my granddaughters.

With special thanks to Lilybet, the one who is about the same age as Lily and Gabby Harper, and who loves country music as much as they do!

Chapter 1

"GABBY, COME QUICK! HOT DAMN, DADDY DONE GOT us a new mama!"

The sound of a little girl's running feet pounded through her head like a longhorn cattle stampede, and her eyes snapped open to see two little blond girls with tangled hair flying out to the sides of their heads as they jumped up and down on the wooden porch, giving Annie Rose the mother of all headaches. The bright morning sun rising above the trees out there on the horizon stung so bad that she frowned and quickly shut them, hoping it was all a bizarre nightmare.

The faint smell of a ranch that wafted to her nose on the morning breeze was one of her favorite scents in the world, but even that wasn't comforting under the circumstances. She felt the rumbling purr of a big yellow cat who had apparently curled up in the curve of her body sometime during the night. Sudden fear, not of the cat, but because she'd slept past daylight, put her into flight mode, and she pushed the cat to the side and sat up.

The porch posts tilted off to the left, and the little girls went fuzzy. She shut her eyes again and muttered to herself, "Where am I? I've got to find an airport or a bus station."

"More important, who are you?" a deep man's voice asked, half-gentle, half-suspicious, and Annie Rose opened her eyes again to look into the concerned green eyes of the handsomest man she'd ever seen in her waking moments.

She glanced down at the torn and dirty bridal gown and the suitcase sitting off to one side of the swing, and it all flashed through her mind like a dying woman's last visions—the terror that gripped her so hard that it nauseated her, the drive across the northern part of Texas, and the last time she checked her rearview to be sure she wasn't being followed. Looking up to see the tree coming right at her, the impact when her left front bumper hit and bark flew, then the long, greasy slide into the muddy water. It was all there in vivid color, right along with Nicky standing across the room from her with a telephone to his ear.

Maybe if she faked amnesia it would buy her a couple of hours. That's all she needed to get cleaned up and get out of here. People did get amnesia. She'd seen it a few times when she was working as a nurse. What she'd dealt with lasted only a day or two, but she'd read case files where it had gone on for much longer. If she could buy herself time to change and catch a ride, that would work out perfectly.

"I'm not sure about anything." She raised her head to look at him and blinked against the light-headedness.

One of the girls sat down beside her on the swing. "It's okay. We'll take care of you. I am Gabby, and this is Lily, and you are our new mama. Daddy married you last night."

"I don't think I married your daddy, honey," she said.

Lily locked her arms around her daddy's waist. "Tell her, Daddy. Tell her that you had a wedding. You must have, Daddy, she's wearing the prettiest wedding dress ever, but Daddy, she sure did get it messed up. That's the big problem with dresses, you know, we keep telling you all the time, Daddy. They ain't jeans, and they don't stay clean. Come on, Daddy, help her remember. Where did you find her anyway? Why did you leave her on the porch and not bring her in the house?"

"Could you tell me where I am?" she asked, looking at the gorgeous man and wishing she could have met him in some other place, at some other time. He looked like he wasn't sure whether to put his little girls behind his back and send her packing, or wrap her up in his arms and rock her to sleep as if she was one of his darlings, or a little lost puppy. For a split second she wished she could have some of that strong male comfort, but she shook that thought away, bringing on a stabbing pain at the bridge of her nose. A concussion, along with hunger and tension, could slow her down, but it wouldn't stop her. It wasn't a very good moment to develop a crush on a handsome rancher who probably already thought she was insane.

"I'm Mason Harper, and you are on my ranch. We need to figure out how you got here, what happened to you, and who you are," the cowboy said with a deep Texas drawl, still looking at her intently.

His hair was dark brown and still had water droplets hanging from it, so he must have just taken a shower. A snowy white tank top stretched over a ripped abdomen and broad chest, and faded jeans hugged his thighs and butt. Annie Rose judged a person by their eyes when she first met them. Looks were deceiving. Words couldn't be trusted. Body language could lie. But the eyes told the truth. She'd learned that the hard way.

His eyes were mesmerizing—mossy green, kind, worried, ready to shift into hardness if he had to protect those two precious little girls. His face had that deep tan of a man who spent most of his time outside, with those crow's-feet at the sides of his eyes that told her he had a sense of humor. The crease between his eyebrows told her he had plenty of worries, and she had the strangest urge to reach up and smooth out that crease and tell him she would be glad to help him carry his burdens. Where the hell did that thought come from? Maybe she really was going insane. A strong chin and positively the most gorgeous mouth Annie Rose had seen outside of a magazine ad finished off the picture, and Annie Rose brought a hand up to her forehead. She really needed to get a grip. This was far more than a concussion; it was dangerous for her to even let such thoughts enter her mind after what she'd already lived through.

Trying to fix everything and everyone was her number one failing and was what put her into nursing a lifetime ago. If there was ever a man who needed fixing, he was standing in front of her, but Annie Rose did not have time to stick around and take care of his problems, no matter how hard her heartstrings tugged. She was on the run for the second time in her life, and she wasn't dragging anyone into her problems.

Lily left her father's side and snuggled up against Annie Rose. "You are our new mama. Daddy got you for us for our birthday that is today. And we're having a party this afternoon, and is that your suitcase? Can I look in it? Maybe we can find you something else to wear. That wedding gown sure is pretty, but it's kind of messed up."

Mason propped a hip on the porch railing and crossed his arms over his chest, making those amazing biceps flex and Annie's mouth go dry. "Phone? ID? Anything?"

Gabby crossed her arms over her chest and stuck out her lower lip. "Daddy, this is not funny, so stop teasing us."

Lily held up both palms. "Joke is over right now. We want a mama like the other kids have. We're not taking to no nannies anymore. Why did you get her for us if you aren't going to let us keep her? That's not nice, Daddy."

Mason pointed at Lily. "Don't you threaten me, young lady, or there won't be any party or presents this afternoon." He turned toward Annie Rose. "Before we can help you, we need to know your name."

"Just tell me where I am, and I'll figure a way out of here."

"We live between Whitewright and Savoy, and we go to school in Whitewright. You are in Texas on the Bois D'Arc Bend Ranch," Gabby answered.

Mason combed his dark hair back with his fingertips. She'd seen Nicky do that when he was really angry, just before he doubled up his fists.

"If you could call a taxi, I'll go to the nearest hotel. I'm very sorry for all this trouble and that I trespassed onto your property," she said.

Lily giggled. "You mean a taxi like on the television in the big places like New York City? And hotels like that, too?"

Annie Rose nodded and kept a close watch on Mason's hands. They were strong and beautiful in that way that a man's work-roughened, muscular hands can give a girl shivers all the way down to her toes. So far he hadn't doubled them up into fists, and his daughters argued with him like they weren't afraid. Annie wasn't feeling any fear either, but even that was ridiculous for a woman in her position. She almost wished she had real amnesia, so she could lie down, close her eyes, and stay here forever.

Gabby patted her on the arm. "Whitewright ain't got that kind of thing. Have you lived somewhere that did? Will you tell me and Lily all about it?"

What in the hell did they mean, no taxis or hotels? Just how far back in the sticks had she driven before the accident happened? She had to get back on the road to Texarkana, where she had another car waiting. She started to stand up, and everything whipped around so fast that she sat back down with a thud that put the yellow cat on the run.

"Did your car break down on the side of the road? Think hard, what can you remember?" Mason urged her. At least she could give him her name, she thought. She'd been Annie the first twenty-six years of her life in Thicket, a little bitty community near Beaumont, Texas. She'd used her middle name, Rose, when she'd started all over in a city of more than a hundred thousand people in Odessa, Texas, two years ago. Now she was in God only knew where in the backwoods of North Texas, and she would be Annie Rose.

"Annie Rose. I remember, my name is Annie Rose," she whispered.

"Well, that's a start. Do you have any idea where you came from? And is Rose your last name or middle name?" Mason asked.

"Annie Rose Boudreau." She touched her aching head. "Ouch! It was nighttime, and I was tired. I broke the heels off my shoes, so I kicked them off, and my feet hurt. I remember the stars and the moon, so it had to be late night. And then I saw your house and the swing. I only meant to rest for a few minutes."

Mason pulled his phone from his hip pocket. "I'm calling Doc Emerson."

Lily and Gabby threw their hands over their cheeks, fell back on the swing, and said in unison, "Oh, no!"

Annie Rose felt a new rush of pure fear. "Listen, I don't need a doctor. I promise I'll be fine as soon as I clean up and find a café or even a convenience store to buy some food."

"He smells awful and he gives shots and he's our doctor and me and Gabby like him in church, but we don't like him to give us shots and make us open our mouths and say, 'ahhh.' His breath stinks," Lily whispered.

"Our new mama is not getting a shot today," Gabby declared.

"Girls, he's going to check her out. It looks like she's been in an accident, and she can hardly stand up, she's so dizzy. We need to make sure she is all right, and figure out where she came from, so we know where to send her. Someone is probably looking for her," Mason explained.

"I'm sorry about all this. If you'll let me use your bathroom, I'll change out of this and be on my way. I've got clothes in the suitcase, and honestly, girls, I really did not marry your daddy last night."

Mason pushed a single button on the phone and said, "Girls, take Annie Rose to the bathroom. The one downstairs—not upstairs. I'll bring her suitcase, Lily, so let go of the handle…oh, hello, Doc. We've got a problem out here at the ranch. No, not one of the girls. A lady with amnesia has shown up on my porch. I know, but could you please come out and check it."

A pause and then he chuckled. "Could be, but you'll know for sure."

"Is he coming?" Gabby asked.

"Yes, he is, and while we are waiting, we're going to let Miz Boudreau clean up," he said.

"Thank you, Mr. Harper. I won't be but a few minutes." Annie Rose managed to keep her legs under her that time, but she didn't rush across the porch.

"I'll take that suitcase inside. You girls go on to the kitchen and fix yourselves some toast or cereal for breakfast."

"You won't take her away while we're in the kitchen, will you?" Lily asked.

"I give you my word that we won't do a thing until Doc gets here," he answered.

The girls skipped off into the house, and he whispered for her ears only, "Lady, if you have a bomb in this heavy suitcase or in your purse, or if you are pulling some kind of scam to get my attention, believe me, you will regret it." His voice so close to her ear would have had her swooning if it wasn't for the threat in his words, but she couldn't blame him at all for protecting his daughters.

She picked up her purse and slung it over her shoulder. Even that motion made her wince, but she'd learned long ago not to whine. "No bomb and no scam. I'll catch a ride with the doctor and be off your property in an hour, I promise. If I could have a glass of juice or some milk, it would help tremendously. I think the major part of my problem is hunger."

Mason followed her and the girls into the house, holding the door open for her and guiding her inside with a firm hand on her lower back. "Not until the doc checks you out, then you can have whatever you want," he said in that deep drawl.

If she fainted at that moment, she would fall right back into his arms. It was tempting as hell but crazier than any thought that had ever gone through her mind. She would have shook her head if she wasn't afraid it really would make her faint—her thoughts about this man would have shocked the little spiky horns right off of Lucifer.

When she reached the door, Lily pointed her to the bathroom midway on the right, down a wide foyer with a semirounded staircase on either side wrapping up to a landing. Several doors were visible at the top. An enormous living room with a rock fireplace on the far wall showed through a wide arch at the end of the foyer.

Mason set the suitcase inside the small bathroom. "Feel free to take a shower, but don't take too long. Doc should be here in fifteen minutes. He lives on the other side of Whitewright, and it's not far."

"Thank you." Annie Rose set her black leather purse on top of the suitcase.

The sooner she got away from there, the better for everyone. She swept the rumpled, stained train of her dress into the tiny restroom and shut the door. The gown puddled around her feet when she pulled down the side zipper, and she held onto the wall as she kicked it out of the way. A full-length mirror revealed a multitude of bruises on her arms, a bump on her forehead that was most likely a minor concussion, and a nice big purple bruise starting to color up where the seat belt had held her tightly as the car hit that big-ass tree. She'd had worse bruises before, and it wasn't her first concussion, either.

She turned the water on in the shower, adjusted the temperature, and pulled off her underpants. The corner rack held shampoo, conditioner, and soap, and she used all three as she made plans. Wyoming sounded nice, and she wouldn't work in a public place ever again. She'd buy some acreage in a place so remote that she went into town only once or twice a year. She'd get back into ranching and run a few cattle. If only she'd had the good sense to keep her ranch, she wouldn't be on the run today.

She put her hands on the shower wall and let the hot water pound against her back as she carefully checked her body for more than bruises. Other than the sore spot on her forehead, she couldn't find a broken or cracked bone or anything that was bleeding. When she'd spent all the time she felt like she dared, she stepped out and wrapped a towel around her head and one around her body, and squatted to open her suitcase. It was her emergency bag and held two pair of jeans, a couple of shirts, socks, underpants, two bras, a small cosmetics kit, a pair of sandals, and a pair of boots, all arranged neatly inside. The weight came from the secret compartments in the top and bottom where she stored fake IDs, stacks of cash, two passports with different names, in case things got so tough she had to leave the country, and three disposable cell phones.

A soft rap on the door was followed by Lily's voice. "The doctor is here and he promised he won't give you a shot, so you can come out, but hold your breath. Daddy said next time I cussed I couldn't swim for a week, but you can guess what he smells like."

Annie Rose answered, "Give me five minutes to get dressed and I'll be out, Lily."

"How'd you know it was me and not Gabby?"

"I just know," Annie Rose said.

She'd learned, like most people who lived in an abusive situation, to pay attention to detail. The slightest nuance could make the difference between a pleasant evening or a beating.

Lily's voice was softer. Gabby's eyes were a little bit rounder and bigger. Lily's hair was finer and Gabby's was a little bit longer. Gabby was an inch taller and five pounds heavier. Lily's hands were smaller and she had fewer freckles across her nose. And apparently, Lily had a potty mouth. Did Gabby have one too?

She dressed in a hurry, towel-dried her hair, and ran a quick brush through it. She hung the wedding dress on the hook on the back of the door and left her suitcase shut and locked, ready to pick up and take with her as soon as the doctor cleared her for travel.

"Did the shower make you remember the wedding? I'm so mad at Daddy for not taking us to the wedding. We would have been good," Gabby pouted and grabbed her hand. "You are pretty even without the dress. I like you even better in jeans and a shirt. I bet Daddy does too, but he should have brought you to meet us before he married you. Folks say that we aren't good girls, but we can be if we want to be. We don't like nannies, so

Daddy has to keep hiring them. We told him if he'd get us a mama we'd be good, but boys don't listen too good, do they?"

"Sometimes boys don't pay attention if they don't like what you are saying," Annie Rose whispered. "Can you girls show me where to go now?"

Their hands felt very small, very soft, and very trusting in hers, and a pang of guilt shot through her like a bolt of lightning. They wanted a mama, but she wasn't mama material.

Mason met them at the door into what had to be his study. A massive desk sat at an angle to a wall of windows facing a play area with swings and a jungle gym and a lovely swimming pool shimmering in the early morning sun rays. A six-foot wooden privacy fence circled the whole area.

Mason made introductions. "Doc Emerson, this is Annie Rose Boudreau, and, Annie Rose, this is our family doctor."

The doctor moved closer and ran his hand over the small knot on her forehead.

Lily was right.

The doctor did smell like shit. Evidently, he didn't take that warning about tobacco seriously, because he smelled like a mixture of cigar smoke and Old Spice aftershave. He had a mop of unruly white hair and deep-set brown eyes that looked kind, and his smile put her at ease.

He pulled out a penlight and checked her eyes. "Don't care much for cigars, do you?"

She shook her head. "How did you know?"

"You were holding your breath," he said. "Feelin' a little dizzy?"

"Yes, sir, but I'm really hungry. I haven't eaten in a long time, and it doesn't have anything to do with your cigar smoke."

"Brides usually get the jitters, and if you had a party the night before, it could be the alcohol wearing off," the doctor said.

"I don't like liquor," she said.

"Little bit of memory there?"

"Yes, sir. I don't like liquor or cigarette smoke, and I'm a nurse, or at least I was at some time in the past. I checked for injuries, and other than dizziness and hunger, I think the concussion is all I have," she said.

Doc nodded in agreement. "It's short-term, Mason. She'll be fine in a day or two. We could take her up to the hospital in Sherman and get an MRI done, but I've seen a good bit of this, especially in rodeo cowboys. I'm pretty sure she hit her head in that car wreck, probably on the dash before the air bags opened or else she was driving an older model car that didn't have air bags," Doc said. "Other than that and a few bruises where the seat belt held her too tight, I can't find a thing wrong with Miz Annie Rose. Bruises kind of goes along with having a wreck and then walking from there to here. Could have been anywhere up the road or down the road, since she don't know which way she was going, but it'll all come back to her."

He put the small penlight into his kit. "This will all be cleared up by dinnertime. Her groom will come along and lay claim to her or her family will put out a missing persons report and we'll know who she is. Or better yet, when she gets something to eat, her memory will return."

Lily popped her hands on her hips and glared at the doctor. "She's ours and we're goin' to keep her."

Doc Emerson nodded seriously. "Okay, girls, she's all yours unless an owner comes along. She might have little girls of her own, and you wouldn't want to keep her from them if she has some, would you?"

———∞———

Reasoning did not work with the twins. It hadn't worked with their mother, and even though they didn't look like her, they'd damn sure inherited her temper and determination.

Gabby took up the fight. "If she already had little girls she wouldn't be marryin' our Daddy, so she is ours and we aren't givin' her back."

Doc winked at Mason. "If you want to fight with your girls, I can take her down to the sheriff's station and one of the deputies can give her a ride up to the bus station in Sherman."

Tears flowed down their cheeks and their chins quivered. Mason hated it when they argued with him, but when they cried, he melted. "Girls, she can stay the rest of today. She can even go to your party if she feels like it after we get her some breakfast."

"Thank you, Daddy," Lily said.

Gabby wiped away the tears with the back of her hand. "Can we please keep her until Tuesday when the new nanny comes? We promise to be good, and we won't even try to drown Damian this year."

"Okay, but only if she's willing to stay." Mason gave Annie Rose a long look. His girls were enthralled with the woman, and if he didn't want a war on his hands, the best thing he could do for all concerned was to buy a little time. As bad as he hated to admit it, she intrigued him too. She seemed lost and brave all rolled into one—he wanted to help her, and he wanted to lean on her both, and if he'd let himself feel it, there was hot chemistry there too. It was downright outrageous for him to feel anything other than doubt, so he damn sure wasn't going there right now.

He looked back at the doctor. "Is she well enough to watch the girls for two days?"

Annie Rose clasped her hands in her lap and prayed silently, *Lord, I promise I'll be honest with him before the day is out. I only need a little while to get myself together. Two days is plenty for me to get a new plan in action.*

The doctor snapped his little black bag shut. "I don't see why not. She seems physically fine other than the bruises, and they'll heal up. It's that concussion that's got her memories scrambled."

Gabby sighed and hugged the doctor. "Thank you, Doc."

"A hug must mean you really want this woman to stay." He chuckled.

"If we can't have a mama forever, then at least we can have one for two days," Lily said. "Now, let's go make breakfast. Do you like toast? You said you were hungry."

"Yes, ma'am, I do," Annie Rose said.

"I'll see y'all at the party this afternoon. Kenna is spending a couple of weeks with us and she can't wait to get here." Doctor Emerson made a hasty retreat toward the door.

Mason took a deep breath and said, "Well, Miz

Boudreau, the doc says it's OK, so we'd be obliged if you would consider staying for a couple of days. Our last nanny left yesterday after I wrote her paycheck. It was too late to call the agency to get one lined up by tomorrow morning, but I can get one here by Tuesday morning." Mason hoped he was telling the truth and that the nanny service had one willing to take a job watching the Harper twins. He looked at a spot right in the middle of Annie Rose's forehead to keep from sinking into her blue eyes.

He cleared his throat and let his eyes shift to her right ear before he went on, "I'm going to warn you that they are not the best-behaved twins, so you might want me to call the sheriff's office and get you a ride into town after all. You are in need of a place to stay until your memory comes back. I don't know you, but I'm a pretty good judge of character and I sincerely hope I'm not making a mistake. If you'd be willing to keep these girls for two days until the service I use in Dallas can get another woman up here, I'd be obliged."

She looked up at him with eyes the same shade as Gabby's and Lily's. "Yes. I'd be glad to work for you today and tomorrow."

"Yes!" Gabby pumped her fist.

"We got a new mama," Lily singsonged.

"What you've got is a new nanny," Mason said.

Lily gave him a cold stare. "She's our mama even if it's only for two days. If you didn't marry her, then God put her on our porch because we've been praying for a mama for a long time. Every Sunday in church we pray for one and God finally heard us."

"I did not marry her," Mason said.

Gabby sighed. "She was wearing a wedding dress. She was on our porch. She's our new mama. Now let's go make pancakes for breakfast, Daddy. No church today, right?"

Mason put a hand on each of his daughters' heads. "No church today, but only because Annie Rose should rest after breakfast and we need to be here with her in case she remembers and then we can take her home."

"I hope she don't never remember," Lily said.

"Coffee?" Mason ignored her comment, turning to Annie Rose and leading the way with his hand on her lower back again. It was to keep her steady, he told himself as they went through the formal dining room and into a cozy kitchen.

A small table for four was situated under a window overlooking a well-kept yard alive with bright red roses surrounded by splashes of purple irises, yellow marigolds, and gorgeous multicolored lilies. A white picket fence separated it from the pasture full of Black Angus cattle.

"I'm still jittery, so I'll pass on the coffee," she said.

He liked a woman who had a bit of common sense. His deceased wife, Holly, lacked in that area, but they'd been happy, and she had taken a piece of his heart with her when she passed. A piece, nothing; she'd taken his whole heart, leaving him empty.

He put thoughts of Holly out of his mind and opened the refrigerator.

"Juice?"

"Love some," she said.

He poured a tall glassful and handed it to her. "Sit down at the table with the girls. I'm not much of a cook, but I do make mean pancakes."

Mason didn't think she'd kidnap his girls and haul them off, and she didn't look like a terrorist or a thief. If she did run away with his girls, in less than a day she'd be willing to pay him to take them back. Nannies had come and gone so fast in the eight years since their mother died that the hinges on the front door were damn near worn out. Few lasted a month. Most were gone by the end of the first week. A couple didn't make it to the end of the first day.

Lily and Gabby didn't like any of them, and the summer loomed ahead for three whole months, which could easily wipe out every available nanny in the service he used. Maybe Annie Rose had been dropped on his porch by angels and would stay on for the summer. Miracles did happen every so often, didn't they?

"I like kids. Just so you know," Annie Rose said softly. "I don't have any, but I like them."

"I'm glad." Mason smiled.

"I can't imagine what must be going through your mind. But I promise I'll be a good nanny," she said.

"I know it," Lily declared. "Your eyes are blue like ours, and your hair is the same color as ours. Yes, ma'am, you will make a good mama."

"Nanny," Annie Rose said.

Gabby smiled sweetly. "Do you like syrup or strawberries and whipped cream on your pancakes?"

"A thin layer of peanut butter and syrup," Annie Rose said.

The griddle sizzled when Mason poured hot batter onto it. "You remembered something else. That's good. Maybe the fog will lift by Tuesday."

"Let's hope so," she said.

Gabby patted Annie Rose's hand. "It's all right, Mama-Nanny. It will all come back, and then you'll tell us how you married Daddy and why your pretty dress got so much dirt on it."

Chapter 2

THE SUITCASE WAS HEAVY BUT NOT NEARLY AS MUCH as the guilt trip eating holes in Annie Rose's soul when she set it down inside a small room on the left side of the landing. She'd lied to Mason and the girls, and they did not deserve that kind of treatment. This was all her trouble, not theirs. They trusted her enough to take her in, feed her, give her a place to rest and even a job for two days, and she'd lied to protect her own skin. It wasn't right, and she wouldn't know a minute's peace until she made it right.

Gabby tugged on her hand. "It was our room when we were babies."

"Then we grew up and got our own rooms. Don't be afraid. We're right across the hall and we'll hear you if you cry at night," Lily said seriously.

"Thank you, girls," she said.

Gabby let go of her hand and said, "Daddy is ordering pizza after awhile because it's our birthday. We'll call you when it gets here, but you sleep until then."

"And we'll show you the way back to the kitchen, so don't worry if you can't remember how to get there. We'll be right here."

They left her alone in a small room with posters of Disney princesses on pale pink walls. A futon with a hot-pink covered mattress was shoved against the far wall. A small white nightstand sat under a window that overlooked the pool area. A matching white chest of drawers held half a dozen pictures of the girls when they were babies, no more than a year old. An overstuffed hot-pink rocking chair that had seen lots of wear was positioned so that the morning sun hit it. Two doors were on the opposite side of the bed. She opened one to find a closet with a few empty hangers on the rack and a white toy box overflowing with baby toys shoved into the left corner.

Expecting the other door to be the second twin's closet, she slung it open and came face-to-face with Mason Harper. Time stood still and her heart thumped in her chest as she waited for his soft green eyes to go rock hard, for him to scream at her to get out of his bathroom, or even for him to raise a hand toward her.

His little crow's-feet around his eyes didn't deepen in a frown but in humor, and her heart went out to him again. "I'm so sorry. I was checking to see if this was another closet and I should've knocked and…" She stopped when he shook his head slowly.

"It's okay. From now on knock, and I'll do the same." He reached for a towel to dry his hands. "I guess you figured out that the room they wanted you to have is their old nursery?"

"Yes, I did, and again, I'm sorry." She hurriedly shut the door and slumped down in the rocking chair, pulled back the sheer lacy curtains, and let the sun pour in on her face. Had it really been only twenty-four hours since she peeked out of the curtains at the runway, getting ready to model a wedding dress?

She was lucky to be alive; lucky to have gotten away from Nicky; lucky that it hadn't been him tailing her when she pulled off Highway 82 and drove south through Savoy. But how long would her luck last?

She finally pulled the suitcase over in front of her with shaking hands. Lord love a duck, as her mother used to say when she was nervous or upset. It had to be the concussion bringing out all the hormones. She'd been so careful to bury any kind of attraction when she ran away and now a tall, sexy cowboy with green eyes had brought them all to the surface. She blinked several times to erase the picture of him standing there before the mirror, giving her a double shot of tall, dark, and very handsome, and then she unzipped the suitcase, hung the clothing in the closet, and put her lingerie and nightshirt in the top drawer of the chest. Then she carefully removed the false bottom and patted the bills. That was security and it had nothing to do with luck.

She made sure the suitcase was put in order, zipped it up, and slid it into the closet beside the toy box. She stretched out on the futon and pulled the soft throw from the back down over her body, but she was too wound up to sleep. Finally she sat up and moved back to the rocking chair.

The adrenaline would take a while to settle, and until then, there would be no sleep and very little rest. What if Mason had been in the shower, or worse yet, standing there naked when she swung that door open? Would he have been so kind then, or would his true colors have come out? And where was the girls' mother anyway? Had she disappeared the way Annie Rose had? Could she be jumping from frying pan into fire? One thing for sure, she'd only agreed to two days. After that, this place would only be a memory for cold evenings in Wyoming.

—•••—

Gabby tapped Lily on the head with the comb. "Be still. I can't get your hair bow in with you wigglin' around like a worm in hot ashes."

Lily grabbed the comb and threw it across the room. "Shit! That hurt and I'm not a worm in hot ashes and you got that from the last nanny and I didn't like her, so don't talk like her."

Gabby crossed the room and picked up the comb. "You'll get in big trouble for saying bad words. Daddy said you done had all the chances he's givin' you. We got to be good today so Annie Rose will stay more than two days. I like her, Lily. She looks like she could be our mama and she's sweet. Damian is wrong. Mamas aren't worse than nannies."

Lily smiled. "Maybe if we help her, then she'll remember that she did marry our daddy. And that Damian is a jackass who don't know shit from mud, Gabby. Don't you dare tell on me for cussin' either, because you would have said it if you'd thought of it."

Gabby nodded seriously. "Yes, I would have. He is that mean, but how are we going to help her remember?"

Lily shut her eyes tightly. After a few seconds, an angelic smile appeared and her eyelids slid open. "We'll make her a how-to book. You know, like that one that Kenna has got that teaches how to make them pretty hair braids. Only we'll make her a *How to Remember* book. Get out the paper and stickers. If she does what it says for her to do, then she might even remember by party time and Daddy will let her stay forever."

———~~~———

Mason leaned back in the recliner and threw his forearm over his eyes. What in the hell had he done? He couldn't hire a nanny for the girls without a background check, especially one who'd just showed up on his porch in a wedding dress and with no memory. Worse yet, one that he could scarcely look in the eye without his heart throwing in an extra flutter or two. Dammit! Life had been going along absolutely fine, even with a set of twins so ornery that the folks at the nanny service shuddered when they saw his phone number. And then in the matter of a few seconds, it had been turned upside down.

He removed his hand and stared at the ceiling as one question after another flooded through his mind. Had she gotten married and then run away from her husband on the way to the honeymoon? Was she one of those runaway brides like in that old movie? Was she trying to find a way onto his ranch to make him the butt of an elaborate scam? Surely to God this wasn't a joke his poker buddies were playing on him, was it?

A nanny had to take the girls to and from story hour, to dental appointments, had to be responsible for them around the pool, and had to be sure that they didn't get into too much trouble during the day when he was running the ranch. Was she trustworthy enough for him to allow her to put his girls in the truck and drive off with them? He couldn't deny Holly anything when she was alive, and he had even less power when it came to telling the twins ' no," so how was he going to dodge this bullet?

Mason's gut said he absolutely could not hire the

woman, but his heart said he couldn't tell her to leave. He'd never seen his girls take to anyone like they did her. Maybe it was the wedding dress or the fact that they really did want a mother more than anything in the world.

The distance from his bedroom, through the bathroom, and to the old nursery door was longer than the length of the Sahara Desert. Knocking would have made better sense, but if Gabby and Lily heard it, they'd come out of their room to see what was going on.

He eased it open a crack and without even looking inside, he said softly, "Hello."

"Come in. I want to talk to you, so I'm glad you are here," she said.

She was sitting in the old comfortable rocking chair that had been used so frequently when the girls were babies that it had his body's imprint in the cushions. And there was the big yellow tomcat, O'Malley, right there in her lap, purring away loudly as she stroked his fur.

Folks said that it was impossible to fool kids and dogs. Did it also work with cats and kids? The twins fell in love with her at first glance, and now O'Malley, who hated everyone but the girls, had adopted her.

"I'd like a word without the girls around," he said.

She motioned him inside. "So would I."

The nursery didn't feel right with a strange woman in it, as if he'd wronged Holly somehow. She tucked an errant strand of blond hair behind her ear, and the gesture reminded him of the way Holly used to do the same thing. Then she looked up at him, chin out like Holly did when she was about to tell him something that she really wanted him to hear, even though she hated telling it. Everything was awkward and felt eerie like the sky right before a tornado struck.

"Please sit, and you talk first," she said.

He propped a shoulder against the doorjamb, looking at her with an intensity that made her squirm, and not because she was nervous. "You go first."

"You could sit on the futon or I'll move so you can have the chair," she said.

"I'm fine," he told her. Yes, he certainly was fine. She shook her head—where did that thought come from? She definitely should not be ogling this man when surely all he cared about was whether she could handle his two adorable spitfire girls until he could get a legitimate nanny brought in.

She dropped her chin and focused on the cat. "I'm sorry I lied to you out there on the porch. I do not have amnesia. I was shocked and startled when I awoke on your porch with those little girls bouncing around and squealing. I grasped at the first thing I could think of and pretended I couldn't remember, so I wouldn't have to explain, especially in front of them. They were so excited that I couldn't disappoint them. They must really want a mother, badly, to take one that looked like I did."

He sat down on the futon and crossed one leg over the other, ankle on knee in a masculine gesture that she caught in her peripheral vision.

"Go on," he said in a low Southern drawl.

"I would like to have the nanny job, but you should know the truth before you officially hire me. My name really is Annie Rose Boudreau. I was raised on a ranch near Beaumont, Texas. I had a nursing degree by the time my parents died and left me a small ranch, which I sold."

"And?" he asked softly when she paused. He didn't seem angry, or like he was going to fly off the handle. He was listening, paying attention, and he was refreshingly calm.

"Right after I sold it, a man came into the emergency room after a minor fender bender. He was charming and I was very vulnerable. I fell in love with the wrong man, plain and simple."

"Until last night, and then you ran away from him, right?" Mason said in a tone she couldn't read.

"No, until he turned out to be a control freak who liked to use his fists when he was angry, which was pretty often. I tried to break up with him, but that didn't work. He was a violent man with a wicked temper, and there was no way out of the relationship with him. So I disappeared. It took a while to put everything in place, but when I walked out of his house, it was pretty smooth sailing. I dropped the first name and became Rose Boudreau and moved to West Texas. Got a job in a library in a different town from where I lived. Yesterday we were having a bridal-dress show for a fundraiser at our library, and he showed up." Even in her own ears, Annie Rose's voice sounded hollow, like it was coming out of a long tunnel.

Mason listened, but the story sure sounded farfetched. His heart felt like he could believe her; his head wasn't convinced yet. "And you became a runaway bride?"

She nodded. "I was wearing a bridal gown, but I wasn't a bride. Believe me, I'm not sure I'll ever wear one of those for real. When I disappeared the first time, I planned ahead, so that if I ever had to do it again, it wouldn't be so difficult or scary. I drove straight to my storage unit and picked up my suitcase. When I got to the Sherman exit, I noticed a black SUV and thought it was following me. So I turned off at the next exit, went through a little town called Savoy, and the SUV kept right behind me. Then he turned off into a driveway and a woman ran out the door to greet him and I knew it had been a case of paranoia."

"Where is your car?" Mason asked.

He was still unsure, but her face seemed to open and she was looking right into his eyes as she told her story. She looked sad, too, adrift, and he knew that feeling all too well.

"There's a lot of curves in this part of the state. I didn't make one and had an up-close and personal talk with a big old tree about a quarter of a mile back up the road. The one right close to a nice deep farm pond."

"That's my property." He nodded, still suspending judgment. She could be a fantastic liar or a damn good actor.

"Well, my car is at the bottom of that pond. I hit the tree, veered off to one side, and barely had time to bail out and grab my purse and my suitcase from the backseat before my car went into the water. I only meant to rest a little while on your porch, but your girls found me before I woke up," she said.

"What is his name? The stalker? I have a right to know that if I'm going to hire you," Mason said.

"Nicholas Trahan."

Mason shook his head. "Nicky Trahan is well known

all over Texas and Louisiana. Everyone knows he's got a temper, and his family calls themselves the Cajun mob. How in the hell did you get mixed up with him?"

"Like I said, he was in the hospital where I worked. He's a smooth talker and a hard hitter, and I had no idea who he was or what he was until it was too late. Nobody leaves Nicky and lives to brag about it. So that's my story, and I was thinking maybe Doc could go ahead and give me a ride to the bus station in Sherman when he comes to the party this afternoon. I've been enough bother to you, and I understand if you don't want me to stay, even for two days."

Mason wasn't afraid of Nicky Trahan. Most men who used their fists on women wouldn't think of raising them to a man, but still he had to think about his girls. He didn't have to make a decision right then. He had a couple of days, and he did know a man who was pretty handy at checking things out. He wanted to believe this woman, who was looking down at her hands. He wanted to protect her and take care of her, and he sure as hell hadn't had that feeling about anyone but his girls since Holly died.

When he didn't say anything, Annie Rose went on, "You can check it all out. Annie Boudreau worked as a nurse in Baptist Hospital in Beaumont. Rose worked as a librarian's assistant in Odessa, Texas. Annie Rose, which is what my daddy called me, will be a nanny if you want her to be. But I understand if you want me to leave. I'm not so sure I'd hire me if I was on the other side of this conversation."

"Do you have a driver's license?"

She picked up her purse, pulled out a small wallet,

and handed a valid Texas license to him. "It's really me. Picture, fingerprint, and name. Address is still the one in Beaumont. I started to change my name, but…" She shrugged.

"I will check this out, and you are welcome to stay here until I do. I've never seen my girls take to anyone like they did you. If you're lying to me, I'll take you up to the bus station in Sherman after the party myself. If not, you have a job for a couple of days or until the girls drive you crazy like they've done to all their nannies. If Nicky Trahan shows up here, I expect you to call me immediately. We might not be a big city like Odessa, but by damn, we've got a police force here that can slam him back into a cell so fast that it'll make his head swim."

He wasn't sure where the words came from. They weren't what he expected to come out of his mouth, but he couldn't ruin his girls' birthday. One day wouldn't hurt, and he really did have a contact to check on her story.

"O'Malley likes you." He stood up.

"He's a sweet old tomcat." She smiled. "I like cats, but it's a good thing I didn't let my guard down and get one or else he'd be starving in a pretty bare apartment out in West Texas."

———

She set O'Malley in the chair and stretched out on the futon. Her eyelids felt like they had twenty-pound weights attached to them, but she still couldn't sleep. Everything about the day before kept playing through her mind as if it was on a constantly rewinding reel. Had

Nicky been so busy with his phone call that he hadn't even seen her? That would be asking for a hell of a lot, but an amazing force seemed to be watching out for her, so maybe, just maybe, she'd gotten away without him even realizing she was ever there. O'Malley left the chair and jumped up on the bed, turned around a couple of times, and curled up beside her.

"Mama-Nanny," Lily's whisper filtered through the door. "Are you awake?"

She swung her legs over the side of the bed and opened the door to find the girls with their hair in neat ponytails.

"We want you to have this before you go to sleep. We think it might help you, and we want you to remember getting married to our daddy, even if he didn't let us go to the wedding. Do what it says, okay?" Lily said.

Gabby handed her a homemade booklet like the ones she and her little friends made when they were children.

"Thank you. I promise I'll sit down right now and read every word, and I will do exactly what it says. You'll wake me up when the pizza gets here, right?"

"Yes, we will," Lily said seriously. "And we'll help you remember where things are until the book works."

Then they were both gone.

She sat down in the rocking chair and looked at the booklet. They'd taken a sheet of notebook paper, cut it into four ragged-edged pieces, and stapled them together. The title, *How to Remember*, was written on the outside in bright red marker and had several cat stickers attached to it.

She opened it and read the steps.

Number 1: *Lay down on your bed with your head on the pillow.*
Number 2: *Shut your eyes real, real tight and don't open them.*
Number 3: *Now put your fingers in your ears so you can't hear anything.*
Number 4: *Think real, real hard.*
Number 5: *Lily says that if that don't work, say, "Well, shit!" and to start all over again. It worked when she couldn't remember where she put her favorite bracelet.*

Annie Rose giggled, and it felt so good that it turned into laughter. She held the booklet to her heart for several minutes before she put it in the secret compartment of her suitcase. Someday she wanted a set of little blond-haired girls exactly like those two.

Twenty kids jumped in and out of the pool, traipsing water all over the deck, eating hot dogs by the dozens, and downing enough soda pop to put them on a week-long sugar high. Girls giggled in groups. Boys bowed up to each other like cocky little banty roosters.

Annie Rose sat with her back to the sliding-glass doors into the house and remembered her ninth birthday party. That was the first one Gina Lou came to, and they'd formed a friendship that lasted through school, college, and right up until the day that she ran away from Nicky. She'd missed her friend the past two years, but they both knew that Nicky had the resources to locate her through Gina Lou, so they'd made a clean break.

A tall red-haired woman pulled up a lawn chair close to her and sat down. "So you are the new nanny? Are you nuts or do you have rocks for brains?"

"I hope neither. Do you know something I don't?" Annie Rose asked.

"Honey, those two girls have been nightmare children since they were born. I had them in first grade. Worst year in my teaching experience. I went home every day cussing and swearing that I wouldn't go back the next morning," she said.

"That bad, huh?" Annie Rose asked. No wonder Mason hadn't tossed her out on her ear.

"Those girls would drive a saint to the asylum. I'm Dinah Miller, by the way. I understand your name is Annie Rose?"

Annie Rose nodded. "Pleased to meet you, Dinah. Does one of the children in the pool belong to you?"

"That little red-haired boy in the blue bathing suit. He's got a crush on Doc Emerson's granddaughter, Kenna. I can't get ready for nine-year-old kids to talk about going out with each other. But at least he doesn't like Lily or Gabby. For that I can be thankful," she said.

"I thought they all hated each other, the way the boys are all jumping in and out of the pool and the girls are all grouped up, giggling," Annie Rose said.

"I'm a school teacher, so we see this all the time. The boys are posturing for them, and the girls are giggling because of the boys," Dinah said.

Lily came running up to Annie Rose's side, holding out a hair ribbon. "Mama, Mama, can you put this back? Matty untied it, and it fell out."

"Mama?" Dinah asked.

"Daddy says she's our nanny, but we've decided that she's our new mama. We found her on the porch this morning. She was asleep on the swing like Sleeping Beauty, but she was wearing a wedding dress," Lily said.

Annie Rose tied the ribbon around the ponytail in a perfect bow. "There you go, sweetie. Go have fun. Your daddy says that you are opening gifts inside the gazebo at four, and that's only fifteen minutes from now."

Dinah laughed. "Kids sure have an imagination, don't they? Nannies don't show up in wedding dresses."

Mason pulled up a chair and sat down beside Annie Rose, giving her a quick wink that kicked up her pulse a notch. Hopefully, Mason and Dinah would think her red-hot cheeks were the result of the hot summer sun, but she knew better.

He chuckled and said, "Oh, yeah, they do. On this ranch, all nannies have to wear costumes. In case you didn't know, Annie Rose wears a ball gown to do housework and a bikini to cook supper and the paparazzi goes crazy when I attend the Oscars."

Dinah nodded toward him. "Hello, Mason. Nice party. The kids always love a pool party. Did you know that Doc bought them real goats for their birthday? And I'll be willing to bet dollars to doughnuts that those two insist on taking them in the house like pets instead of barn animals. Oh, I must go talk to Mrs. Emerson about Kenna. See y'all later." She was up in a flash and making her way across the patio before Annie Rose found her voice.

"Goats?" Annie Rose asked.

"I'll get even with him, damn his old black soul. Just wait until his granddaughter has a birthday," Mason groaned. "Dinah is right. They'll want to make house pets out of them."

Annie Rose patted Mason on the arm. "I've got the cure for that problem."

"Believe me, you'll be worth every dime I'm paying you if you can tell them no."

"I don't intend to tell them no. They can bring the goats in the house if they want to, but that's only if they really get them. Dinah could be saying that to get a rise out of you. But if it's the truth, I'll tell the girls the rules, and they can decide what they want to do. Sometimes it's best to let them decide rather than fighting with them."

"Mama-Nanny," Gabby sang out across the patio. "I wanted some punch, and it's all gone. Is there any in the house?"

"I'll check," Annie Rose said, putting her hand on Mason's arm as if they'd known each other for a decade instead of a day, and then wishing that she hadn't been so impulsive when her fingers tingled. "Trust me, Mason. I did see extra punch in the refrigerator, didn't I?"

"There's at least two more gallons. I don't know how they drink that watered-down stuff," he said.

"They are kids." She smiled.

~~~

"Good-lookin' nanny you got." Frank Miller sat down in the chair Annie Rose vacated. "You sure a young one is the right way to go? We seem to do better with one who's at least fifty and pretty firm with Damian. The younger ones let them get away with too much."

Frank was one of those mousy guys who walked in his wife's shadow, spoke when she allowed it or when he could get away from her, and had a perpetual frown. But then if Mason had to live with Dinah, he wouldn't be grinning about much either.

"The girls like her," Mason said, his heart warming a little about how he liked her too.

"Damian told me that they found her on the porch in a wedding dress this morning." Frank shoved his empty beer can into the trash can and reached for another. "I told him that Lily was pulling his leg, so there could be a fight. Thought I'd give you a heads-up not to get too comfortable about this party. It could turn in a second if your girls get angry at my son."

Mason scanned the area, located Gabby in her purple bathing suit on the diving board, and Lily, in her hot-pink suit, whispering to Kenna. It had been going so well, and he'd hoped that there wouldn't be any more drama of any kind that day. But the girls didn't like Damian, and if he said something hateful, the fight would be on.

"Excuse me. I want to see Gabby do this dive," Mason said.

Gabby did a cannonball into the water and Damian came up from the bottom, sputtering. "You did that on purpose. You almost drowned me when you jumped right on top of me. You are as mean as your lying sister. She said that woman over there came here in a wedding dress, and my daddy said she was pulling my leg."

Gabby drew back her fist, and the noise stopped. Everything was eerily quiet as the people waited for her to black his eye or worse. Mason took another step toward the pool and noticed that Lily was shaking her head furiously at Gabby, who glared back at her with the meanest look he'd seen between them in years.

Finally she dropped her fist and swam to the shallow end of the pool. "Hey, Daddy, can we open presents now?"

Mason breathed a sigh of relief and said, "It's your party. If you are ready to open presents and then blow out your candles, you sure can."

Now he'd have to watch them extra special at church, at the library, or anywhere Damian might be. Calling Lily a liar was purely fighting words. The boy didn't have any idea how much trouble he'd gotten himself into. Mason hoped Annie Rose had told him the truth and would be willing to stay longer than two days. He'd wipe up the whole state of Texas with Nicky Trahan's sorry ass if he showed up on the Bois D'Arc Bend Ranch, just to have a nanny that the girls liked enough to be good—even for one day.

Frank was at his elbow again. "How did you find her?"

"I've got a service out of Dallas," Mason said honestly.

"Care to share? Damian needs a part-time nanny for the summer, and Lily told Kenna that they were being good for the new mama-nanny. I could use a woman like her."

Mason raised an eyebrow. "But Dinah is home in the summer."

Frank nodded. "But she'll be crazy if she has to deal with Damian every day. He whines if he's bored, and Dinah needs time for herself after teaching all year. We could make do with three days a week with light cleaning tossed in. And I'd pay extra if she could do some cooking."

Mason pulled a pen from his shirt pocket and wrote the name of his nanny service on a napkin, folded it, and tucked it into Frank's pocket. "They're not cheap, believe me."

Frank flashed one of his rare smiles. "Money isn't an issue. My sanity is."

Doctor Emerson yelled over the noise of the children gathering up around the present table to watch the girls unwrap their gifts. "We would like to be first in line to give them our present."

He swung open the gate, and Kenna led two half-grown Toggenburg goats by wide pink satin ribbons into the pool area.

"Happy birthday to Gabby and Lily," she singsonged.

Gabby squealed. "Look, Mama-Nanny, this is the best birthday ever. We got you, and now we got goats. Look, he's already growing a beard! And I'm naming him Djali."

"Jeb!" Lily screeched right behind her. "I love him, Kenna. You have to come over and play with us and the new goats sometime."

"Don't worry, Mason," Doc Emerson called out. "They'll eat anything that they can get in their mouth, but they don't use a litter pan, so you might want to build them a pen rather than letting them stay in the girls' bedrooms."

The whole birthday crowd laughed. Mason grinned and said, "Thank you so much, Doc, but remember, paybacks are hell!"

"They really did get live goats." Annie Rose poured another gallon of punch into the empty bowl and stuck nine candles on each end of the rectangular cake. "I thought maybe your friend was pulling your leg."

"No, ma'am," Mason said with a sigh. "I hope you can fix it as well as you think you can." He'd known the woman only a few hours, but when she looked up at him with that smile, it seemed as if they'd grown up together right there in Whitewright, Texas.

She handed him a long candle lighter she'd found in a kitchen drawer. "I guarantee my medicine works, so don't you worry. If it doesn't, you don't have to pay me a dime for my services for the next two days."

"You are pretty sure of yourself," Mason said.

Annie Rose didn't look a thing like Holly, but the way they were working together and the warm feelings he was developing towards her reminded him of his late wife, and he felt as if maybe he was cheating on Holly's memory, even though he was talking to Annie Rose about goats. He backed up a step and took a deep breath. He'd dated. He'd slept with a few women. But he never cheated on his wife's memory and he wasn't about to start now.

Doc guffawed and pointed his finger like a gun. "Remember this the next time you clean me out on poker night."

"Come on, Djali, I'll open presents and you can eat the paper," Gabby said.

Mason picked up the camera to take pictures of the girls opening the rest of their gifts. He let the pictures of the women he'd dated the past seven years filter through his mind in a flash. He'd kissed them and even bedded them, but none of them put him on a spin cycle of heat and guilt the way Annie Rose had done since the girls found her on the porch.

Annie Rose sat down beside him. "It'll be a tough

night if they really want to take them in the house, but it will only be for one night, and it will be their decision not to ever bring them inside again."

"How tough are we talking about? What's involved?" he asked, breathing in her scent. Holly had a liked a floral perfume that he'd bought for her on their first anniversary, while Annie Rose smelled fresh and crisp, like apples and cucumbers and fresh air all blended together.

"You got an old playpen in the attic? Maybe one the girls used when they were babies?"

"There's probably more than one up there."

"That's even better. If they put up a fuss to keep them in the house, then bring two down, and we'll make a makeshift cover for them, so the goats can't get out. Then they have to put it beside their bed with the rule that they will take care of the goats all night and clean up whatever mess is in the playpen before breakfast tomorrow morning." She smirked at him, and Mason couldn't help but crack a smile.

"That sounds like the voice of experience talking," he challenged.

She nodded. "One night with a smelly goat bawling and then cleaning up the playpen the next morning and I was more than ready to take my goat out to the pen with the other goats."

"You are a wise woman, but are you big enough to make them actually clean up those playpens? They are tough and there are two of them."

"Yes, I am. This could be an interesting summer if you still want me after Tuesday."

"You must be pretty sure of those credentials I'm checking out," he said.

"I am. Can you get a real pen built for them first thing tomorrow morning? It should be right outside the yard fence, so the girls can get to them easily and yet I can keep watch from the kitchen window. Make it big enough for two goats and two girls to romp and play in it."

Chapter 3

THE LAST OF THE PARTY CROWD KICKED UP A CLOUD OF dust as Doc Emerson drove away from the ranch. The girls and Mason waved good-bye at the gate, and then Gabby tugged at his arm. "Daddy, we can't leave our goats here, because they'll fall in the swimming pool and drown, and we can't put them in the yard, because they can get out of a rail fence."

"We'll put them in the pasture with the new calves until tomorrow. I'll get Skip to build a pen for them right next to the yard tomorrow morning," he said.

"But, Daddy, they will be scared of those big old cows," Lily fussed.

"What do you want to do, sleep with goats?" Mason asked. "Have you smelled them? And remember, they don't use a litter pan like O'Malley."

"Not in our beds." Lily rolled her eyes.

"We was thinkin' maybe in the bathtub just for tonight," Gabby said.

Annie Rose stopped shoving wrapping paper into an oversized black leaf bag and asked, "What if they accidentally turned on the water and drowned because they couldn't get out of the tub?"

"Well, that ain't going to work, is it?" Lily said quickly.

Mason's phone vibrated in his hip pocket and he quickly removed it, held up a finger to the girls, and walked away from wrapping paper, presents, goats, girls, and Annie Rose.

"Hello, Jeremiah. I wasn't expecting to hear from you until tomorrow," he said.

"It only took a couple of phone calls. Annie worked as a nurse in Beaumont. Rose worked as a librarian assistant in West Texas. The rest took a little longer, but we got it sorted out. Nick was dating her when she was Annie and they were even engaged but then she disappeared. According to my sources, he was furious and said that she'd pay for embarrassing him. But about six weeks ago he found a new playmate, who organizes fundraisers for various organizations. That is probably why he was out there in Odessa. Candy James, honest to God, Mason, that is her name, was in charge of that bridal showing in Odessa that your girl was a part of. It's possible that he didn't even pay attention to the models, but even if he did, scuttlebutt has it that he's quite taken with Candy and has finally gotten over Annie," Jeremiah said.

"What's your gut feeling?" Mason asked.

"My gut feeling says that Nick has a nasty reputation and that she'd be smart to lay low until Nick and Candy get a lot more serious in the relationship. But if I was you, I'd hire her on the spot. She's got nurse's training and she's been raised on a ranch and she was a librarian, so she's kind of like a teacher, a tutor, and even knows ranchin' business all rolled into one woman. And you said that the girls are taken with her. So I think it's probably a win-win situation," Jeremiah answered.

"And if Nicky comes around here?"

"Nicky is mostly all belt buckle and no cowboy, but if he does come around Whitewright, shoot the bastard."

Mason chuckled. "Send me your bill."

"Sure thing. And good luck."

—∿∿—

Annie Rose tied the top of the garbage bag shut and set it to the side. "I need one more bag."

"I'll go get it for you, Mama-Nanny," Gabby said and yelled back over her shoulder as she ran across the patio. "Lily, you watch my goat and don't let him eat my new Barbie doll's hair. Kenna got one at her last party and her goat plumb ate every bit of its hair before we saw what was happening."

Lily nodded seriously. "And it ate up a Monopoly game too. Daddy, can we please, please, please keep our baby goats in the house?"

Mason put his phone away and said, "It's not up to me. I'm going to offer Annie Rose the job as the new nanny around here for as long as she wants to stay with us. So you have to ask her about goats in the house."

Gabby came back with the trash bag and handed it to Annie Rose, who went right on sorting through the paper to make sure no toys or books were lost in the trash pile.

"Gabby, Mama-Nanny is staying. Daddy said she can stay as long as she wants!" Lily yelled so loud that the goats stopped licking at paper scraps and huddled together.

Annie Rose shoved her foot into the bag, stomped down the paper, and then crammed more into it. When that was done, she folded the plastic tablecloth around all the messy plates, empty cups, and half-eaten hot dogs, and forced it into the bag too.

"Room and board plus minimum wage if you'll do light housekeeping and some cooking," he said.

She wiped her hand on her fanny and stuck it out. "Deal."

After the thoughts that had snuck through her mind all morning, she wasn't a bit surprised at the reaction skin-on-skin contact brought about. Thank goodness the extra beat in her pulse didn't radiate through her fingertips.

He shook. "You hear that, girls?"

"Yay!" They high-fived each other with their left hands.

"So now you've got a new nanny, and she'll make the rules about the goats."

Lily crossed her arms. "Can't we call her Mama-Nanny?"

"You'll have to talk to her about that. Since she's the one y'all have picked out, then you can work out the details with her." Mason winked at Annie Rose.

Annie Rose shrugged. "It's fine with me, but remember, before you decide to call me Mama-Nanny, know that a mama can boss you even more than a nanny. So you might want to think it over or at least talk about it first."

Annie Rose kept stuffing paper into the second trash bag without even looking up, knowing that if she met Mason's eyes, she'd spontaneously combust. He was a damn handsome man, and when he winked at her like that, her insides flat-out turned to mush.

Lily nodded. "We understand."

"Okay then, I'll be your Mama-Nanny if that's what

you really want me to be," Annie Rose said. Lord, how did anyone tell those two darlings "no" about anything?

"If a Mama-Nanny can act like a mama and make decisions like a mama, then I want to talk about them dumb old piano lessons this summer. I want to play the fiddle like Grandpa did," Lily said.

"No one around here can teach you, and I'm not driving to Dallas for fiddle lessons every week," Mason told her, crossing his eye-candy arms over his gorgeous chest.

"Grandpa's fiddle is here. You could hire someone to come to the ranch and teach us," Lily said.

"You got a fiddle in the house?" Annie Rose shouldn't stay, not with the way Mason Harper affected every sense in her whole body, mind and soul.

Mason nodded. "We have my grandfather's, and his banjo too."

Gabby threw up her hands then quickly grabbed for the ribbon around Djali's neck before the goat took off. "Don't look at me. I don't want to play anything. I want to be a rancher and raise cows and sing. Lily is going to grow up and play the fiddle, and I'm going to sing in the band. We aren't going to let Damian play the drums, though. He's not any good. And if Lily don't have to go to piano, then I don't have to either, right?"

Annie Rose smiled at the girls. They were going to be a handful, but she'd been taught by the best. Her mama had been a damn fine teacher when it came to discipline and raising an ornery child.

"I could give Lily a few fiddle lessons, just for the summer, and then if she didn't like it, she could go back to piano lessons, but that's your decision, Mason. I'll make the one for the goats. You have to make the one for the music lessons."

"You play?" he asked, raising his eyebrows and looking at her appreciatively.

"Since I was four. Not the violin, the fiddle, as in country music," she said.

"Like Alison Krauss. You play like her?" Lily's cute little bow-shaped mouth formed a perfect O.

"Honey, I'm not nearly that good, but I could probably teach you the basics," Annie Rose said. "And, Gabby, I don't sing, but maybe you could practice your singing while Lily is learning to play. If that's okay with your dad."

Mason thought about it long enough that both girls grew impatient; forgot about the goats, and threw their arms around his waist and begged in unison, "Please, Daddy, please, even if it's only for the summer."

Just when her heart had resumed its normal thump, he winked over the top of the girls' heads at her. Where was her resolve to never let another man charm his way into her heart? Had it sunk to the bottom of that farm pond along with her car?

"Okay, but only if you really practice hard. Your mommy wanted you to play the piano like she did, but if you want to take three months off, I'll let you," he said.

Annie Rose fussed at herself. She really needed to learn when to keep her mouth shut and quit trying to fix every problem. Talk about what goes around comes around; now it was her turn to listen to the screeching whine of the fiddle during practice sessions like her mother had to when Annie Rose was a little girl and wanted to play like Charlie Daniels.

Gabby took a deep breath. "Okay, Daddy. I'll make her practice every day."

"And you have to practice your singing, too," Mason said.

Now that was double-damn-duty punishment. One playing. One singing. At least Annie Rose's mother only had to listen to the one playing, but then she'd told Annie Rose that she'd have to pay for her raising someday and it would be with high interest.

"Can we start tomorrow?" Lily asked.

How could a woman get so drawn into a family in one day? She'd vowed after the fiasco with Nicky that she would never trust another soul, and she'd already offered to give lessons, clean house, and cook for less money than she'd ever made in her entire life. That involved trust, didn't it? Trust that Mason wasn't another Nicky who would wind up mistreating her. Trust that she could actually corral those two little feisty blonds and teach them something at the same time. Trust that she could still read people enough to know that these were good people.

That was one hell of a lot of trust.

She could almost hear her mother saying, "It's all in the eyes. They are the windows to the soul, and if you are honest, you'll see the person through his eyes."

She wished she'd done that when she fell for Nicky. Looking back, there had always been a veil over his eyes that never lifted. And no matter how hard she tried to be what he wanted, she couldn't fix the problems that he had with control and anger that were worse than a drug addiction. Mason's eyes were warm and she could not only see but feel the love and worry in them when he looked at the little girls.

"Well?" Lily asked.

"Of course we can start tomorrow," Annie Rose said.

"Oh, Djali!" Gabby stomped her foot.

The goat was rooting around inside the still-open garbage bag. When he raised his head, there was pink cake icing on his beard and a piece of paper dangling from his mouth.

"Jeb!" Lily squealed and dashed off to the side of the pool where Jeb was kneeling to drink the chlorine water. "You can't have that. It will make you sick." She tugged at his ribbon leash and it broke. The momentum caused her to fall into the pool, and the goat took off toward the jungle gym, bleating like someone was trying to kill him.

Mason chuckled, then he laughed, then he guffawed so loud that it bounced off the clear blue sky and echoed off the far reaches of the state of Texas. Annie Rose's dad had laughed like that and she always loved hearing it, but this man sure wasn't her father. No, sir! He was a gorgeous cowboy who wore his jeans just right and had lips that begged to be kissed and a body that... dear God in heaven, he couldn't even laugh without sending her thoughts spiraling into places they had no place going. He probably had a girlfriend or maybe even a fiancée, and even if he didn't, she was the nanny and that was all.

"It's not funny, Daddy!" Lily swam to the far end of the pool.

"Yes, it is funny. Let's get those pesky critters out in the calf pen, and then we'll move Annie Rose into the nanny apartment."

"Which is where?" Annie Rose asked.

"Last door on the left off the foyer. It's yours as long as you want it."

Annie Rose smiled. "If I like the job at the end of the month and if the girls still like me after tonight and you still want me to stay, we'll shake on a new deal then. I don't want you to offer something you'll regret later."

"If you last a month, it will be a miracle."

"So do we get to keep the goats in our room, Daddy?"

"Ask Annie Rose about goats in the house. She's the new Nanny-Mama," Mason said, shaking his head and still chuckling quietly.

"And it's Mama-Nanny. Mama comes first," Gabby said.

"How far is it from their bedrooms to my apartment?" she asked.

"Down the stairs and across the foyer," he answered.

"Your dad says there are a couple of old playpens up in the attic that he will bring down for you. Jeb will go in one beside your bed, Lily, and Djali goes in one beside your bed, Gabby. If you bring them in the house for the night, they are your responsibility. You have to take care of them and then clean out the playpens tomorrow morning before breakfast. Understood? Your father is not going to clean the messy playpens, and neither am I. You still want them in the house?"

Gabby tilted her chin up a notch. "A nanny's job…"

Annie Rose laid a finger on her lips. "A mama's job is to teach her children responsibility. They can stay in the pen with the calves or you can babysit them all night and clean the pens tomorrow morning. Those are your options, and you have to get a bucket of soapy water and clean the dust and spiderwebs off the playpens first if you want to use them."

Annie Rose had turned into her mother. Elizabeth Boudreau's spirit had been resurrected inside her the minute that she took on the job of taking care of those little girls.

"But it's our birthday," Lily said.

"And they are your goats. I don't want to sleep with them in my room, and I don't want to clean up after them tomorrow morning or listen to them whine all night. So you have a choice. Calf pen or playpens," Annie Rose said.

Gabby and Lily put their heads together and whispered, gestured, frowned, and Annie Rose's sharp ears picked up a couple of swear words. She finished cleaning the patio, tied another plastic garbage bag shut, and handed it to Mason.

"How about some cowboy hash and vegetables for supper?" she asked. "The girls have had enough junk food for the day."

"Corn and green beans?" he asked.

"If you'll show me around the kitchen enough so that I can find things, I bet that's doable," she answered.

Mason slid the glass door open and stood to one side. "Sounds good to me. You girls come on in when you make up your minds."

"We've decided to clean up the playpens, Daddy," Gabby said seriously.

"But only if you say it's okay to keep them in the playpens at night for more than one night. They can play in their outside pen in the day, but we don't want them to get lonesome at night," Lily declared.

Mason winked at Annie Rose and it slammed right into her heart, no matter how hard she tried to ignore it. "The playpens can stay in your rooms as long as you clean them every morning and don't fuss about having to do it. And it has to be the first thing you do, even before breakfast. And you have to take care of the goats at night. Annie Rose and I aren't taking that job on."

"Okay," Gabby sighed.

"Right now they are going to the calf pen so you can open your present from me and we can have supper. Then when the pens are cleaned, I'll bring the goats inside and carry them up to your rooms. I don't want them outside the pens while they are in the house. I catch one in your bed, and he's going to the auction barn Thursday night."

"Okay," Lily agreed. "Now can we open our present from you?"

"Yes, you can." He handed each of them a card with a note inside.

Lily hugged Mason tightly after she'd opened her envelope containing her birthday present. "Oh, Daddy, this is the best day in my whole life."

Gabby's hands trembled as she held the paper to her chest. "I can't believe it. I can't believe we are really going."

Annie Rose crumbled hamburger meat into an iron skillet and hoped to hell if those envelopes contained tickets to Six Flags over Texas that she wasn't expected to go with them. June was one of the biggest months at the amusement park and that many people milling around in the Texas heat was not her idea of a good time. Especially not if she had to ride something that shoved her right up next to Mason Harper.

"Mama-Nanny, we're going to The Pink Pistol and Daddy is giving us each a hundred dollars to spend in the store and we get to eat at the Dairy Queen in Tishomingo, Oklahoma, and I know that Miranda Lambert has bought ice cream in that very Dairy Queen." Lily danced around, waving the envelope in the air. "This is the best present ever. It's even better than Jeb, and I love him to pieces. Do you think Miranda will be in The Pink Pistol that day?"

"I'm going to buy a pink cowgirl hat with a diamond hatband and a belt to match." Gabby's voice was still only an octave below a complete squeal.

"Mama-Nanny is going too, right, Daddy?" Lily said.

"Of course she is. That's part of the nanny's job," Mason said.

"What is The Pink Pistol?" Annie Rose asked. He'd defined her place with one sentence. That other crazy stuff would disappear in a couple of days. It was all the result of adrenaline, fear, and then finding safety, mixed up together like a margarita in a blender.

"It is a shop in Tishomingo, Oklahoma, that Miranda Lambert owns. *People Magazine* published an article on it last year. She sells all kinds of Western things. The girls have the article taped to their mirror," Mason explained.

"Where is Tishomingo?"

"About an hour and a half northwest of here."

"Duh!" Lily said. "It's where Miranda Lambert and Blake Shelton live."

"Well, duh!" Annie Rose said right back at her. "I knew that. I just didn't know about a Pink Pistol store."

Annie Rose peeled four potatoes and cut them up into

the browned hamburger meat, put a lid on it, and found a couple of sauce pans in the cabinet for green beans and corn. "I bet you've got time to get those playpens out of the attic while I get supper ready, Mason. And the girls might even have time to get started on cleaning them. Check close for spiders. This is the time of year when they hide in corners."

———

Mason propped a hip on a stool in front of the bar dividing the kitchen from the dining nook, where four chairs circled a small, round pedestal table. "They are out in the front yard with buckets of water, doing their part of the job. This should prove interesting. That smells really good."

"Just hash and vegetables. They've had a lot of sugar. This should settle them down for the night. I appreciate you giving me this job. I really do like kids and I like to cook, but it's no fun cooking for one person," she said.

It was the way she dumped the can of green beans into the pan that brought him up short. Holly had tapped the bottom of the can to get out the very last bean like that. He shut his eyes and could visualize her red ponytail swishing around as she prepared supper and her green eyes dancing when she held her hand under a spoon as she carried a taste of whatever she was cooking to him.

"The girls like you." He blinked away the memories.

"It could be a passing thing." She laughed.

Thank God her laughter wasn't anything like Holly's. His wife had sounded like a little girl with a case of giggles. Annie Rose sounded like a three-hundred-pound trucker. But they both ducked their head the same way when they got tickled and he had to get away from it all in a hurry. He had to clear his mind, figure out what it was about this woman that caused him such feelings when others couldn't or at least hadn't.

"I'd best go make sure one of them hasn't drowned the other in the bucket of water," he said.

"Supper will be ready in about twenty minutes, but if you want them to finish the job before they eat, I can keep it warm until they do," she told him.

Holly would have said that supper would be ready in twenty and he'd better be at the table or she'd pour it in the trash can.

"I'll see how the job is coming along," Mason said.

He wandered out onto the front porch, scratching his head and trying to analyze the day. Annie Rose had been hurt, both physically and mentally, so the protective side of him wanted her to be sure that she was safe on his ranch. But the part that kept his wife's memory alive in his heart wished that he hadn't hired her. It could be that he'd be the one who put Annie Rose off the ranch, not the girls.

The apartment was quite a bit larger than the one-room-plus-bath efficiency she'd rented out in Midland, Texas. She'd played it smart. Work in one town. Live in another town. Keep the getaway car, cash, and papers in another. That's the way she'd kept her sanity.

She could hear bleating goats, but the sound was faint. It certainly wouldn't keep her from sleeping in that big old queen-sized bed beckoning to her. It hadn't taken long to repack her things into the suitcase and move them from the tiny upstairs room down to her new digs.

The *How to Remember* book now rested on the nightstand in her bedroom. She sank down into a rocker recliner and threw the side lever to prop up her feet. The air conditioner clicked on and cool air flowed from the vent right above her. She shivered and grabbed for the small quilt draped over the side of the love seat right beside her.

Love seat! Made for two people. Would she ever find a real love seat? One where she and someone else would sit together every evening, no matter what the day brought?

It was doubtful. But then miracles did happen sometimes. She'd proven that when she woke up to the sounds of two squealing little girls and wound up not only with a job but a place to live. And she hadn't touched a dime of the banded thousands of dollars hidden in her suitcase.

A gentle knock startled her. Expecting one of the girls to tell her that they wanted rid of a goat right then, she said, "Come on in."

The door opened wide and Mason filled the entire opening. He wore orange Texas Longhorn lounge pants with a white tank top stretched over his broad, muscular chest. The scent of manly soap wafted across the room to send her senses in another twisting spiral to areas where it had no business going. She reminded herself for the umpteenth time that she was a nanny and that was all.

"I made a pot of tea. Would you like a cup?" he asked.

"I'd love one. In the kitchen?"

He nodded and turned his back. She followed him

into the kitchen to find a little white teapot and two cups on the table. He pulled a chair out for her and she sat down.

"Shall I pour?" she asked.

That look of pain she'd recognized earlier crossed his face and settled into his eyes, but he nodded.

She filled two cups and said, "It's very good. I would have never taken you for a tea drinker. I would have figured you'd be a strong black coffee man."

"I am in the morning. Late at night when I can't sleep for bleating goats, I like a cup of tea. Blame it on my late wife, Holly."

Just the mention of her name brought a change in the air, something sad and lonely, an aura that hauled out every one of Annie Rose's fix-it tools.

"You said late wife. Then your wife has passed. A car accident?" She thought of those sharp curves and the one she'd missed.

"She died with a brain aneurysm. She kissed me on the cheek and headed out the door. She worked in Whitewright at a real estate agency. She didn't even make it off the porch and was gone before I could get to her," he said.

"Their birthday brings it all back so vividly, doesn't it?" she asked.

He nodded and sipped his tea. "We were high school sweethearts, moved in together in college, and married the week after we graduated. My folks gave us the ranch for a wedding gift with the stipulation that I could never sell it, but it has to go to my children or the child who loves it, so that it'll stay in the family. I got my degree in business agriculture. Holly got hers in business administration and went straight into real estate and insurance."

"Do the girls look like her?" Annie Rose sipped at the hot tea and then added a spoonful of sugar.

"Oh, no. Holly had red hair with curl that gave her fits and green eyes. The girls have my mother's blond hair and blue eyes, which did not sit well with Holly at first. She and my mother never did get along."

"Red-haired temper?" Annie Rose asked.

If he needed to talk, then she'd listen. That was part of her fix-it nature and sometimes talking did more good than anything, even if it was to a stranger he'd met only that morning.

"No, not her temper, although Holly did have one, and so does my mother. It was blond-haired control issues. Mother thought Holly should help me run the ranch and raise our children and be happy doing it. Holly had more modern ideas. She would have smothered to death on the ranch, day in and day out, so we hired a nanny and a housekeeper and Holly worked at the agency in town," he said.

She waited, but he didn't go on, so she asked, "Do the girls remember her?"

Mason shook his head. "They have pictures, but they were only a year old when she passed. I'm sorry, Annie Rose. I didn't come down here to dredge up depressing things. I figured with the sound of a barnyard in the house that you couldn't sleep either and maybe you'd like a cup of tea. I never talk to strangers about my personal life."

"It's the birthday season, and besides, now we aren't strangers. We've shared a cup of tea. That makes us friends," she said.

No wonder he had never remarried. A woman would be battling an impossibly rocky slope. Add that to a couple of ornery little girls who had learned the art of making even a nanny's life miserable, and he'd probably never find happiness again. It was time to pull out the change-the-subject tool from her bag of fix-it tricks.

"Listen to those goats carrying on up there. If we're awake, so are they, and the more they fuss with the goats, the easier tomorrow morning will be when they put them outside permanently," she said.

"Gabby is fussin' with the goats; Lily is cussin' at the goats." He finally smiled but it didn't reach those striking green eyes of his. "I'm glad you are here, Annie Rose. They would have steamrolled right over me and the goats would have ended up living in the house. You'll be good for them."

"I promise to be good to them, but they aren't steam-rolling anything over me." She laughed.

"Well, thank you for listening. I'm going to sleep on the sofa in the den tonight. It sounds much worse up there than it does down here. Good night, Annie Rose."

She carried both cups to the dishwasher. "Good night, Mason. Tomorrow night will be much quieter, I promise."

Chapter 4

THE AROMA OF BACON, MUFFINS, AND COFFEE BLENDED together and rose up the stairs as Mason headed for the kitchen early that morning. Previous nannies might pour cereal in a bowl for the girls if he didn't have the time or inclination to cook breakfast. None of them ever had things under control, were fully dressed with a smile, and poured a cup of coffee for him before he even said "good morning."

She barely came up to his shoulder, and with her blond hair up in a ponytail, she looked more like the girls' older sister than she did their nanny. He tried to remember her birthday on the driver's license that she'd flashed at him, but he'd been too worried about who she was and what she was doing on his porch to pay close attention.

"Did the goats keep you up all night?" he asked.

"No, sir. Slept like a baby. First half in the recliner and second in the bed. I fell asleep watching CMT videos, woke up in the middle of the night, and went from chair to bed. How about you?"

He covered a yawn with the back of his hand. "The sofa was better than my bedroom, but I did consider going out to the hayloft or taking a blanket to my truck when Lily raised her voice. It was almost daylight when she told her goat if he shit again, she would haul his sorry little goat ass out to the calf pen right now. And then there was something about that stuff not smelling like roses. I'm pretty sure you are a genius."

Annie Rose giggled at first and then she laughed so loud that it echoed off the walls. She was so darn cute with her blond hair twisted up and her rounded fanny filling out those jeans just right. She had that purely beautiful skin that didn't need a smidgen of makeup, and her laughter cheered up the whole house.

She wiped at her eyes with a dish towel. "I know she shouldn't cuss, but it's so damn cute coming out of her precious little mouth. Are they awake?"

He nodded. "I don't think they've gotten much sleep. I want you to keep them awake all day. No naps. It'll teach them a lesson."

"Oh, I will. It's all part of the goat process, as my mama said," she promised. "We're going to do Monday morning laundry and dusting today, a fiddle and singin' lesson this afternoon, and then we might have an hour to swim before we cook supper, and since I'm cookin', they get to do the dishes."

"We have a dishwasher." He pointed.

"We have two, and they're plenty old enough to learn. They might not like it at first, but later, they'll appreciate having to learn to do for themselves."

"They might fire you," he said.

She turned around to check on something in the oven. When she bent over, he couldn't take his eyes off the back seam in her jeans that ran right down the middle of that perfectly rounded butt.

"I wasn't lookin' for a job when I found this one. I expect I could find another one without too much trouble," she said.

"If you're fryin' eggs, I like mine over easy," he said hoarsely as he shut his eyes tightly. Still the image of her cooking breakfast in faded jeans lingered on and on.

"Two over-easy eggs comin' right up, boss man. You got a problem with me makin' the girls learn to work, tell me now before I make them mad."

"It didn't kill me and I'm not *boss man*. I'm plain old Mason. Did you ever think hard work was going to make you wither up and die when you had to work on the ranch where you grew up?"

She broke two eggs into an iron skillet. "Couple of times, but I was wrong. Didn't your housekeepers or nannies make them do chores?"

"Honey, there hasn't been anyone mean enough to make them do much of anything since their mama passed. I have the nanny service in Dallas on speed dial, if that tells you anything," he said.

Eggs, bacon, biscuits, and hash browns covered the plate she set before him on the table, and then she removed a pan of muffins from the oven and shook powdered sugar on the tops. He forced his eyes on the plate rather than taking another peek at her rear end, but now her breasts were close enough that he could reach out and kiss one. He quickly snapped his eyes shut and counted to ten before he opened them.

"Muffins will be cooled enough to eat by the time you finish that." Her voice was laced with honey and soothing, even if her laughter was loud and rambunctious.

"This is a special breakfast. Is it going to happen every morning?" he asked.

"Let's see if I've still got a job before I answer that question. I hear them coming down the stairs. You might need to get out that speed-dialing business here in a few minutes."

Gabby marched through the kitchen like an army general, with Djali in her arms. Stopping at the back door, she shoved her feet down in bright pink rubber boots and slammed the screen door on her way outside. Lily followed with Jeb thrown up over her shoulder like a baby, his pink rhinestone-studded collar sparkling with every step.

Mason left his breakfast and hurried to the kitchen window where Annie Rose watched the show with a smile on her face. She giggled when Djali got loose and Gabby had to chase him down. Her little, short nightgown flapped in the morning breeze and her boots flashed in the early morning sunlight. Lily marched through the open yard gate, carried poor old Jeb straight to the nearest calf pen, and set him down.

From her body language, Lily was giving Jeb a stinging lecture, but he wasn't paying attention to her gesturing and mean looks. He bounded out into the pen, sniffed noses with a couple of calves, and then shot right back toward her like he was going to climb over her to get away from the nosy black calves.

But then Gabby sat Djali down inside the pen and Jeb and his buddy romped around in the pen like they'd been set free from prison, using a bale of hay for a trampoline as they frolicked in the fresh morning air.

The girls slammed the gate shut together and headed to the house. Mason and Annie Rose turned to get back to the business of breakfast so fast that they bumped into each other. Annie Rose froze and threw up her palms.

"Hey, it's all right. I would never hurt you," Mason said.

Annie Rose dropped her hands to her sides and murmured, "Reflex. I'm sorry."

Mason stepped back out of her space and said, "You have no reason to apologize, Annie Rose."

He was sitting at the table, enjoying breakfast, when the girls stormed into the kitchen and flopped down into chairs.

Annie Rose went to the sink and filled two small plastic buckets with soapy water.

"I'll have muffins and milk," Gabby said.

Annie Rose set a bucket in front of each of them. "Not until the pens are cleaned. If your goats are coming in every night, then you'll have this chore to do every morning before breakfast. If they're staying outside from now on, once the pens are cleaned, your dad can take them back to the attic. And then you will have eggs, toast, and biscuits. Muffins are for breakfast dessert. The easy way is to clean the poop out with paper towels, put them in the bathroom trash, and then wipe down the playpens with the soapy water. Then you can pour the nasty old dirty water in your bathroom sink, wash it out and dry it with paper towels, and empty your trash in the big can beside the back door. I don't want that smelly goat poop in the house all day."

"You clean the pens. We had to put up with them bawlin' babies all night long," Lily said. "I'll have bacon and scrambled eggs with picante sauce on top."

"Pens first. Breakfast afterwards," Annie Rose said as matter-of-factly as if she'd told them there were clouds in the sky.

"We don't like you. We aren't doin' it," Gabby said.

"You're fired," Lily said.

"Sorry, darlin'. You voted me in as a mama, not a nanny, remember. You can fire a nanny, but you don't get to fire a mama. The rule, and you agreed to it, was that you would clean those pens before breakfast, so get out of here and don't come back until they are cleaned spotless. Then your dad can put them away if you are leaving the goats outside," she said.

"Well, shit!" Lily said.

"Lily Harper." Mason drew his eyebrows down in a frown.

Lily threw her hands over her face and groaned. "Damian said that mamas were worse than nannies. Guess he was right. Come on, Gabby. I bet she makes us start scoopin' the litter pan for O'Malley next."

"You mean you don't already? Well, we'll add that to the chore list. You can do it today, and from now on, you take turns," Annie Rose said.

"Chores! Good God! Daddy, fire her. She's the devil," Lily gasped.

"Sorry, girls. You decided you wanted a mama. Now you got one. And I don't know if you realized it before now, but the daddy and the mama do not disagree with each other when it comes to raisin' the kids."

"Oh, no!" Gabby said.

"Oh, yes," Mason said. "Now your job is to pick up those buckets and go take care of the pens. And one other thing, girls. You are only as good as your word, so be careful what you say you'll do or won't do from now on."

"She tricked us," Lily said.

"The pens aren't going to clean themselves," Annie Rose said.

They trudged out of the kitchen with their buckets, their heads hung down, and each one with a roll of paper towels under their arm.

It started as a chuckle down deep in his chest but soon erupted into laughter. Neither of the twins thought it was funny and they threw dirty looks over their shoulders to prove it. Annie Rose loved the sound of it. Any man with a genuine laugh like that had to be honest and decent. Nicky had a tight little laugh with a mean edge that matched his temper. And Nicky never did fill out a knit shirt like Mason did, or wear tight jeans or cowboy boots.

"Thank you for backing me up. It can't be easy to make those little angels do something they don't want to do."

"Not until now, but it helps to have someone around that they like even a little bit. Great breakfast, by the way." He wiped his eyes with a napkin.

"Kids and ranchers need a good solid breakfast so they can do a morning's worth of chores," she said. "Do you have a problem with anything I've done so far?"

"Not a single one." Mason finished his breakfast and washed his hands in the kitchen sink, reached over and stole the tea towel from Annie Rose's shoulder, and dried them. He tossed it back at her shoulder, missed, and grabbed for it at the same time she did.

One second she was reaching for a falling towel, the next she was looking up into the softest green eyes in all of Texas. Time was suspended for a minute while Annie Rose held her breath. She was drowning in those sensations, and they were close enough to kiss when the alarm bells went off like fire engines in her head.

No, no, no. You can't trust him or anyone else, the voice in her head yelled loudly as flashes of Nicky those first weeks went through her mind. He was charming and wonderful in those days. It wasn't until he'd trapped her in his web that he made a hundred-and-eighty-degree flip around.

His finger shot across her shoulder and he pointed to a paper on the front of the refrigerator. "This is my cell phone number in case you need something today. If I don't hear from you, I guess dinner is at noon?"

She took a step backwards and said in a tight, thin voice. "Dinner at noon. Supper at six unless you are busy in the hay field or wanting to use daylight another hour to finish up a chore, then if you would call me, I'll hold it off until you get here. Mama always said that a rancher's supper was the most important part of the day. They could spend some good time with their family and everyone could talk about their day."

Dammit! She always talked too much when she was nervous. It was her second failing, coming in right behind her desire to repair broken hearts and fix problems.

"How old are you?" he asked abruptly.

"What did you ask?"

"How old are you? Simple question. I need a simple answer." His voice was gruff but not scary. When Nicky's voice went that low, it meant trouble was coming and it would be painful.

"How old do you think I am?"

"Twenty-one, I hope," he said.

"Thank you, but I'll be twenty-nine in October. And you?"

"Thirty-one," he said.

"Why would my age matter? Surely you've hired young nannies before now."

"It doesn't. Not really. I just wondered. Now I'm going to go put two playpens back in the attic, and then I'm going out to work until noon," he said.

"How much crew comes in with you to eat?" she asked.

"Just me. The ones that live in the bunkhouse have their own cook and go there. The temporary help that comes from Savoy and Whitewright eats with them." He waved over his shoulder as he started up the stairs. She heard the clatter of two playpens as he wrestled them back up to the attic, and then the front door shut. She braced her hands on the cabinet to still her emotions and reminded herself again of her position in the house. The girls might call her mama, but she was really a nanny.

"It was awful." Gabby threw herself into a kitchen chair and put her head in her hands.

"I'll get your eggs started. Scrambled or fried?" Annie Rose asked.

"Hard-boiled like Easter eggs," Gabby said.

"That wasn't an option. Scrambled or fried?"

Gabby put her hands over her eyes. "This mama business isn't easy."

"She likes them fried with runny yellows," Lily said. "I want mine scrambled."

Gabby shot her sister a dirty look and said, "We poured that yucky water down the bathroom toilet and flushed it three times. And our bathroom still stinks."

"Does that mean the goats are living outside?" Annie Rose asked.

"Yes, and if we have to scoop that litter pan,

O'Malley may learn to like it real good out in the yard," Lily answered.

"Where is your cat?" Annie Rose asked.

"He comes and goes," Gabby said with a wave of her hand.

"O'Malley don't like nobody but us," Lily said.

"He likes Mama-Nanny," Gabby reminded her.

"Well, I like him too. Yellow cats have always been my favorite kind." Annie Rose set their breakfast before them. "Eat it all and you can have a muffin. Better not waste a bit, because you are going to need the energy. After breakfast you are going to strip your beds and bring down your laundry. Today we wash clothes, and since it's such a lovely day, we're going to dry the sheets on the line out back."

"You've got to be kidding me," Lily groaned.

"No, ma'am. I'm not kidding. When the laundry is done, we're going to make cookies and a cake for dessert. If you don't whine about chores, then you can help with the baking. Then after we eat at noon, your dad will go back out to do ranchin' and we're going to do some more chores and have a music lesson."

"You meant what you said this morning? I thought you were teasing," Gabby said. "We don't do chores. We don't work. We play. We are kids. We are not slaves."

"Well, then when you get to be grown, I will choose your husbands. If you don't know how to do anything, he'll have to be really rich. And since you won't be trained in how to be ladies, he'll have to be kind of slow-witted and see only your beauty instead of your smart little brains. But it's your choice, girls. You can play and I'll pick your husbands when you get to be about forty."

"Forty!" Gabby gasped.

"Or maybe a little older, since you won't know how to do anything but watch television and play with video games and feed goats. Maybe there's a big old dumb boy out there who will be satisfied with a wife who knows how to feed goats," Annie Rose said seriously.

All little girls must be cut from the same bolt of denim, because she'd had the same conversation with her mother in a slightly different form once upon a time.

Lily popped her hands on her hips. "I'm going to be a country music singer. I don't need to know all that."

"You are going out on the stage in stinky clothing with bed bugs in your hair because you don't know how to do laundry? I don't think you'll be very popular, my lady," Annie Rose said.

"All right!" Gabby plopped down in a chair. "Life sure ain't easy when there's a mama in the house."

Lily joined her. "You got that right."

Chapter 5

MASON HAD NO TROUBLE DATING OR EVEN SPENDING a night with a woman. He'd even entertained marriage one time, until the woman talked about putting his girls in a boarding school back East. And during all of it, he'd never had the guilt feelings that had fallen on him that morning when he wanted to kiss Annie Rose in the kitchen.

"What was I thinking? I've known the woman twenty-four hours and she's the new nanny." He turned on the radio in his tractor and found a country station.

"Rule number two. Never get involved with the nanny. Rule number one. Never get involved with a woman in the house, no matter who she is. That's why they make babysitters and motels." He talked above the radio noise. "Besides, she reminds me of Holly. She doesn't look a thing like Holly, but in every motion she makes, I'm thinking about Holly all over again. I've never even liked blonds, so what is it about this woman that has me in a spin?"

At noon, he stopped the tractor at the edge of the field, walked a quarter of a mile back to the house, and took off his dirty boots on the back porch. Sheets flapped out on the clothesline. Goats were happy in their new pen. Everything seemed to be in order, so maybe his daughters hadn't strung the new nanny up by her blond braids.

The aroma of fried chicken and hot bread wafted

through the kitchen and into the mud room. He stopped at the wall-hung sink beside the washer, and heard the hum of it running through a spin cycle. Busy sounds of a ranch house like he used to hear when he was a kid and his mother had charge of everything. He felt a sense of place and contentment he hadn't felt in so long he couldn't remember the last time.

"Daddy, Daddy! Guess what?" Lily's bare feet slapped against the floor.

Gabby was right behind her. "We got to help make dinner."

"Is that right?" he asked.

He looked up to see Annie Rose with a hint of flour on her forehead, an apron tied about her small waist, and a smile on her face. She winked at him like Holly used to do when she was happy. And his heart swelled the same way it used to—seeing his woman happy just about made him burst. Wait a minute, wait a minute, Annie Rose wasn't "his woman"—holy Lord, what was he thinking? Was he losing his mind out of sheer relief to have someone who seemed capable of looking after the twins?

"You're still here," he said.

"I've made it four hours, but I've got a ways to go to beat the record," she said.

"Okay, girls, what did you make me? Cold cereal or toast?"

"Fried chicken," Lily said. "And me and Gabby made the biscuits. Mama-Nanny let us do it all by ourselves."

"And we set the table too. Did you know the knife is supposed to face the plate so you are ready to use it when you pick it up, but that we don't have to cut our meat if there's a bone, like in chicken legs? We can pick them up and eat them with our fingers if we remember to wipe our hands on the napkin and not on the front of our shirts," Gabby said.

Lily tugged at his hand. "Come on, Daddy. We've got it on the table because we saw you comin'."

"Thank you," he mouthed at Annie Rose.

She smiled her answer and followed them to the table.

The girls chattered all through dinner and didn't even argue when Annie Rose reminded them not to talk with food in their mouths and to use their napkins. Maybe it was the mother instinct in her that reminded him so much of Holly.

"Mighty fine dinner, and especially the biscuits. I could eat those every day." He pushed back from the table and picked up his tea glass.

"We have dessert," Lily said.

"You should have told me that before I ate that last chicken wing," Mason said.

Gabby cocked her head to one side like Holly used to do when she was on the verge of an argument. "We worked all morning, so you can at least taste it."

"Yes, ma'am. Maybe half a serving now and then more tonight," he said.

Annie Rose removed the empty chicken platter and set a lopsided, three-layer chocolate cake in the middle of the table. "From a mix, and two little girls couldn't leave the oven door shut, so it's leaning a little bit to the left," she whispered for his ears only. He'd never had a nanny in the house who got excited over an ugly cake or who made his girls love to work or one who had such gorgeous blue eyes.

"Well, would you look at that? We won't be ordering cakes from the bakery for your birthdays anymore if you two can cook like this," Mason said.

Annie Rose cut a small slice, laid it on a saucer, and handed it to Mason. He picked up a fork and tasted a small bite. "Hmmm? It looks like cake and it tastes like cake. Guess I'd best have another bite or two before I pass judgment on the quality."

Annie Rose watched them as they waited impatiently, with a sweet look of pure excitement in her eyes that matched his girls' expressions.

"Delicious. Absolutely delicious. I can't wait until supper to get a fatter piece," he said.

The girls threw up their palms and high-fived each other. Annie Rose carried his plate to the sink and he snuck a peek at her butt swaying from side to side as she walked away from the table.

She brought back a cup of steaming black coffee and set it in front of him, her breasts barely brushing his shoulder. Other women had done the same thing, but none other than Holly had caused the reaction that Annie Rose did. Guilt washed over him again for feeling that way about any woman, but most especially about one who lived under the same roof with him.

"Okay, ladies, how much cake do you want? Like your daddy's or bigger?" she asked. "And remember, you are washing dishes while I put everything away."

"Like Daddy's and yes, ma'am," they said at the same time.

He picked up his cup and pushed back the chair, "You girls want to have dessert by the pool? I would sure love to stretch out my legs in a recliner lawn chair while I have coffee. Is it all right if they do the dishes after I go back to work, Annie Rose?"

"There's no hurry. We all get a break at noon, no matter if we're hauling hay or baking. I'll put your cake on paper plates and you can pour your tea into plastic cups. Be careful and don't spill it," Annie Rose said.

Mason settled into the chair and Annie Rose pulled up another one beside him. The girls were ten feet away at the patio table.

"They are fast learners," she said.

"You are amazing. I'll pay you double if you'll sign a year's contract." Where in the hell had those words come from? He couldn't hire a woman like Annie Rose for a year. He couldn't bear the guilt that being in the same room with her brought about. He held his breath as he waited for her answer.

"One month at a time," she said.

———

The rooms were usually a cross between a dump ground and what happens when a tornado hits a toy store when Mason went in to kiss the girls good night. That night everything was in its place and Gabby was propped up against the headboard on pillows with a book in her hands.

"I'm reading this book that I got for my birthday yesterday and Mama-Nanny says that it was in her library and that I should read it. We get to read thirty minutes before we have lights-out now, and we're on the honor system. At nine thirty, we have to put the marker in our book. See?" She held up a piece of paper with stickers plastered on it. "Me and Lily made one this afternoon.

Mama-Nanny showed us how to make it and she taught us how to use measuring cups and cook and she says she trusts us to turn off our own lights at nine thirty."

Without having to pick his way across the floor to avoid stepping on a Barbie, an electronic device, or a hair bow, he quickly crossed the room and sat down on the edge of her bed. "So you think maybe you'll keep your mean old nanny?"

Gabby sighed. "We would fire her if she was a nanny, but since she's a *mama*"—she emphasized the word—"we are going to keep her. We had so much fun today, Daddy."

"I thought you had to do chores," he said.

"Well, we thought chores were work. We didn't know they were fun." Gabby yawned. "I'm glad Djali is in his own bed tonight. I really didn't like all that carryin' on last night."

Mason kissed her on the forehead. "So today was a good day?"

"The best ever." Gabby smiled.

"I'm glad to hear that."

Lily looked up from her book when she heard him coming through the connecting bathroom between her and Gabby's room. "Daddy, come and smell my sheets. They smell like springtime. Mama-Nanny says that we can hang them on the line every Monday if it's not raining."

Mason crossed another clean floor and stuck his nose in Lily's pillow, inhaling deeply. "They do smell nice. What are you reading?"

"It's called *Winner Bakes All*, and it's about a little girl my age who likes to be a tomboy, but she likes to cook too. Mama-Nanny says when I read it all, me and Gabby can make cupcakes and put our own decorations on them and we'll have them for dessert when you come home at noon."

"Then you had a good day and you like this idea of turning off television and games so you can read before you go to sleep?" Mason asked.

Lily twisted her mouth to one side. "Well, I didn't think I was going to like it one bit, but Mama-Nanny says that if we know where our things are all the time that it makes everything work better."

"So we're not going to fire her?" Mason asked.

"Hell, no! I mean heck, no! Mamas are better than nannies, so me and Gabby were right all along," Lily answered.

Mason kissed Lily on the forehead. Two calm girls who didn't want thirty more minutes of Nick-at-Nite or thirty more minutes of games on their tablets—no one could tell him that miracles didn't exist in today's world.

The faint squeak of porch-swing chains sent him outside. Hopefully there wasn't another woman sleeping out there. If so, he was going to take the swing down and store it out in the barn.

A full moon hung in the sky right above Annie Rose's head with bright twinkling stars gathered around it like subjects around a reigning queen. She moved to one end of the swing and patted the empty space beside her.

"Plenty of room for two," she said.

He sat down on the other end of the swing, and an instant wall went up between them. It was as if Holly was right there between them, reminding him that she still had a place in his heart. And yet, there was Annie

Rose with her amazing ability to love his girls, a body that he yearned to wrap his arms around and protect, and eyes that could see all the way to the bottom of his soul.

"Girls asleep yet?" she asked.

"No, but they are watching the clock. Honor system, Gabby said."

"It worked for me. I didn't let them swim today, because water makes them sleepy and they were about to drop by midafternoon, so we told stories and folded clothes before the fiddle lesson. Lily has a good musical ear and she's going to be a quick study. The piano lessons helped. She's already playing a simple little two-chord song by ear. Gabby has a beautiful voice. She and Lily harmonize well, but Gabby has the better voice. I promised them that every Friday night they can show you how much they've learned. It'll be like a concert in the living room, so get ready for it."

"I'd like that," he said.

He'd cleaned up for supper, and the remnants of soap and some kind of masculine-smelling shaving lotion mixed with the night air was a heady combination. A plain white T-shirt stretched over the tight muscles in his chest, and the sleeves strained over his bulging biceps. Mason had arms and a body that were the result of hard work and not a set of expensive machines in the private gym in the basement of an expensive house in Beaumont. Somehow, it was a helluva lot sexier than the toned body produced by trainers and weights.

Mason wore his shirt on the outside of his snug-fitting jeans. She blushed when she realized that she'd stopped scanning his body where the shirt ended midway down the zipper of those tight-fitting jeans. She quickly followed the faded denim to his feet. He'd kicked off his boots and even his bare feet were gorgeous.

Her body screamed, *yes, yes, yes, you can trust this man. He's a good person who would never be mean to a woman.* Her mind continued to yell, *no, no, no, look what trust got you into.* Her poor heart cringed and hid from the voices.

Quickly coughing to cover the squeak that came out when she tried to speak, she covered her mouth with her hand and then asked, "So have you lived here on this ranch your whole life?"

"I was born in that room where my bedroom is now. My great-grandpa started the ranch. Grandpa built it up further, and then my dad and mother made it grow even bigger. I inherited it when I married the girls' mother when I was twenty-one years old."

"Only child?" she asked, glad that he was staring out across the land and not at her.

"Oh, no! I have three brothers, all older than me and all hate ranching. When my folks retired, they traveled for two years, seeing everything that they'd missed while they were tied down to ranch and family, then they settled in Florida right on the beach. Mother loves it and Dad stays active on the golf course, and he still works with the National Angus Association, so he gets to be involved in enough ranchin' to keep him happy."

"Do your brothers live near them?" She wanted him to keep talking, not so she'd know everything about his family, but his deep Southern drawl was so soothing.

Mason shook his head. "My middle brother lives

in Germany. He's career military and will retire in a couple of years. Right now, he plans on joining the folks in Florida when he retires. The oldest one has an oil business in Houston. And the youngest one, who is eight years older than me, is in California. He's in the movie industry."

"And they all grew up right here? I'm surprised none of them stuck around. This place is so…" She stopped.

"So what?" he asked.

"So peaceful and beautiful and"—she paused again before she finished with—"and soul satisfying. Sounds kind of crazy, but it is."

Mason nodded. "They were eight, ten, and twelve when I was born, and not a one of them liked the business. Mother said God gave me to them so the ranch would survive. I loved dirt and cows from the time I could crawl, or at least that's what she says. What about you?"

"Only child. Adopted."

For the hundredth time since she'd sold the ranch, she regretted it again. It had only been a section of land, six hundred and forty acres, with a one-story ranch house, but it had been home. And now she wished that instead of a suitcase full of money and a bank account she'd never touched, that she had the dirt and cows.

She inhaled deeply and went on to say, "I was raised on a small ranch outside Thicket, that's not far from Beaumont. Daddy grew Angus and dabbled around with some fancy breeds for fun. They were well into their forties when they adopted me, and they died within six months of each other when I was a senior in college. I sold the ranch a few weeks after Mama died."

"You sound wistful," he said.

"After a day with the girls, I am," she admitted.

"If you hadn't sold the ranch, you wouldn't be where you are today."

She smiled. "Philosophical, are you?"

"If I am, then it's because life made me that way. I didn't know jack shit about babies when Holly died. Barely knew how to change a diaper, but I learned real fast. Mother offered to come live with me, but she and Dad deserved their retirement, and I wanted to prove that I could run a ranch and raise two kids all on my own. Sometimes I felt like Holly was laughing at me. I talked to her—especially that first year, and"—he stopped for a full minute before he went on—"on occasion, I still do. It took a few months, but one morning I woke up and realized I was making it work all by myself. Maybe not a good job, but I was getting it done. It's been a long time since I liked a day as much as I have today, Annie Rose. Guess that was a lot of information all at once. When I'm nervous, I tend to use forty words when four would do the trick."

"So do I. It's my second-biggest failing," she said.

"What's the first?" he asked.

She wiggled her eyebrows. "I'd tell you, but then… well, you know the rest. And you've got two kids that adore you and need you."

The silence that surrounded them wasn't uncomfortable. It didn't need to be filled with words or stories. Even the tension that had been between them when he sat down was more relaxed now that they were talking. He chanced a glance over at her. The moonlight danced on her blond hair as the swing moved back and forth and took her from shadows into light.

"I should tell you," he finally said, "that the investigator I hired to check out your story told me that Nick Trahan had a new girlfriend. She's the one that set up that bridal thing you were in, and it's a probability that he was there to see her."

Annie Rose sighed. "He vowed if I ever left him he'd hunt me down and kill me."

Mason laid a hand on her shoulder and she didn't flinch. "You're safe here on Bois D'Arc Bend."

"Thank you for everything. I should be going inside now. Good night, Mason."

"Good night," he said. "I'm going to sit here a little longer. I'll lock up when I come in."

Chapter 6

HOW IN THE HELL TWO GOATS COULD BE SO WILY WAS beyond Annie Rose's wildest imagination. She and the girls had finished setting the table for dinner and everything was staying warm, either in the oven or on top of the stove, when it sounded like a whole wagonload of cats got into a major fight in the backyard.

She tossed her apron on the cabinet and took off toward the back door with both girls right behind her, screaming that O'Malley had come home and was into it again with his arch enemy, the wild barn cat. It would have been a good thing if it had been two old tomcats having a showdown with fur flying and claws out.

But it went way further than that scenario. There was old O'Malley halfway up the porch post, hair all standing on end, tail puffed out, and eyes that were nigh unto popping right out of the sockets. Djali must have thought the cat's tail was a big ball of cotton candy, because he was standing on his hind legs trying to eat it. Jeb was right behind Djali, fighting for a chance at the cat's tail.

Lily stomped her foot and screamed, "Jeb, you get your sorry goat ass back in your pen or I'm going to butcher you for supper."

"I think you'll have to drag him to the pen," Annie Rose said. "He's sure not going to turn around because you are yelling at him."

"You catch him, and then I'm going to sell his ass at the auction. I'm tired of being a goat owner," she said.

"He's your goat. Not mine. If he kills your cat, then don't come crying to me. I'm going back in the house to put dinner on the table." Annie Rose turned around in time to see Mason crossing the yard in long strides.

Lily had Jeb in a death grip by his collar, dragging him back to the pen, with Gabby right behind her, manhandling Djali. O'Malley jumped down from his perch, shot across the yard like a tornado, crawled right up Mason's frame as if he were a pecan tree, all the way to his shoulder, and jumped off into the pickup bed.

"What in the hell happened?" he hollered.

"The goats got out of their pen and treed O'Malley. Lily is of the opinion that she doesn't want to be a goat herder anymore, but I vote that she has to keep him a good deal longer to learn her lesson." Annie Rose held the door open for him. "By the time you get washed up, they'll have them back in the pens."

"You are the Mama-Nanny. I'll support your decision." He adjusted the water in the mudroom sink and washed his hands. "Is that roast that I smell?"

"It is, and the girls helped make the yeast rolls. They're a lot of fun, Mason."

"Even when the goats get out of the pen?"

"My God, you are bleeding. It's spotting your shirt. Take it off so I can clean the wounds. Cat claws are dirty and can cause a fever that's miserable." She grabbed him by the shoulders and turned him around to unbutton his shirt. She had to tiptoe to pull it over his shoulders and toss it over on the washer. Quickly, she lathered up her hands with soap and cleaned each puncture wound dotting his hard body from belly button to up over his shoulder and halfway down his back.

"Where is the medicine cabinet?" she asked.

He nodded toward the cabinet above the sink. She rinsed her hands and reached for the familiar brown bottle and a tube of ointment. She wiped the soap away with a clean washcloth, then flushed the claw marks clean with hydrogen peroxide before she dotted each one with an antibiotic ointment. "I'd put Band-Aids on each one, but I think the bleeding has stopped now, and it would be better for them to air out."

"Yes, Dr. Annie," he said.

"Here they come. You'd better go find another shirt. They'll kill that cat if they think he hurt their daddy. They've already threatened both cat and goats," she said. And besides, touching his hard body had her in a fizz that would take a few minutes to settle.

The girls washed the goat smell from their hands in the sink, and Annie Rose held her own hands out to see if they were shaking as badly as her insides. To her surprise, they were steady as a rock.

Mason changed into a pale blue pocket T-shirt that hugged his body like a glove, every taut muscle begging to be touched. Annie Rose was glad that Gabby started to talk to ease the silence in the room.

"Them damn goats got out of the pen and treed poor old O'Malley on the porch post and that's why O'Malley was running away. He must have thought you were a tree, Daddy. Did he hurt you?" Gabby asked.

Mason shook his head but couldn't get a word in edgewise before Lily started.

"And Mama-Nanny says that I can't sell Jeb at the

auction next week. I swear to God, Daddy, that goat is more trouble than he's worth, and I don't know why I even wanted one for my birthday."

Gabby started while Lily caught her breath, "We can't sell them, Lily. It would hurt Kenna's feelings, and besides, if we did, Doc might give us a shot just to get even, since he gave them to us."

"Well, shit. I'm not even going to apologize for saying that, Daddy, because it's the way I feel," Lily said.

Mason sipped at his sweet tea and raised an eyebrow toward Annie Rose.

She shrugged. "Just another day in paradise."

—~~—

Gabby and Lily were reading.

Mason was in his office.

Annie Rose slipped out the front door.

The swing had become her friend and called to her to come out and play. Evening had always been her favorite time of the day: a time to sift through the happenings and save the sweet memories for another time when there might not be any, to giggle again at the antics of two girls, two goats, and a rangy old tomcat named O'Malley.

Mason surprised her when he sat down on his end of the swing. Her reflexes were getting entirely too lax if someone could sneak up on her like that. She glanced his way to see that he was wearing lounge pants, a tank top, and no shoes. The darkness couldn't cover a five-o'clock shadow or erase the scent that was a mixture of soap and something far more personal that belonged to Mason and no one else.

"So did you like this day in paradise?" he asked.

He handed her a longneck bottle of beer so cold that the sides were sweating. She rolled it around on her forehead before she twisted the cap off and took a long gulp. "Thank you. That really hits the spot on a hot night. And yes, boss man, I liked this day."

His mouth turned up in a slightly crooked grin. "Not boss man. Just Mason. I told you that. Here's hoping you stay here for a long, long time." He tipped his bottle over to touch hers.

"That's my intention right now… Mason."

"I talked to the girls and kissed them good night. They told me how they made that delicious mousse that we had for dinner. Lily says she might be a chef when she's not touring with her country music band." He chuckled.

"It'll take a little more than instant pudding, whipped topping, and chocolate curls to turn her into a chef, but it's a start. We practiced the fiddle today for an hour and you're going to be surprised on Friday night."

"What is she going to play?" he asked.

"Well, it's not 'The Devil Went Down to Georgia,' but it could be in a few months. She's really got an ear and a handle on how to play that thing. You sure she hasn't been sneaking it out of your room?"

"Honey, I'm never sure of anything when it comes to those two. My grandpa could make that thing do everything but tell you bedtime stories. Maybe she picked up the ability to play from him. She's sure pestered me a long time about it, but her mama wanted them to take piano lessons, so I tried to steer them in that direction."

Annie Rose put the swing in motion again and tucked

her feet up under her, sitting cross-legged and facing Mason. "I showed her three chords yesterday. I figured I'd have to show her again today, but when I put the lyrics and music in front of her, she remembered, and she's pretty damn good at knowing exactly when to change."

"So I might have a country music star and a chef?" he teased.

She took another sip of her beer and set it on the porch. "The sky is the limit where those two are concerned."

He was ten steps past sexy in that gauze undershirt. They called them wifebeater shirts, but something down deep in her soul told her that Mason Harper was not a wife beater. He might argue and raise his voice, but he'd never lift his fist to a woman he loved. It was in the eyes, like her mama said.

"You ever get mad enough to hit a woman?" she asked bluntly.

"Yep, I have. Lots of times. But I didn't. I walked out, slammed the door, and kept walking 'til I got to the barn."

"What'd you do then, hit a bale of hay?" she asked, imagining those big arms hugging her close rather than slinging punches at a hay bale.

"No, I usually worked like a fiend, cleaning stalls that didn't need cleaning or else I crawled up on a four-wheeler and drove it out to Nash's place so recklessly that only the grace of God kept me safe. Nash and I would sit on his porch, sometimes without saying a word until I cooled down, and then I'd come back home."

"Nash is your friend?"

"More than that. He's my foreman Skip's granddad. He was the foreman before Skip, and he's a wise old fart." Mason's handsome face lit up in a smile that rivaled the stars in the heavens.

"So Holly could make you that mad?" Annie Rose asked.

"Yep, she had red hair and a temper to go with it. We argued and we disagreed, but we loved each other. I would have never, ever hit her."

"What did you do then? After you came back into the house?"

"Well, we'd both cooled off enough by then to talk about the problem."

"Which was?"

"It's hard to explain now, but it was important to both of us that we had our own way, but that wasn't enough. The other one had to approve and like the decision. Her temper got worse about six weeks before she died and we had some really big arguments, mostly about nothing. I chalked it up to her job and two feisty girls needing so much attention at night. Now I wonder if it wasn't that thing in her head all along."

"The brain is a tricky little thing and aneurisms are crazy. We don't know what kind of effect they have before they decide to explode."

"Tell me about Nicky." He changed the subject so quickly that she had to think fast to keep up.

Annie Rose scratched her left eyebrow. Failing number three—messing with her eyebrow when she didn't want to talk about something, but Mason had been open about his wife, so she should reciprocate.

Therapy is talking to strangers about personal things.

Gina Lou, her best friend, had told her to find a damn good therapist when she disappeared, but fear kept her from doing it. What if Nicky had found her because she'd sought out a doctor? But talking to Mason wasn't difficult at all. It was like she was talking to a friend.

"You are so strong and wise. Why would you ever fall for a playboy?" Mason asked.

The laughter that escaped was more sarcastic than happy. "A strong, wise woman would have seen through him, listened to her heart and her friends. I didn't do any of those things, so it's hard to trust my judgment about anything anymore."

Mason waited.

"He had a minor fender bender and came into the ER where I was working. Looking back, it was most likely my predecessor who got tired of his shit and tried to run him off the road. In my defense, he was damn good-looking and a charmer, even when he was whining about a few bruises on his pretty face. And I was in a very bad place in my life. My folks both died within six months of each other. I was on a guilt trip for selling the ranch, and I'd broken up with my boyfriend of three years a month before."

"And he asked you out?"

"Not that night. We put an IV in his arm, filled him up with fluids and medicine, and sent him home with a couple of prescriptions. I got a dozen roses the next day with a lovely note thanking me for saving his life."

Mason's hand touched hers and she immediately jerked hers away. She tucked it firmly under her thigh.

"And?" he asked.

It took effort but she forced herself to unwind. Talking about Nicky always brought about the same knee-jerk reactions. "The next day he sent another dozen roses and a card asking me if he could call me. Ten minutes after the flowers arrived, the ER phone rang, and it was Nicky. That's when he asked me out."

"And you said no?"

"I said yes so fast that he probably wondered why he wasted his money on the second vase of roses. He was a smooth talker, and six weeks later we were living together. The third month after our first date, he gave me an engagement ring. On the fourth month, he gave me my first black eye."

"I'm sorry," he said.

"No need for apologies. After that first one, he was careful not to leave bruises where they could be seen. I made excuses for him until one morning I woke up and realized that the diamond ring on my finger had bought me a life of hell. That's the day I started planning my escape. It took several weeks and a lot of patience before I could leave, but when I did, I never regretted my decision."

"Therapy?" he asked.

She shook her head. "You?"

"Couldn't do it. Mother thought I should, but how do you tell your darkest secrets to a stranger?" Mason asked.

"Exactly, and yet here I sit doing just that."

"Hey!" He patted her on the knee and she didn't tense up. "We have lived through goats and tomcats and cleaning two little girls' rooms. I'd say that makes us pretty good friends."

"It does, and friends can tell each other anything."

"Almost. I'm not going to tell you about the first time I got drunk." He laughed.

"Oh, honey, I'm not so sure we'll ever be that good of friends that I'd discuss my first drunk with you," she told him.

He stood and pulled her up with him. "I should make sure the honor system is working tonight."

"Me, too."

He took one step then stopped." I like talking to you, Annie Rose."

"Me, too," she said again.

"Let's go make sure the lights are out. Maybe we'll run into each other again out here on the porch."

"It's my favorite part of the day. That swing and I are pretty good friends now," she said.

Lights were out.

Mason disappeared into his room and closed the door softly.

Annie Rose padded down the stairs, went to her tiny little apartment, but she was too wound up to sleep. She folded the throw from the back of the sofa and put it over the recliner, picked up a leaf she'd tracked in from the porch, and put it in the trash. Then she saw the *How to Remember* book on the coffee table.

Frowning, she picked it up. She hadn't moved it from her bedside table, so how did it get from there to the sitting room?

"Oh!" She smiled.

It wasn't her *How to Remember* booklet but a brand-new one with stickers of horses, cows, and even goats and cats scattered among the words on the front: *How to Be a Rancher*.

She opened it up to find the steps outlined in Gabby's handwriting.

Number 1: *You got to love animals but you got to never let your kids bring goats into the house. Not even if they fight with you and use cuss words. Goats stink.*

Number 2: *You got to wear jeans and boots. Lily says that since you already do that you are doing good.*

Number 3: *You got to like living in the country. Ranchers don't live in big towns with taxis and hotels like those places on television.*

Number 4: *You got to know that dirt sticks to boots and sometimes it comes in the house.*
Lily says there's other rules but we are tired and that's all for tonight. We love you, Mama-Nanny.

She held the booklet to her heart. It started as a soft giggle but pretty soon it turned to sobs as the dam let go and she truly mourned her past. Now if only she could find closure and let it go.

Chapter 7

ANNIE ROSE COULDN'T BELIEVE THAT IT HAD BEEN SIX days since she'd been awakened by little girls squealing on the front porch, or that tonight those same little girls were playing and singing for their daddy in the living room. The girls were giddy with the preparations and had changed clothes a dozen times, traipsing up and down the stairs for her opinion on what they should wear for their first concert.

She had planned on a one-song show after only a week of fiddle playing and singing. But that had stretched to two numbers, and now it was up to three songs, one with fiddle accompaniment, and two with the karaoke machine providing background music.

Supper involved more wiggling, whispering, and squirming than it did eating. The show was to start at seven o'clock, and it was already after six, so the excitement was mounting fast.

"Do I need to get out my tux or will my Sunday suit do for this show?" Mason teased.

"Oh, Daddy, it's a country music concert. You can wear your jeans and shirt, and Mama-Nanny can wear jeans too. But y'all have to clap even if we miss a note, and at the end of the summer we might even get matching T-shirts for us all, like at the Miranda concerts," Gabby said.

"I'm very good at applause. I took that class in college," Annie Rose teased.

Mason caught her eye above the girls' heads and smiled. "Did you pass it?"

"Made a hundred on every test," she said. "Did you take it too?"

"No, I'm self-taught. Trained in how to clap my hands by two little girls when I taught them to play patty-cake," he answered.

"Daddy!" Lily exclaimed. "Don't laugh at us. We're going to knock your socks off."

"I'm sure you are, but right now could we finish supper? I'm really hungry, and you don't want my growling stomach to be louder than your music. Have you forgotten that tomorrow is the Angus Association picnic and the next Saturday is the trip to The Pink Pistol? And speaking of rodeos, the Saturday after that, let's take the girls to the Resistol Rodeo down in Mesquite." Mason made plans as he ate the rest of his supper.

Lily threw a hand over her forehead. "One thing at a time, Daddy. We have to concentrate on our concert right now, then all three of us girls will plan out what we'll wear to the picnic."

"Picnic? Tomorrow?" Annie Rose asked. Surely the nanny didn't attend every one of those affairs, and if she did, what was she going to wear?

"It's the one family affair that we have each year. We alternate ranches where we have it. This year it's Lucas Allen's turn. His ranch is up near Savoy, not far from here. He supplies the brisket. We all bring a covered dish. There's a cheesecake from Cheesecake Factory in the freezer. That's what I always take," Mason said.

"We're done. May we be excused, Mama-Nanny?" Gabby asked.

"Of course, and we'll use the dishwasher because you two are concert stars not ranchin' women tonight." Annie Rose's head was in a spin. A picnic and she only had two outfits and a dirty wedding gown. If only the dates had been reversed, she might have found something decent at The Pink Pistol store.

"We'll be ready in fifteen minutes, Daddy. You best get in line at the door, or you'll miss the first number." Lily tossed back her hair on the way out of the kitchen.

"I dread it when they're sixteen," he said.

"You have every right to dread their teenage years. Am I really supposed to go to all those places you mentioned? I'm the nanny. I can stay home."

"Yes, ma'am, you are going. A nanny could take the day off, but since you are the mama, you have to go."

"How far is it into Whitewright?" she asked.

"Five minutes, tops. Why?"

"Because I have two pair of jeans and a torn, dirty wedding dress. If I'm going somewhere with you and the girls, I'd like to look decent," she answered.

"The keys to my truck are hanging on the rack beside the back door. They're the set on the keychain that says World's Best Dad. Don't have to tell you what I got for Father's Day last year, do I? I'm not so sure what you can find in Whitewright. Seems like there is a new women's store across from the library, so you might have to do a quick run up to Sherman."

"Thank you. And now you'd better get on out of here and let me clear off the table so I can set up the refreshments," she said.

"Refreshments?" He cocked his head to the side in a gesture that made him even more attractive. Green eyes twinkled and a smile tickled the corners of that absolutely delicious-looking mouth.

"Since this is their first concert, they are giving open backstage passes. We will be serving coffee, sweet tea, and cupcakes immediately after the concert. Just a reminder, you should ask for autographs on the paper napkins," she leaned in to say softly and wished that she could taste, just one time, his lips after he'd sipped sweet tea. Even thinking about it was more intoxicating than a shot of whiskey.

Mason pushed back his chair. "I keep saying the same words, but I don't know any other way to say it: you are amazing, Annie Rose."

"You might want to wait to say that until after the concert. I don't even know what they are doing after the fiddle song. The other two are with Lily's karaoke machine," she whispered.

Mason leaned down and kissed her on the cheek. "This week has been incredible."

She didn't get the pleasure of a real kiss, but she felt like a teenager who'd been kissed by Blake Shelton at a country music concert. She had to hold her hands tightly in her lap to keep from touching her cheek to hold the kiss there forever.

"It's been the most fun I've had since I was a kid," she said.

"Daddy!" Lily yelled through the closed door. "Do you have your camera to film us?"

"Yes, princess, your filming crew is ready," he said.

"Is the refreshment table ready?" she asked.

"It will be in five minutes," Annie Rose yelled back. "And in exactly nine minutes we will be in our seats and ready."

"Beers after they are in bed tonight?" Mason asked.

"I'll be the one on the swing in my bare feet," she said.

"I'll be on the lookout for you." He smiled.

Mason and Annie Rose waited until the clock struck seven to open the doors. Jar candles were on the coffee table, the end tables, and defined an area around the part of the living room designated as the stage. They'd gone to a lot of trouble setting up a metal stand with music and a fiddle, a karaoke machine, and two bales of hay. How they'd gotten that hay into the living room was a mystery. Annie Rose thought she'd kept a better watch on them than that.

She and Mason took their seats and managed to keep a straight face when they saw gray duct tape holding a sign on the chair beside the music stand. Written in bright pink crooked letters, it read *Welcome to the first concert of the Famous Harper Sisters*.

The door swung open and they made their appearance, walking slowly into the living room and waving at Annie Rose and Mason. Gabby was dressed in a pale blue gingham-checked sundress that matched her eyes. Lily wore a hot-pink skirt with a petticoat making it stand straight out, and a cute little tank top. The bling on her hot-pink cowgirl belt glittered in the candlelight.

"Welcome," Gabby said in a big voice. "Thank you for coming. We've got a show that y'all are goin' to love. We'll get started with the fabulous Lily Harper playing on the fiddle and accompanying me while I sing "I'll Fly Away.""

Lily picked up a microphone from the music stand and

said, "Afterwards you are invited to a backstage party held in the dining room. Refreshments will be served, and we will be giving out autographs. Now sit back and enjoy the first-ever Famous Harper Sisters concert."

Mason leaned over and whispered into Annie Rose's ear, giving her a warm tingle all the way down her spine. "No way can she play that already."

"Be prepared for a surprise," she whispered back, her lips close to his ear.

Lily laid the microphone down, picked up the fiddle, tapped the bow on the strings twice, and then drew it down in a whine before she started. She did a perfect chord progression of DGDDAD as a prelude, nodded at Gabby, and then started over again.

"Some glad morning when this life is o'er," Gabby sang into the microphone held at the right distance from her mouth like Annie Rose had shown her.

She made the last note last long enough to let Lily change chords and then went on. They only had one small glitch, and that came on the last stanza when Lily was supposed to put the fiddle down and harmonize with her sister. She started the next chord procession with the D chord instead of dropping the fiddle. She realized immediately what she'd done, and Gabby covered for her by flipping her hand backwards and saying, "Play it, Sister."

Lily repeated the prelude and then joined Gabby in the last chorus, harmonizing beautifully for two little nine-year-old girls. When they got to, "When I die, Hallelujah by and by... I'll fly away," they were right on key and in sync.

Annie Rose didn't know if she was prouder of them

for covering the mistake like pros or for their fantastic job. She jumped to her feet and applauded.

"Wow! I don't believe it. I didn't even hear her practicing," Mason said.

"Practice time is for an hour or two after you go back to work in the afternoon. But I have a confession that I'm not supposed to tell you. She's been sneaking that fiddle out and practicing for weeks. She gets chords from the Internet and even read some how-to articles on beginning fiddle playing. She's a quick study, Mason."

"And now if everyone will take their seats again, we have two numbers picked out to sing to you," Lily said.

The first chords of Jason Aldean's "She's Country" came through the karaoke machine, and they both picked up a microphone.

"Dear God," Mason gasped.

Gabby strutted across the stage as she sang about being a hot little number in her pickup truck. Lily came in when the lyrics said she was a Georgia peach with a big Southern drawl. They had the choreography down to a T, winking and pointing at each other as they sang about being born that way.

When the song ended, they held hands and bowed and then popped right up in time for Lily to take the lead on "If I Die Young," by The Band Perry. She sang that if she died young then the Lord should make her a rainbow. Gabby took first place on the second verse and winked at her daddy.

Annie Rose could feel his tears without even glancing his way. The girls had no idea that any song of dying young would open up raw emotions that were still buried inside his heart. She reached over and covered his hand with hers, hoping that it brought him a measure of comfort and that he didn't let the dam inside his soul break in front of the girls.

"And this one is because we get to go to The Pink Pistol next week and we love you, Miranda, wherever you are tonight." Gabby held the microphone up in a salute.

Background music for "Hell on Heels," by the Pistol Annies came through the karaoke louder than the other songs. At the end of the prelude, both girls came in to sing about being hell on heels. Then Lily said that she was made pretty and Gabby said she was made smart and they both did Miranda's part about having a pink guitar.

Mason laughed and drew his hand out from under Annie Rose's to clap. His whistles rocked the room, and the girls beefed up the performance more with every bit of his applause.

Annie Rose swore she could hear Miranda's grit in Lily's voice. Mercy sakes, that child might have a tour bus someday if she could learn to play that fiddle like Alison Krauss and sing like Miranda. Gabby brought her voice to the mix and the two of them didn't miss a beat when they clapped along with the background singers on the karaoke tape.

"And that ends our show. Your backstage passes are on the table, and there will be refreshments and autographs," Lily announced.

Mason and Annie Rose applauded until the girls were out of sight.

"The little imps. Look at this. We've got passes with our names on them, and they're good for drinks. Thank you, Annie Rose. I've never seen them so happy."

Mason hugged her tightly. She spontaneously looped her arms around his neck and hugged him back.

"Daddy!" Lily's voice floated into the living room.

"Your adoring audience is on the way," Annie Rose yelled.

"Is this our first date?" Mason asked.

"I don't know. Did we go as friends or as a couple?" she asked.

He flashed a brilliant smile. "I'm not sure. What's the difference?"

"Would you kiss a friend?"

He threw an arm around her shoulders. "That's putting it pretty straight."

She smiled and led the way into the dining room, where the backstage passes had to be shown before they could get through the doors. The party lasted half an hour and then the girls had to give up their celebrity status, but they didn't fight with Annie Rose when she said it was time to clean up the mess in the living room and get ready for bed. Mason volunteered to haul the equipment up so they wouldn't miss out on their reading time. Annie Rose said that she'd take care of the cleanup in the kitchen.

"I don't know if I'll ever calm down," Lily sighed. "That was so much fun."

"Will you come tuck us in, Mama-Nanny?" Gabby asked.

Annie Rose glanced at Mason, who had a dollop of chocolate cupcake icing in the corner of his mouth. That was his time with the girls, so she didn't know what to say. She cocked her head to one side in a question.

He nodded his approval and licked the icing from his

lip. She would have gladly taken care of that for him. All he had to do was give her a sign. He didn't even need to ask.

Good God! What am I thinking? It's the excitement of the evening that's gotten to me. That and the kiss on the cheek, but I'm not a teenage hussy. I'm a full-grown woman who's been hurt too many times to be thinking like this.

"I can do that," she finally answered. "I'll get your pillow all fluffed up and then your dad can come in and do the final tucking."

"I'd like that," Lily said. "It'll be the perfect ending to a perfect day. Both parents saying good night."

Mason sat down on the stairs. He wanted to go outside and talk to Annie Rose on the swing. He'd looked forward to that part of the day from the time he got up in the morning. The concert had been wonderful and it was so nice to come home to happy kids and routine. And tonight of all nights, he should go talk to her, tell her again how much he appreciated the way she had turned his life around for the better in a week.

But hugging her had felt strange, again as if he was disrespecting Holly. Maybe it was because he was breaking both of the first rules he'd set up when he decided he could run a ranch and raise two girls all alone. He stood up slowly and made it halfway down the staircase before he stopped. He went to the kitchen to get a couple of bottles of beer and found her sitting at the kitchen table, her knees drawn up under her chin, a pot of hot tea in front of her.

"It's steeping. It'll be ready in one more minute if you want a cup," she said.

"No swing tonight?" he asked.

"Nope. My friend isn't calling my name tonight, so I decided to have a cup of tea."

"Mosquitoes?"

She checked the clock and poured tea into her cup. "Get a cup if you want some."

He pulled one from the cabinet and set it on the table. She filled it and handed it to him.

"Have a seat and relax," she said. "And it's not the mosquitoes."

"Then what is it?" he asked.

"It's this thing between us. The thing that we've been sidestepping all around rather than talking about it."

He set his cup on the bar and hiked a hip on a stool. "Kind of hard to talk about something that neither of us can even define."

Annie Rose stood up, walked over to him, wrapped her arms around his neck, rolled up on her toes, and kissed him hard right on the lips. It didn't feel strange and there was nothing but a tingling feeling in the pit of his stomach when she pulled away.

"Now we've talked about it," she said. "Good night, Mason. See you at breakfast."

"Good night, Annie Rose," he said.

When he heard her door shut, he said, "Well, I'll be damned. She sure don't kiss like Holly did. Not better. Not worse. Just a hell of a lot different. And I like the way she talks about things."

Chapter 8

ANNIE ROSE HAD NEVER SHOPPED SO FAST AND FURIOUS in her entire life. Flutters danced in her gut like they had the night before when she closed the door to her apartment. The old Annie Rose, the one who trusted her own judgment, had kissed Mason and enjoyed it immensely. But then that morning at breakfast he'd acted like it had never happened, and now she wondered if she'd made a colossal mistake by breaking every rule she'd set up for herself after the Nicky episode in her life.

She didn't have time to analyze and pick apart every nanosecond of the impulsive kiss. She had to shop for something to wear to the ranch party. The girls were dashing from one thing to another, and her head swam trying to make decisions.

Finally, she bought two maxi dresses in bright summer colors at the little eclectic dress shop, and she let the girls each pick out a bracelet to wear to the picnic. She was about to pay out when she saw a gorgeous soft, light blue shawl that would work to tie around either dress for church. The owner of the shop told her how to get to the Dollar Store so she could purchase hair spray, a curling iron, and a few makeup items. She and the girls dashed through the store in less than twenty minutes, where Lily picked out a new lipstick for Annie Rose and Gabby picked out just the right hair spray.

"Next year it's at our ranch and we'll be ten years old

and Daddy says that for our tenth birthday we can get our ears pierced," Lily said as Annie Rose drove back toward the ranch.

"Oh, no!" Gabby gasped.

"What? It won't hurt but only for a minute. Kenna got hers done last year," Lily said.

"No, I'm not afraid of needles. You are, but I'm not. I remembered that Damian is going to the picnic and I almost drowned him last week. He's going to be out to get even, and he called you a liar, so I might have to whup him," Gabby said.

"You know what Daddy says. Ladies don't throw the first punch. But if he hits one of us, you can bet your Texas ass we will finish the job," Lily said.

Annie Rose didn't think those were the exact words that Mason used, but she had to agree with Lily. That little red-haired shit would do well to cut his pride losses and stay away from her girls or she might help them finish the job.

—◦◦◦—

Mason had never had to wait on the twins before. They usually whined at him to hurry up, but that morning they were closeted in the nanny's apartment with Annie Rose and it was already five minutes past eleven.

The foyer held three pieces of furniture. A mirror hung above a semiround table that caught everything from mail to car keys. All that had been pushed aside that morning and a boxed cheesecake waited to be taken to the picnic.

Farther down beside his office door was an antique hall tree with hats on every hook, boots lined up on both sides and sitting on the bench seat, and two pairs of pink flip-flops in front of it.

In between the two was an old wingback chair that was seldom used for anything except another catchall. He pushed a plush throw and a jump rope to one side and sat down to wait. Brad Paisley's old song about waiting on a woman came to mind and put a grin on his face. Brad talked about one woman; Mason had three and for the first time he could possibly be late to the picnic.

He heard the door open, and there they were. If he would've had to speak or drop dead, it would have been lights-out. His mouth felt like he'd packed it with alum and his eyes grew dry from not blinking.

Shit! Shit! Shit! And dammit, too!

She wore a long, flowing dress with splashes of light yellow, green, and baby blue the exact same color as her eyes, and she'd done something with her hair that made it all soft and curly. By the end of the day she'd have a date for every Friday and Saturday night for the next ten years and all because he'd dragged his feet.

His eyes started at her hair and traveled slowly down to pale pink toenails peeking out from the ends of sandals. And then they started back up again, stopping a few seconds at the slight cleavage, and stopped dead at her lips.

"Too much?" she whispered. "Maybe my jeans and boots would be better."

"You are gorgeous," he managed to spit out hoarsely.

"And look at us," Lily said.

Clones of Annie Rose! They wore sundresses that they usually reserved for Sunday morning, white sandals with pink polish on their toenails, and their hair had been styled exactly like hers.

"You are both beautiful," he said.

"Smell us. Mama-Nanny let us use some of her perfume and her hair spray so we'd smell like her. What are we waiting for? Let's go and, Daddy, if Damian throws the first punch, he's toast," Lily said.

They ran out the front door in a gallop, long, skinny legs reminding him of newborn colts instead of princesses in their finery.

He held out his arm to Annie Rose and picked up the cheesecake with the other hand. "Don't let any of those other cowboys steal you today."

"Is that a pickup line, Mason Harper?" Even her voice sounded like the old Annie Rose, the one that had confidence and loved a good time.

"It might be. Is it working?"

"Maybe. But I don't think you have to worry about any of the other cowboys. They'd have to go through Lily and Gabby, and no one is that brave, not even if he wears size-thirteen cowboy boots and his cowboy hat would hold ten gallons of water," she said.

"They sure look pretty today. You've done wonders with them. Even that little shit Damian might be so awestruck, he'll forget to be a mean little bastard."

Annie Rose looped her arm in his. "I do believe his mama and daddy are married. But I could agree with you if you called him a sumbitch."

A deep chuckle came out of Mason's chest. "His mama is that. Sometimes I feel sorry for poor old Frank."

"Amen," she said.

"Daddy! We're going to be late, and Kenna is already there. She called fifteen minutes ago," Lily hollered from the pickup window.

"And it's hot in here," Gabby said right behind her.

"Far be it from me to keep the two tomboy princesses from their friend," he said.

"Or to cause them to sweat off their lip gloss," Annie Rose whispered. Her arm in his made him feel like he was ten feet tall and wore size-fifteen cowboy boots.

If it walked like a duck, it was a duck. If it meowed like O'Malley, it was a cat. If it got into everything like a mischievous goat, it was probably Djali and Jeb. So if it felt like a date, then why wasn't it?

Because, her inner voice said, *you are not on a date even though you flat-out laid a kiss on him last night just to see how it would feel.*

She didn't feel nearly as spicy when she got into the truck and Mason shut the door behind her. Gabby reached over the seat and patted her on the shoulder. "Don't be nervous, Mama-Nanny. It's a big old ranch like we live on and you done already met some of the folks that will be there. Just remember the book we gave you about bein' a rancher, and you'll be all right. Doc Emerson and Damian's mama and a lot of them were at the birthday party."

She inhaled deeply and let it out slowly. Through the rearview mirror she could see Mason putting the cheesecake in the toolbox in the bed of the truck. He wore a green-and-yellow plaid, Western-cut, short-sleeved shirt that morning, brown boots, and a brown belt with a big silver buckle.

Everything that she liked in a man. Everything that Nicky Trahan was not. Lord, why couldn't she stop comparing Mason and Nicky? It was apples and oranges and could not be put in the same basket.

One minute her inner voice was lecturing her about liking Mason too much. The next it was fussing at her for thinking of Nicky. She wished it would pick a side and stick to it. Life could be so damn confusing!

It was the shortest ten-minute drive that Annie Rose had ever had in her entire life. It scarcely gave her heart time to settle down from the compliment Mason paid her and the way it felt to loop her arm in his. There sure wasn't time to get calmed down from the way his arm brushed accidentally against her breast when he opened the truck door for her and the masculine scent of his shaving lotion wafting through the truck when he reached across the seat and buckled her in.

Listening to the girls' lively chatter in the backseat about the story they were going to tell Kenna about the pesky goats took her mind off Mason for a few seconds at a time. It didn't last long, because every time she glanced across the console where his summer straw hat rested, the flutters in her stomach started up again.

The minute the truck came to a stop out in a pasture with dozens upon dozens of other vehicles, Kenna dragged the girls off toward a shade tree in the front yard. They quickly put their heads together to whisper about goats and their concert and whatever else little nine-year-old girls giggled about behind their hands. Dinah and Frank parked three trucks down, and a red-haired streak that Annie Rose recognized as Damian created a blur as he ran toward a group of little boys.

"Hey, Mason," Frank called out. "Did you bring your famous cheesecake?"

Mason held up a hand. "Stayed up all night making it. Dinah make potato salad?"

"Oh, yeah! Straight from the Walmart deli section." Frank laughed.

Dinah covered the distance from their truck to Mason's quickly, and Frank was right behind her, carrying a big container of potato salad.

"How does this work?" Annie Rose whispered to Mason.

"I'll take the cheesecake to the dessert table and come back for our lawn chairs," he said.

"How about I take the cheesecake and you take the lawn chairs right now? Something tells me I don't want to get too close to that woman. We may have a fight later if Damian hits one of our girls and it'll be easier to snatch her bald-headed if she's not my friend," Annie Rose said.

"They're wearing pretty dresses and have their hair all done up, so I'm hoping they'll act like ladies, but that might be too much to ask. Maybe they'll wait until another day to wipe up the dirt with Damian." His words came out of the side of his mouth as Dinah got closer and closer.

Our girls? Her inner voice yelled: *Since when are they our girls?*

She argued back: *Since I had to do nails and fingernails this morning and since I had to put up with pesky goats and since I could name dozens more things.*

Annie Rose put an end to the internal argument and flashed her brightest smile. "Good morning, Dinah. You look lovely today."

"So do you. So you've lasted a week. Gawd-almighty,

that will put a gold star on your resume at the Dallas office," Dinah said.

"Come on now!" Mason picked up four green webbed lawn chairs from the back of the truck. "Lily and Gabby aren't that bad. Hell, they aren't a bit worse than that red-haired demon of yours, Dinah."

Dinah tucked an errant strand of red hair behind her ear and nodded. "Don't you bring my son into this. At least the church house doesn't hold its breath when he walks through the doors on Sunday morning."

"If it could hoist itself off the foundation, it would run like hell when it sees him coming," Mason teased, but there was an icy edge to his voice.

Annie Rose fell into step beside Mason, cheesecake in her arms. Dinah was on the other side, keeping up as if she was a long-lost friend.

"He's a boy, for God's sake. You're raising girls. There's a difference, and your two girls make him look like a saint with a halo," Dinah said.

There were two long tables of desserts with women behind them cutting pies and cakes into slices or wedges. Dinah clapped her hands and everyone stopped talking.

"Folks, this is Annie Rose. She's the new nanny over at the Bois D'Arc Bend Ranch for those of y'all who didn't make it to the twins' birthday party last week," Dinah said loudly.

"She is not!" Lily yelled from across the yard. "She's not a nanny. She's our new mama, so don't you be calling her a plain old nanny."

Annie Rose nodded toward the women. "I'm pleased to be here today and to meet all of you. Maybe in a little while I'll even get names sorted out with faces. The girls call me Mama-Nanny. One of y'all is the lady of this ranch?"

A blond-haired, very pregnant lady raised a hand. "That would be me. I'm Natalie Allen, but I've only been the lady of the ranch since Christmas."

"Well, I want to thank you personally for hosting this. It's not easy, especially when it's hot summertime and you've got a baby due soon," Annie Rose said.

"Thank you for that. But I'm not due until October," Natalie said.

Annie Rose handed her the cheesecake. "Bless your heart!"

Natalie patted her round stomach. "It's twins. Came as a shock to us, since our son, Josh, will just be a year old when they're born. But we've got lots of help and we're excited about having twins. They're girls. I'm hoping they're blond-haired like Mason's girls."

"Maybe you can steal Annie Rose from Mason to be their nanny," Dinah whispered.

Gabby had left her friends and was standing right behind Dinah. "Ain't nobody stealing Mama-Nanny from us, but we know all about how to take care of twin girls and we'd love to take care of the babies for you."

Dinah rolled her eyes and headed toward the salad-and-casserole table.

Gabby threw her arms around Annie Rose's waist. "You aren't going to let Miz Natalie steal you, are you?"

Natalie laid a hand on Gabby's shoulder. "Darlin', I'd have to fight with the grandpa, great-grandpa, and foreman of this ranch to ever hire a babysitter, but I appreciate the offer. And another person might be able to steal a nanny, but never a mama, so you don't have a thing to worry about."

Annie Rose didn't need to turn around to know that Mason had walked up behind her. She had that antsy feeling that made her all jittery when he was near. Then he laced his fingers in hers and whoosh, heat traveled like a Texas wildfire from her toes to her cheeks. Where was one of those cardboard church fans when a woman needed it? And how in the devil had she gone from a candidate for that *Fear Factor* show on television to a blushing teenager in such a short time?

"How about a walkin' tour of the ranch before they ring the dinner bell?" he asked.

"If the girls want to go, I'd love to," she answered.

"We're going to sit on Kenna's blanket and tell her all about our concert. She can play the keyboard pretty good, so we're thinkin' about letting her join our band," Gabby said. "Besides, we don't want to walk through the pasture and ruin our toenails. So can we stay here, please, Daddy?"

"No fights. And that means no matter what," he said sternly.

"The boys are playin' hide-and-seek, and we don't want to play with them anyway. They don't play fair," Gabby said.

"Okay then. You're on the honor system," Mason told her.

--~~--

Mason opened the yard gate for Annie Rose, but he didn't let go of her hand. The sunlight sparkled like diamonds in her hair and her eyes were the exact same color as the sky. If he thought about it for a few seconds, he could still feel the kiss she'd laid on his lips the night before, and it sent a shot of warmth, not unlike Jack Daniel's through his body. It was strange how that one minute he felt so guilty for having such feelings for a woman other than Holly, and the next he wanted to make out with her like a high-school boy out on a dirt road with his girlfriend.

"What is this all about, Mason?" Annie Rose chewed at her bottom lip. ·

Holly had done that, and it brought him up short, but he wasn't willing to turn around and go back to the crowd.

"It's about me bringing a pretty woman to the picnic for the first time since Holly died, and there being lots and lots of talk. It's about getting away and giving the women time to gossip and the men time to be jealous."

"No pressure there, huh?" She smiled.

Mason squeezed her hand gently and pointed with the other one. "We can talk about something else so the pressure won't bother you. That is the chicken pen where I understand Natalie killed a snake. And she also put a coyote to rest when it threatened some puppies. Her husband is Lucas. His father is Jack and his grandfather is Henry. Their foreman is Wyatt, and they've all bragged about how good she is with her pink pistol."

"Pink Pistol? I thought that was a store owned by Miranda Lambert in Oklahoma."

"It is, but Natalie owns a real one. You'll like her when you get to know her. Lucas is head over heels in love with her," Mason said.

"Is she from around here?" Annie Rose asked.

He could feel the tension leaving her body as her hand relaxed in his.

"No, from out in the Panhandle. They met online through a mutual friend and it was an Internet relationship to start with. Funny thing is that Lucas used to bitch and moan about all that Internet shit. It came right back around and bit him square on the ass."

Annie Rose wanted to ask another question, but she couldn't think straight. One kiss had set her hormones into overdrive, and she wasn't even sure how to handle that gear anymore. She wasn't a teenager. Hell, she wasn't even a twenty-six-year-old woman who trusted a charming man and then suffered the consequences. She was looking thirty square in the eye and should know better.

He pulled her into a big hay barn and pointed to the ladder leading up to the loft. "Best way to see a ranch is through the doors in a hayloft," he said.

She planted a foot on the bottom rung and scampered up the ladder, unhindered by the dress length. Coming back down would pose more of a problem and she'd have to be careful not to get tangled up in the flowing material around her ankles.

He followed her. "You do that like you've done it before."

"It ain't my first rodeo or my first hayloft," she said.

It was clean except for a couple of small rectangular bales sitting far enough back from the doors to serve as chairs. She sat down and gazed out over rolling hills, mesquite, scrub oak, cattle, and even a working oil well. Memories of a barn in Thicket, Texas, came flooding back to her mind.

There was a scene of her mother looking for her, calling out her name frantically when she was about five years old. She remembered having a straw stem in her mouth, just like her father, and watching her mother for several minutes before she inched over to the edge and hollered at her.

She learned that she didn't like heights that day when she got dizzy and fell out of the window into a wagon-load of loose hay and lost her breath.

She'd lost her virginity in a hayloft. She was seventeen and he was eighteen. He worked for her father that summer and she'd fancied herself in love. Then summer ended and he went away to college somewhere in Arkansas.

The hayloft was where she went to cry over her mother's death and shed tears again over selling the ranch. But through it all she'd never, not one time, spent even one minute in a hayloft with Nicky Trahan.

"You sure are quiet." Mason sat down beside her.

"I was thinking about what stories these walls could tell if they could talk," she said.

"Probably better for Lucas that they can't." Mason chuckled.

One hand went around her shoulders and the other one tipped her chin up. For several seconds he lost himself in her blue eyes and then his lips found hers in a lingering kiss and both her arms went instinctively around his neck.

"I've wanted to do that all morning," he said.

"I've wanted you to do that all morning," she whispered. "I guess we don't need to talk about this thing anymore now."

"I'm ready to do lots of things, Annie Rose. Talk is not anywhere on the list."

He pushed her hair back and buried his face in the curve where neck met shoulder and strung kisses all the way to the cleavage showing above the neckline of the dress. One hand slid from her knee up to the top of her thigh and all she could think was *please don't stop*.

She moved a hand from around his neck to his broad chest and unfastened two snaps so she could inch inside to feel skin. Fine dark chest hair tickled the sensitive skin on her fingertips. She was inching her way down to where the hair traveled beneath his belt buckle when he groaned.

Good God Almighty! She had to get ahold of herself fast.

She had been about to undo his belt and go exploring. She'd known him less than a week and only found her lost confidence the night before. As fast as the relationship with Nicky had been, she'd known him longer than that before she fell into bed with him. She sat up so fast that it gave her a head rush.

"Whoa, hoss." She grabbed her head with both hands.

"What?" Mason asked hoarsely.

"We've got a picnic to get back to," she said.

"I'll be the one with a smile on my face all afternoon."

"I'll be the one with a blush," she said.

She had a worse case of nerves than the night she said good-bye to her virginity, but her voice came out strong and determined. That night she'd thought she knew everything and was more than ready to enter into the world of sexual adulthood. Now she wasn't nearly so sure about anything, except that Mason had sure turned her life around in a short time.

He brushed a sweet kiss across her lips and stood up. "After you, m'lady."

She turned around backwards and started down the ladder, amazed that her weak knees were working properly. A scampering noise off to her right caused her to stumble, but she quickly righted herself.

"What?" he whispered.

"Probably a wild mama cat," she mumbled.

His long legs and butt followed her. A very nice butt indeed, all packed down into those tight jeans. She had to keep her mind on the ladder or she would fall backwards and then she'd be explaining a sprained ankle or broken wrist to everyone at the picnic.

Mason pulled the tab on a can of beer and sat down beside Lucas Allen. Colton Nelson was on his other side with Greg Adams beside him. His friends surrounded him, but he kept a close watch on Annie Rose in his peripheral vision. She'd opened up a whole new world for him and he still wasn't sure that he was ready for it.

"So you finally find someone who can tolerate Lily and Gabby?" Lucas asked.

"Finally found someone that they can tolerate," Mason answered.

He was ready to rescue Annie Rose if he felt that she was getting swamped by questions and gossip. But she seemed to be holding her own, and he'd heard her laughter more than once.

"You're shittin' me," Colton said. "They like a nanny. I thought they lived to make a nanny miserable, so you'd fire her."

"Ahhh, they want a mama, not a nanny," Greg said. "Gabby told me that Annie Rose is not a nanny but she's their new mama and that they found her on your porch in a wedding dress on their birthday last week. Sorry we missed all the fun, but Emily and I were in Dallas for the weekend."

"Wedding dress?" Lucas's eyebrows shot up.

"So you got a nanny and they got a mama and they are being good? Don't tell me there's no more miracles in the world," Colton said.

The words were barely out of his mouth when Natalie rang the dinner bell and asked Henry, Lucas's grandfather, to say grace.

Henry removed his hat and waited for the noise to die down before he bowed his head. "Dear Lord, thank you for this beautiful day for our picnic. It's good to gather with friends who raise cattle and ranch like we all do. Lord, we're glad that we've got friends when the big corporations are looking to take over the little guys' ranches. And here on our ranch we're right glad that we're seeing the next generation coming on. We're thankful for Josh and for the prospect of new baby girls. Bless this food and the hands that fixed it all up for us. Amen."

He settled his hat back on his head and said, "Now let's eat before the food gets cold and the women get mad at me for prayin' too long."

Mason hadn't made a step toward the food table when movement over to his left took his attention. Before he could even get turned to look that way, Annie Rose ran past him in a flash of bright colors and flowing blond hair. Dinah was right behind her with Frank coming in a close third. He dropped his beer and beat all of them to the dog pile of kids on Kenna's blanket.

Frank got ahold of Kenna, but she managed to kick him in the shins before he could drag her backwards and then she was right in the middle of the fight again. He went after her while Dinah tried to dig her way through little girls to get her squealing red-haired son out of the swinging fists, but she wasn't having much luck.

Annie Rose finally got a firm grip on Lily's ear and one on Gabby's. She brought them up, but it wasn't easy because they kept kicking and screaming that they were going to pull every one of the hairs off his head and then they were going to put soap in his mouth.

Mason wondered what in the hell Damian said that was so vile that Lily, of all people, would put soap in his mouth. He waded into the melee and looped an arm around Gabby's waist and one around Lily's, brought them up to waist level like two fighting roosters, and whispered loudly, "That is enough. You are ruining Annie Rose's first time to meet all these people. And you gave me your word you would be good."

Kenna had a firm hold on Damian's hair and it took every bit of Frank's power to pull her free. Damian sat up, digging at his streaming eyes and bawling like a lost calf.

"They attacked me. I sat down on their quilt, and they started beating me up," he sobbed.

Dinah wrapped her arms around him and shot daggers at the three girls. By that time, Doc Emerson had joined the adults around the quilt and Frank set Kenna down. Mason thought it was safe enough that he followed Doc's lead and put his girls' feet on the ground.

Kenna narrowed her eyes and in an instant was on top of Damian again, knocking Dinah backwards in the process. "You're a lyin' sumbitch, Damian Miller. We didn't do nothing, but if you're going to accuse us, then we'll beat the shit out of you and take our punishment for doing it."

Doc grabbed Kenna's arm and jerked her backwards. "That's enough fightin' and enough cussin' for one day."

Kenna broke free again, and all three girls piled on Damian. Dinah's hands went to her hips and she yelled at Frank.

"Can't you big men do anything? They're going to kill my son. They're demons, every one of them," she screamed.

Annie Rose let out a shrill whistle and everything went dead still and quiet. Damian ran to his father and hid behind his skinny legs. Lily and Gabby clenched their fists, stood up, and glared at him. Kenna crossed her arms over her chest.

"Grandpa, he called their Mama-Nanny a slut. He said he saw her and Mason up in the hayloft kissing, and she wasn't a nanny, she was a slut," Kenna tattled.

"Did not!" Damian yelled.

"Did too!" the twins said in unison.

"Where did you hear such language?" Frank asked.

"Mama said it last night. She said that Mason was bringing his slut to the picnic today and that he was lyin' about her being a nanny, that she was his slut and that's something real bad," Damian whined.

Annie Rose burst into laughter that echoed off the mesquite bushes and came back around like a boomerang. The folks in the yard didn't pay a bit of attention to what was going on out near the parked vehicles. Evidently fights among a bunch of kids occurred often.

Mason finally gave way and guffawed with her.

Doc Emerson shook his head. "Funny how amnesia works. You are remembering something, aren't you?"

"Yes, Doc, I've remembered almost everything, but that's not why I'm laughing." She bent forward and dried her eyes on her dress tail. "I was wondering if every woman who kisses a man is a slut. If so, there are probably a whole lot of them here today."

Dinah stuck her nose in the air, grabbed her son by the arm, and pulled him toward the truck. "Come on, Frank. We're going home. I don't have to stay here and be insulted like this."

"No one insulted you. You insulted Annie Rose," Doc said.

"I'm going home and you are coming with me, Frank."

Frank shrugged. "Sorry about all this. You know how she is."

"Don't worry about it," Annie Rose said. "But you two…" Her eyes went to Lily and Gabby.

"He threw the first punch," Kenna said quickly. "Grandpa, you always told me that I can't start a fight, but if someone else does then I can whip the shit out of them."

Doc pushed his glasses back up on his nose. "Guess I did say them exact words, but you aren't supposed to repeat what I say, Kenna."

"He hit Kenna and we had to help her," Lily said.

"And then he kicked Lily and said she was a slut too.

What is a slut, Mama-Nanny?" Gabby asked. "Is that like a hooker?"

"Yes, it is," Annie Rose answered.

"Well, then I'm not sorry. If I get punished then it'll be worth every bit of it. He's a lyin' little sumbitch. I'm not a hooker. I'm a country star," Lily said stoically.

"Let's go have some dinner, and there will be no more fighting today. If someone says something you don't like, you come tell me," Mason said. Holly would like it that Annie Rose laughed about the whole thing and made Dinah so mad that she left. Holly never did like that woman.

"Yes, ma'am. I'm sorry I cussed. Now I'm hungry. Come on, Kenna, let's go get some ribs," Lily said.

Off they went. Three little girls with hair ribbons all tangled up in their hair, dresses wrinkled, and grass stains on their elbows and knees.

Doc Emerson patted Annie Rose on the shoulder. "Don't worry about it, honey. If the Harper kids and my granddaughter don't get into trouble at least once at any gathering, the folks would think the kids were terminally ill. Have you begun remembering how and why you got on that porch last week?"

"Yes, sir. Most of it is clear as a bell now," she said.

"That's good."

He ambled off toward the food tables, leaving Annie Rose and Mason alone under the shade tree with a rumpled quilt at their feet.

"Why did you laugh?" Mason asked.

"It was funny as hell," she whispered. "I've never had anyone take up for my honor like that before."

"It's my biggest fear that one of the girls will grow up

and date him. I probably should go on and wring his neck now. Save everyone a lot of trouble," Mason growled.

"He was only repeating what he heard," Annie Rose said.

"His mama's sorry neck should be wrung too," Mason said as he tucked her small hand into his.

"My mama said the more you stir a pile of cow shit, the worse it smells. I knew Dinah wasn't going to be my friend from the first time she talked to me, so it's no big loss. It's her privilege to say or think whatever she wants. It's mine to ignore her. But I do like Natalie. Now let's go have some dinner. If we don't hurry, those three girls are liable to eat all the ribs."

Chapter 9

ANNIE ROSE WAS SO PROUD OF HER GIRLS THAT MORN-
ing that her heart swelled with pride. They didn't do
anything spectacular, like sing for the whole church,
but Lily and Gabby were good. They sat there like little
angels, one on either side of Annie Rose through the
whole service. Their singing was lovely. They bowed
their heads for prayers and didn't even fidget. They listened to the sermon, which was more than Annie Rose
did. She was almighty glad that a child separated her
from Mason. If she was plastered up against Mason,
keeping her X-rated thoughts from setting the church on
fire would have been impossible.

Mason's eyes never left the podium, but he stretched,
slung his arm around Gabby, and his fingertips brushed
against Annie Rose's bare arm. She wished again for
one of those old-fashioned cardboard fans. The air-
conditioning in the church couldn't keep up with the
heat flowing from his hand through her body.

The preacher finally wound down his sermon. From
the bits and pieces that Annie Rose caught in her fu-
tile attempt to keep her eyes and mind off Mason, she
thought that he'd sermonized about not casting stones at
glass houses. She wondered if Dinah had a big rock in
her fancy purse, hoping for the opportunity to throw it
at Annie Rose.

The closing amen was finally said. The noise level

in the little country church went from an occasional muffled cough to rock-concert loud in seconds. The girls skipped off to talk to Kenna. Annie Rose quickly scanned the church to see exactly where Damian was. She breathed a sigh of relief when she finally located him leaving with his parents.

Mason introduced her to the few people she hadn't met either at the birthday party or the ranch party the day before. She smiled, shook hands, greeted each one, and still kept one wary eye on those three girls over beside the piano. The glitter in their eyes when they came running with Kenna in the lead said they were planning something.

"Daddy, please, please can we go home with Kenna? Doc says it's all right with him and Miz Doc and we need to go practice our band stuff and…"

Gabby picked up when Lily stopped to catch her breath. "And Doc says he'll take us to the Pizza Hut to eat, and we can play and sing after that."

Doc Emerson laid a hand on Mason's shoulder. "We'd love to have the twins for the rest of the day. Kenna gets lonely with us old far…" He chuckled and didn't finish the word. "We'll have them home in time for bed. I thought we'd take them to that new Disney movie playing up in Sherman after they get their band practice done. It's a late-afternoon matinee, and afterwards we'll have a KFC picnic at the park."

"If you are sure," Mason said.

"I've got your cell phone number if there's a problem, and I *am* a doctor." He chuckled again.

Mason clapped a hand on his shoulder. "I trust you, Doc. But after an afternoon with all three of those girls, you might need to call a doctor for yourself."

"If it gets too bad, I'll take a nap and trust the wife to hold down the fort," Doc said.

Kenna grabbed Lily's hand with her right one and Gabby's with her left and off they went in a run down the aisle next to the wall. After only a week, Annie Rose could read their little minds. If they could get to Doc's van and close the doors, then the adults wouldn't change their minds.

Then it hit her!

She and Mason would be alone for the whole afternoon and evening.

———

Mason picked up Annie Rose's hand and looped it through his crooked arm. "Guess that means we get to have dinner wherever we want and not at McDonald's today. What's your fancy?"

"We could go home and I could cook," she said.

He took a couple of steps forward, following the crowd toward the door where the preacher shook hands with everyone as they left. "I love your cooking, but the Bible says that I'm supposed to take you out to dinner on Sunday."

Annie Rose's big blue eyes locked with his and he felt as if he was drowning. "I'm racking my brain to remember a verse that says you should take me out for Sunday dinner."

"Blessed are they who hunger and thirst after righteousness," he quipped. "You've been to church and I know you are hungry."

"But the blessing should be for the hunger and thirst, not for fried catfish," she said.

"All a matter of interpretation. So catfish, huh?" he asked.

"I was making a statement."

"I like catfish and I know a good place to get it in Denison. Ever heard of Huck's?"

"As in Finn?" she asked.

"Yes, ma'am. Sound good?"

"Do we eat it floating down the river on a raft?" she asked.

He patted her hand. It was smaller than Holly's had been, but then Holly had been a tall woman, a basketball player in high school and college and she'd been—he bit the inside of his lip and shook his head. He should not compare Annie Rose and Holly... they were two entirely different women.

"What about a raft?" he asked.

"Can we eat catfish while floating down the Red River on a raft?" she asked.

"No, but we can eat the catfish first and then we'll float down the river. I've got a couple of big tractor-sized inner tubes. Sun is out, and it's plenty hot," he said.

"I didn't bring a bathing suit, but it is tempting. I haven't done that in years."

"That's no excuse." He hadn't seen a woman blush that crimson in years and years. "I don't think there's a biblical blessing for skinny-dippin' thoughts, but it sure puts a pretty picture inside my head, especially if we share an inner tube."

"I was not... well, shit! It's not right to lie in church, and we aren't outside yet. I was thinking about skinny-dippin' since I don't own a bathing suit, and now you made me use a bad word too."

He leaned down and whispered in her ear, "And I bet you didn't listen to the whole sermon either, did you?"

She shook her head. "Did you?"

He grinned. "No, ma'am. My mind was on you."

Just exactly how erotic and exciting had he let his wanderings go? She'd bet that her imagination had been a hell of a lot hotter than his had been. There was no way she looked better than he did in those creased jeans, that crisp plaid shirt, and those polished boots.

"Did you think about a certain hayloft?" he asked.

"Did you?" she asked.

"Guilty as charged."

"I'd love to float down the river on inner tubes if you'll let me have ten minutes to find a bathing suit," she said, trying to banish all crazy thoughts of skinny-dippin' from her mind.

"Make it the darkest one in the store, and you've got it," he said.

"Why the darkest one in the store? Maybe I want a pure white one."

"You'll understand when you see the Red River. It's not a pretty little bubbling stream of clear water. And pick up a gallon of sunblock while you are in the store, because your fair skin won't take the afternoon heat."

Before she could answer, they'd made it to the church doors and the preacher stuck out his hand. "Good mornin', Miz Annie Rose. We met at the picnic yesterday. I'm Lucas's grandpa. I don't usually preach at this church, but the minister wanted to take his family on a vacation, so I volunteered to help out."

She pulled her arm free from Mason's arm and shook hands with him. "It was a lovely picnic."

"Yes, it was. Did you meet my great-grandson, Josh? He's the king of the ranch."

Mason reached for the preacher's hand when he dropped Annie Rose's. "Yes, he is, Henry. But when those twin girls come along, he'll have some competition."

Henry's smile erased a multitude of wrinkles. "We'll spoil them all when they get here. We're hopin' for a dozen or more, but don't tell Natalie. We're workin' on easin' her into the idea."

Mason let the next people in line move up to shake hands with Henry and he ushered Annie Rose outside with a hand on the small of her back. He opened the truck door for her, reached across her lap and fastened the seat belt, brushed a quick kiss on the tip of her nose, and whistled all the way around the front to the driver's side.

Floating down the river might not be a real, official, honest-to-God date, but it sure felt like something more than a way to pass off an afternoon with no girls underfoot.

"We'll go to the house first. I'll load up the inner tubes and grab a few things. Then we'll go to Huck's for the best catfish you've ever eaten." He talked as he backed the truck out of the church parking lot and headed south toward Whitewright. A picture of her in a bathing suit of any kind flashed through his mind and put a big grin on his face.

"And then I can buy a bathing suit and a gallon of sunblock, right?" she asked.

His quick scan up and down her body sent shivers from hair to toenails.

"Maybe only a little bitty bikini and only a small tube of sunblock, then it will take longer for me to smooth it out over all that pretty white skin." His drawl was just shy of seductive.

"Is that one of your pickup lines?"

"Never know. It might be my best one ever if it's working."

"We'll see after you put the sunblock on my back," she teased.

Annie Rose stopped in the foyer and wrapped her arms around herself. The chill had nothing to do with the air-conditioning vent right above her and everything to do with the doubts flooding through her mind. What in the hell did she think she was doing? She should ask Mason to drive her to the nearest car dealership, buy the oldest model on the lot, and leave while the girls were away. Leaving without saying good-bye would be the coward's way out, but a good clean cut would be best for everyone.

He took the steps two at a time, calling out over his shoulder that he'd have his things thrown into a bag and be back in five minutes. She went straight for her quarters, crammed what would fit into her suitcase, and left the rest in the closet. Money, driver's license, insurance verification on a vehicle that was sitting at the bottom of a pond, and enough clothing to get her to the next stop—that's all a woman on the run needed.

She'd checked the weather that morning on the television before they'd left for church, but she'd forgotten to turn it off in her haste to get the girls' hair all done. The picture now filling the screen stopped her dead in her tracks. There was Nicky at his finest, all tanned, a brilliant smile showing perfectly even white teeth, dark hair brushed back, and brown eyes as evil as they'd always been.

She quickly turned up the volume. Hopefully, he was announcing his engagement to the woman that he'd come to see at the bridal fair.

"In a tragic accident this morning, Nicholas Trahan, his girlfriend, Candy James, and two other unnamed people were killed in a plane crash. Trahan was flying from the Texas Panhandle to southern Louisiana when his plane crashed into a field in Beaumont, Texas. All four people in the plane were pronounced dead at the scene. Names of the other couple have been held pending notification of relatives."

Annie Rose listened to the news on two different stations before Mason rapped lightly on the door.

"Hey, are you about ready?"

"Give me one more minute." Her voice sounded strange and tense even in her own ears.

She shoved the suitcase back into the closet and opened the door to find him right outside, his face not six inches from hers. He laid his hands on her shoulders and pulled her close to his chest.

"My God, Annie Rose. Are you okay? You look like you saw a ghost."

"I did. I'll tell you about it on the way to the restaurant," she said.

His arm around her shoulder as they left the house was all that kept her upright. The world seemed to be listing off to the left about fifteen to twenty degrees.

"Okay, now about this ghost," Mason said when he was buckled into his seat.

"Nicky Trahan was killed this morning in a plane crash down by Beaumont," she said. "I saw it on the news."

"So your troubles are over, right?" Mason started the engine and drove down the lane toward the road. "Want me to haul your car up out of the pond now?"

She shook her head. "No, I can't believe that it's over and that I don't have to run anymore. I can live a normal life without looking over my shoulder."

Mason reached across the console and laced his fingers in hers. "Yes, you can. Please don't tell me you're leaving. The girls love you, and I want you to stay."

She could go anywhere, even back to Beaumont to work as a nurse again, but the thought of leaving Lily and Gabby put a lump in her throat that she couldn't swallow down. She'd been crazy to think that she could pick up her suitcase, buy a used car, and drive away, never to see those two little faces again.

"Of course, I'll stay until June is over. I gave my word for a month at a time," she said.

"Your color is coming back. A catfish dinner and a long float down the river will be good for you."

She snapped her fingers. "Just like that, it's over. It's surreal."

He squeezed her hand. "Understandable. Tell me again how long ago that you disappeared."

"Two years."

"It'll take a while to get the jumpiness out of your body, but one day you'll wake up and it'll all be gone."

"How do you know?"

The smile was forced, but he got credit for trying. "Today is not a good time to talk about that."

"Why? We're talking about Nicky. Let's hang everything out on the clothesline."

He chuckled. "That sounded so much like my grandmother that it's not even funny."

"It was one of my mother's favorite sayings. We'd hang out whatever was bugging us on the virtual clothesline and then we'd forget it. Mama was in her forties when she and Daddy adopted me, so it was like being raised by grandparents."

"Little old to be taking on raisin' a kid," he said.

She nodded slowly. "The story Mama told me when I got old enough to ask was that her cousin in Lafayette knew a teenage girl who'd gotten pregnant. Boyfriend had joined the Army and was coming home to marry her, but he was killed. The girl decided to give the baby up for adoption, and Mama's cousin convinced her to let Mama and Daddy have me. So they paid the hospital bills and the teenager signed over her rights to them with the understanding that someday, when she was ready, she could come see me. Later, when I was about five years old, they got word that she had joined the Army and was killed in Iraq. And I'm rambling again."

"You want to go to Nicky's funeral for closure?"

She jerked her head around to stare at Mason. He looked normal. He hadn't grown two heads, and there weren't alien tendrils coming out of his head. So why did he ask a damn fool question like that?

"You'd be sure that it was over if you saw the casket going into the ground," he said.

"Hell, no! I do not want to go anywhere near him or his family."

"Well, that's definite enough."

He turned off the highway and parked in a crowded lot next to a building with a big sign on the front announcing that it was Huck's. Sunday-afternoon crowds usually marked the best places to eat, and her mouth watered at the thought of good fried catfish and maybe some decent hush puppies on the side.

"Table for two for Mason Harper," he told the hostess.

"Right this way, sir," she said.

"You made reservations?" Annie Rose asked.

"We'd have been waiting in line for an hour if I hadn't. I called when we were at the house. I haven't been tubing down the river since the girls were born. I don't want to waste time waiting to eat when we could be enjoying the sun and water," he answered.

The hostess seated them in a booth and handed them menus. "Your waitress will be Lori. She'll be with you in a moment. Could I get you something to drink?"

"Sweet tea," Mason said.

"I'll have the same," Annie Rose said.

She nodded and rushed off to seat a family of four who also had reservations.

"Now it's your time to hang things on the clothesline," Annie Rose said.

"Guess it is," Mason nodded. "The first time I kissed a woman after Holly was gone I felt guilty. The second time not so much. It got easier until you came into the picture. You remind me of her. Not in looks, but in actions. The way you hold a spoon. The way you walk, but believe me, I don't think about Holly when I kiss you. Then it's just me and you and the world disappears. It's the first time I've felt like that in a long time. And I don't know how to handle it, Annie Rose. I want to move on, but I feel guilty doing it."

Annie Rose picked up the menu and hid behind it, trying desperately to sort out her own feelings. Nicky was dead. She'd only known Mason a week, but if the time was factored in, it had been twenty-four hours a day, seven days a week, which meant if she'd been dating him, this could be about the tenth date.

Lord, what am I doing? I should be dancing a jig in a pig trough that I'm free at last, not thinking about a relationship.

"And for you, ma'am?" the waitress asked.

"How big is a full order?" Annie Rose asked.

"It's huge," Mason answered. "I get half an order."

"Then that's what I'll have. Half order of catfish. French fries and coleslaw. And could I get an extra order of hush puppies?"

"Yes, ma'am. Appetizers?"

Annie Rose looked over the top of her menu at Mason.

"I ordered a combination platter to munch on before the food gets here."

"Can we share?" she asked.

"Oh, yeah." He grinned.

Why did he have to be so nice? One big, hellacious fight where he told her that she was a crazy bitch would make leaving so much easier.

The waitress arrived with a tray in her hand. She set one glass of tea in front of Annie Rose and took half a step toward the other side of the booth, stumbled on her shoelace, and dumped the whole glass on the table. Annie Rose popped up in the booth like a preacher about to deliver a Sunday-morning sermon. Mason scrambled to the other end but still got a few drops on his shirt before he joined Annie Rose, standing up with a hip propped on the back of the tall booth seat.

The mortified little waitress turned as red as her hair, apologized profusely, and saturated two napkins before she finally covered her face and ran to the kitchen. The manager came out with a mop and a thick towel, quickly cleaned up the mess, and apologized again.

"We will definitely make this right on your ticket," he said softly.

The restaurant had gone as quiet as a funeral and all eyes were on Annie Rose, standing up, holding her dress tail up above her knees. Mason had a brilliant grin plastered on his face, and his green eyes twinkled. A man who didn't get angry at an incident like that was well worth trusting, even if she had to help him get past his guilt issues.

"Yes, we'll gather at the river, the beautiful, the beautiful river," she singsonged.

A deep chuckle came from the far corner and Henry stood up in his chair and picked up where she'd left off. "With its crystal tide forever... flowing by the throne of God."

Instantly the whole restaurant turned into a mob singing the old hymn with others bringing their voices to the mix. Annie Rose caught Mason's eye on the last verse as they sang together, "Soon we'll reach silver river... soon our happy hearts will quiver with the melody of peace."

Henry led the applause when the last note died and everyone, including Annie Rose and Mason, sat down. He reached across the squeaky-clean table and covered her hand with his.

"Probably a good thing that Nicky is gone," he said softly.

She raised an eyebrow.

"I saw at least a dozen phones filming the singing."

Her eyes popped wide open so fast and furious that it gave her a pain right in the middle of her forehead. "I don't know why I even started that. All those people were staring, and it was funny as hell. I've never been on a date and wound up standing in the booth."

It was his turn to raise an eyebrow.

"Oops! Is this not a date?" she asked.

His smile lit up the whole noisy restaurant. "My pickup line worked."

She pulled her hand free and the red-haired waitress carefully set two more glasses of sweet tea on the table. "I'm so sorry, but I could hug you for the way you handled that. You could have gotten me fired."

"Mistakes happen," Annie Rose said.

"Well, you are a blessing and I'll never forget you."

"I agree with what she said," Mason whispered.

Chapter 10

GETTING UNDRESSED AND INTO A BATHING SUIT IN THE backseat of a pickup truck was no easy feat, but in minutes Annie Rose was wearing a cute little neon blue-and-black polka-dotted, two-piece suit that looked like it came right out of *I Love Lucy*. All she needed was one of those turban swim caps, and she'd be thrown back fifty years in time.

She carefully wrapped her underwear inside the dress, shoved it into the plastic bag that her swimsuit came in, and stowed it in the backseat of the club-cab truck. She slipped a pair of cheap rubber flip-flops on her feet and stepped out of the truck into blistering hot sunshine.

Mason's face lit up in a brilliant smile. "Oh, yes, you certainly do need sunblock."

"Are you saying that I'm not a tanned beauty?"

"No, ma'am, I'm saying that you are not tanned. Darlin', anyone that says you are not a beauty is stone-cold blind or dumber than a box of rocks."

"You are a charmer, Mason Harper. I bought a big tube of sunblock. Will you please do my back and then I'll do yours? I reckon we can both get to the other parts just fine."

His sigh was heavy, but the grin didn't fade. "I guess the day can't be absolutely perfect or else we wouldn't believe it was true."

She handed the sunblock to him, turned around, and shut her eyes to enjoy every second of his hands on her bare skin.

"I'd say that the sweet tea incident already fixed that perfect issue," she said.

His hands started at her neck, smoothed the cream down over her shoulders, and then traveled down her back, reaching under the strap of the bra top and on down to the waistband of the bottoms. She had to remind herself to breathe in through her nose and out through her mouth or she would have gotten light-headed.

She could testify, with her right hand raised up to heaven, that the swoon had not died with the ending of the Civil War, and it was still a very, very real word and should have a place of honor right there on the dictionary page. Maybe they should even put a picture of her right beside it.

Her hands trembled when it was her turn to put the sunblock on him, but she vowed, by damn, that he wasn't getting ahead of her. She squirted a healthy amount of white cream onto his bare back and followed his lead. Starting at the nape of his neck, she massaged the tense muscles as she applied the sunblock. Working her way down his back to the two dimples below his waist right above where his cutoff jeans rode low on his hips, she made sure that there was not a single square inch of skin left to the ravages of sun rays.

"My God, Annie Rose, your hands are like silk," he said hoarsely.

"Feel good?" she whispered.

He groaned. "Let's forget the river and you can do that all afternoon."

She squirted out another handful and sat down on the tailgate of the truck. "Oh, no, cowboy! I'm going tubing right after I take care of the rest of my body."

"I could do that for you," he offered.

"If you did, we'd spend our afternoon doing something other than floating down the river."

He wiggled his dark eyebrows. "Sounds like a wonderful plan to me. I have a quilt and I see a really nice shade tree."

"And I see chiggers in those pretty weeds under that shade tree," she said.

"Party pooper."

"Maybe so, but I avoid chiggers like the plague."

"How about a fancy hotel room? Do you avoid those too?"

She handed him the sunblock. "Don't see one right now. I do see two big inner tubes and a lot of river water. But to answer your question, yes, I do avoid fancy hotels. They cost too much."

"You are a hard woman, Annie Rose Boudreau. Maybe the hot sun will soften you up this afternoon and you'll change your mind about the quilt when we get to our destination."

"Which is where?" she asked.

"On down the river." He flashed another beautiful smile.

He leaned in and kissed her, only their lips touching. His hands did not snake around her body to draw her closer and his fingers didn't tangle themselves into her ponytail to steady her head as his tongue slipped inside her mouth. It was the beginning of a trip that promised an adventure beyond her wildest dreams, and she looked forward to it with a racing heart.

When he took a step backwards, she had to catch herself and open her eyes quickly or she would have fallen on her face.

"About that quilt?" he murmured.

"About those chiggers." She giggled.

"Guess there's nothing to do then but get into the water."

"Guess not."

―⁓―

Mason hooked an arm into each of the two big rubber doughnuts and carried them to the edge of the water. He'd envisioned Annie Rose in a skimpy bikini, but what she had picked out was so damn cute he couldn't keep the grin from his face. And it felt damn fine to be smiling like that.

The Red River was calm that day, flowing along slowly like an old man stopping to smell every rose on his way to church. The sun was high in the sky and only a few white puffy clouds dotted the clear blue canvas.

"Okay, m'lady, you want to get wet first or fall into the tube?" he asked.

She waded out into the water until it was knee deep and reached for the first inner tube, did a cute little bounce, and landed in it perfectly; legs and arms dangling over the sides, butt in the water, and head using the black tube as if it was a feather pillow.

"How long until we reach that destination?" she asked.

He had pushed his tube out into the water and flipped his body into it. "Well, shit! I forgot something."

In his haste to get into the water, he'd forgotten the rope and the floating cooler. No way could they spend the whole afternoon in the heat without something to drink, and if he fell asleep, he wanted to be damn sure that their tubes were tied together. What if she got into trouble and he couldn't hear her?

"Hold on to my tube and paddle so you don't float away." He rolled out of the tube, getting thoroughly wet when he splashed into the water. Then he jogged back to the truck, grabbed a rope and a red-and-white cooler, and ran back.

"What are you doing?" she asked.

"Hitching us together. Don't you want to be hitched to me?"

"I'll have to think about it. We've only known each other a week," she teased.

Most women would have screamed and thrown a fit at the sweet-tea incident, but she'd turned it into a party. Not many women would have darted in and out of a clothing store to buy a bathing suit in five minutes. And now there she was, holding his inner tube close to hers and paddling with the other hand to keep from drifting away with the current. He waded out into the water and quickly tied the two tubes together with the rope, leaving enough room between them to hook the tail of the rope through the handle of the floating cooler filled with ice, beer, and water bottles.

Waves slapped against their legs and arms as the flow carried them downriver in a slow, lazy fashion. The sun's rays were warm. Mason had eaten a big dinner of fried catfish and all the trimmings, and soon his eyes were shut behind his sunglasses. Instinctively, he held on to the sides of the tube as the river gently rocked him to sleep.

—⁓—

Annie Rose listened to the soft regular snores coming from the other side of the rope. She carefully opened the cooler and removed a bottle of icy-cold water, took a few sips, and put it back. The sun was downright hot on her face and she knew that if she didn't remove her big, bug-eyed style sunglasses she'd get a tan around them. She tucked one of the ear pieces into the waistband of her bathing suit bottoms and shut her eyes.

Thousands of memories of Nicky flashed in bright colors against the backside of her eyelids. That first time she'd met him, when he'd checked into the hospital and she had served as his nurse. He'd been charming in those days. Flowers, little presents, phone calls, text messages by the dozens. Afterwards she'd realized that was the tip of the iceberg in his seductive and controlling skills. As the time went by, incident by incident, month by month, until that last time when he was so violent. She should have gone to the emergency room, but every time he hit her it was worse than the time before. She feared that if he found out that she'd gone for help, he'd kill her for sure.

The final picture of the charred remains of a small private plane flashed and then it all ended, leaving nothing but a black screen like the end of a movie when the credits have finished rolling. It was over and now she was free. She started to open her eyes, but they were so heavy that she didn't even fight sleep. Deep, calming peace filled her heart and soul as she gave herself to dreams of the twins romping in the pen with their pesky goats, of them helping her cook in the kitchen, and their

music lessons in the afternoon. That segued off into a
video of Mason joining her on the front porch swing
after the sun had gone down.

As if in a time machine, she shot backwards through
the years to her childhood. Her mother was in the kitchen
and it was the last day of school for the year. It must have
been when she was in the third grade, because she was
carrying a report card with a big number three on the front.
Surprisingly, she looked so much like Lily and Gabby that
it was amazing. Her mother gave her a hug, poured a glass
of milk, and put half a dozen still-warm chocolate chip
cookies on a saucer and set it all in front of her.

"How did your day go?" her mother asked.

"I got in a fight with that mean girl again. She said
you aren't my mama and that you found me in a ditch."

"Who won the fight?"

"I did. The principal made her sit in his office."

"Did you hit her?"

Annie Rose smiled in her sleep at the memory. "I
slapped her face and she pulled my hair."

The picture faded and Annie Rose's eyes snapped
open. Good Lord! Her poor mother had had to raise a
child just like Lily. She'd never realized what a chore
her mother had taken on when she adopted a baby late
in her life.

"Good mornin'," Mason said.

His deep voice brought her back to present time in an
instant. The past and bits of the past week had flashed in
her mind, but no visions of the future. Did that mean that
Mason wasn't a part of it or that a higher power wasn't
letting her peek at what might happen? If not, she'd
still be grateful for all he'd given her, beginning with

letting her stay on the ranch and going right through to the kisses that proved a kiss could just be a kiss. It didn't have to be a prelude to a bruise or a reward for doing something right instead of wrong.

"It's late afternoon, not morning," she said.

"I'm horrible company. I napped when we should have been talking."

"I took a nap too, and it was wonderful, Mason. I've been enjoying the ride," she said.

"Want a beer?"

"Love one."

He opened the cooler, removed two bottles, and handed one to her.

She twisted off the top and tossed it back in the cooler.

"This ain't your first trip to the river, is it?"

She shook her head. "No, and I've stepped on those things at the bottom of the creek too often to be the sorry culprit who throws a bottle cap in the water."

"What time is it?" he asked.

"The beauty of a tube float is that there is no time. I'd guess four o'clock, but that's only a guess by the sun's position. How are we getting back to the truck?" she said.

"We aren't. Skip drove it to our destination and parked it. We should wind up north of Telephone, with the truck parked right there waiting for us at the edge of the water."

"Telephone?"

He tipped back the beer and took a long gulp before he answered. "It's more like a community, but it still has a post office. About twenty minutes north of Bonham, and been there for more than a hundred years."

"Why'd they name it that?"

"Rumor has it that the man who owned the general store had the only telephone in town and when he applied for a post office, he submitted Telephone, and they took it. You'll see it if you don't blink when we drive back to the ranch."

She sipped at the icy-cold beer. "Thicket is like that. Just a wide spot in the road."

"Population?" he asked.

"Little more than a thousand."

"Telephone only has about two hundred." He chuckled.

"Bet the people there are cut from the same bolt of denim," she countered.

"Probably so."

She trailed her free hand in the river water and said, "We should do this with the girls sometime."

"You are a brave woman. Think about how bored they'd get. It would be a constant chatter of how far is it, when do we get there, I'm going to starve before we get out of this, why don't we have a motor on these tubes so they'll go faster?"

She splashed water on his bare belly. "But wouldn't it be fun."

He sucked air. "Damn, that's cold on my hot skin."

She peered over the edge of her oversized inner tube. "Holy shit, Mason! You missed a stretch of skin right above your waistband. You're burned."

"Are you going to kiss it and make it all better when we get to the truck?"

"Vinegar, not kisses, is what you're going to get when we get home."

"Well, dammit! No quilt. No fancy hotel. And smelly old vinegar. You're worse than my mama," he whined.

Her laughter echoed off the willow trees lining the banks of the river. "Come morning, you'll be real glad that you put vinegar in a cool bath."

"Your kisses would heal it."

She wished she could see his eyes, but he still wore his sunglasses. "If my kisses didn't make it hotter, I wouldn't be a very good date, and you don't want it hotter. You want it to cool off so you can wear your jeans tomorrow morning."

"Maybe I want a good reason to go naked."

"Are you flirting with me?"

"Maybe. Are you flirting with me, Annie Rose?"

"A woman doesn't give away all her secrets, Mr. Harper."

The thirty-minute drive to the ranch took forever. Dusk was settling when Mason opened the door into the ranch house for Annie Rose. The second it closed behind them, he pinned her against the wall, but her blue eyes went wide with fear and her whole body stiffened. She pulled backwards, slipped to the floor with her hands over her head. So much for that jolt of confidence she'd enjoyed for almost twenty-four hours. One little show of force and she went into the protective fetal position.

He sat down in front of her and gently laid his hands on her shoulders. "I would never hurt you, Annie Rose, or force you to do anything you didn't want to do. I'm sorry."

She raised her head. The total chilling fear was gone, but tears rolled down her cheeks, leaving irregular spots on the T-shirt she'd bought as a bathing suit cover. "I know that. It's reflex. You are the first man who's even touched me since then. And I mean even touched as in the very simple word, not as in sex. I thought I was past the fear, but it paralyzed me when you held me like that. It's me that should be apologizing. I've flirted with you all day and now I revert back to this."

He tipped her chin up and kissed each eyelid before he very softly touched his lips to hers. "It takes time to heal, and we've got time, Annie Rose."

He could feel the tension leaving her body as she uncurled and leaned in to lay her head on his chest. "Thank you, Mason."

A car door slammed and it sounded like a herd of full-grown elephants stomping across the front porch, screaming all the way. "Daddy. Mama-Nanny. Where are y'all?"

"Dammit! They're going to know that we went to the river and whine all evening because we didn't take them," he said.

Like a flash, she was on her feet. "Follow me."

"Where?"

"Just trust me."

He followed her through his office and into the pool area. They could hear both girls running up the stairs and back down, searching in the kitchen and dining room as she pointed toward the pool.

"Jump," she said.

When the girls found them, Mason had his elbows propped on the edge of the deep end of the pool. Annie Rose was on a float with an arm over her eyes.

"Hey, y'all are home early," he hollered when the girls shot through the den door.

"Mama-Nanny got a bathing suit!" Lily stopped at the edge of the pool. "I like it."

"Well, thank you. I thought if we were going to swim this week, I'd best have something proper." Annie Rose wasn't surprised that her voice sounded normal. She'd perfected that trick when she was with Nicky. If she cried, it made him furious. If her voice trembled after he'd been abusive, he would go into another raging fit.

Doc waved from the door. "Hey, we got a call that Kenna's parents are on their way to pick her up. The last trip didn't take as long as they thought, so I brought the twins home early. Y'all don't get out. I can't stay. I'll let myself out. Looks like Kenna's folks will be home for a month this time. Maybe next time she's here the girls can get together again."

"Were they good?" Annie Rose asked.

"Couldn't have been better. Mason, you'd best be figuring out a way to keep this woman. She's worth her weight in gold. Got to go now and, Annie Rose, if you get tired of living on a ranch, Kenna's mama would hire you in a heartbeat," Doc said.

Mason waved back. "Let us know when Kenna comes back, but you don't want to try to steal Annie Rose. The girls will make your life miserable."

"Yes, we will," Lily said.

"Can we swim too?" Gabby asked.

"Sure. Go put on your suits and you can have an hour to play before showers and bedtime. Did your band practice go well?" Annie Rose asked.

"Yes, ma'am. Let's go, Lily. I betcha I beat you back to the pool."

"No, you won't. I'm faster than you," Lily squealed

and looked like a streak of blond hair and long legs as she ran toward the open den door.

"That was some fast thinkin'," Mason said.

"Woman's got to do what a woman's got to do. Figured it would cool both of us off. What's this about Kenna's parents being gone and then home for a month?"

"I didn't want to get cooled off that way," Mason said.

"Me, either, but evidently I haven't let go of past issues enough to take this to that level yet."

"Like I said, we've got time," Mason said. "And about Kenna's folks. They do missionary work in the summer, and sometimes if it's safe, they take her along, but if it's not, then Doc and his wife take care of her."

Lily did a cannonball off the side of the pool and yelled at her sister, who was six feet behind her. "I beat you. I told you I was faster than you."

Annie Rose paced from one end of the tiny sitting room to the other, did a snappy military turn, and repeated the motions. She'd been at it for fifteen minutes, solving nothing but wearing out the carpet under her feet, when someone knocked and startled her into fight or flight mode. Since she'd learned early on in that Nicky was bigger and meaner than she was and fighting back only made things worse, flight mode put her heart into double time, and her whole body went stiff.

"Annie Rose," Mason whispered.

Her heartbeat eased back to normal. The adrenaline rush would take a few minutes to settle. She opened the door wide and said, "Tea?"

"No, but I'll make a pot if you want some. I'd like to talk. May I come in?"

"Of course. Please sit down." She left the door open and motioned toward the love seat.

He patted the place beside him. "Sit with me, Annie Rose."

Leaving several inches between them, she sat down and drew her legs up under her. "Are the girls all right? Did something happen today that they didn't tell us?"

"This is about us, about me maybe more than you," he said.

"Okay," she said slowly, letting the last syllable out in a long gush of air. "As a boss, friend, or what?"

"As a boss, there is only praise and no complaints or pink slips. This is about the what. I want to say that I would never, ever hurt you physically or mentally. I'm not that kind of man. There's something like strings between our hearts that keeps tugging me back to you, even though your actions sometimes remind me of Holly. I think we can be good for each other, and I'm willing to take it slow." He reached down to the side of the love seat and threw a lever, bringing the footrest up on his side.

"I didn't know that it did that," she said. A love seat recliner, how great was that?

"Lots of things you still got to learn about the ranch, I guess. Try it. You'll like it." He smiled at her as he stretched out.

She popped up the footrest on her side and unwound her body. "Thank you."

"For letting you in on the love seat-turning-into-a-recliner secret?"

"For coming in here and talking to me. I've been pacing back and forth, trying to get up the nerve to knock on your door." She reached over and slipped her hand inside his.

He brought it to his lips and kissed each knuckle then held her hand in the space between them. "I love floating in the river, but that hot sun and the water sure wears me out."

She glanced over at him, but his eyes were shut. She looked down at their hands intertwined together. Her heart was thumping away at a normal, merry little pace. It felt right and she didn't want it to end, but she didn't know what to say to keep him there.

Then he crossed his legs at the ankle and snored ever so slightly. She got comfortable and thought about how lucky she'd been when she found a porch swing to sleep on a week before.

A thin orange streak on the far horizon brought form to the mesquite trees and the backyard fence, and sent enough light through the window to wake Annie Rose the next morning. Her hand was still in Mason's and his big hand covered hers. He'd rolled to his side, facing her, and was staring at her with the softest expression in his green eyes.

"Good morning, beautiful," he said.

"Good morning."

"I slept like a baby. How'd you do?"

"No dreams. Just good sleep," she answered.

"Comfortable love seat, ain't it?" He smiled.

"That and good company. I reckon it's time to start breakfast. We've got a couple of girls who'll be hitting the floor soon."

"That's right, we do."

His emphasis on the word, *we*, put a smile on her face.

"Thank you for the sleepover." He let go of her hand, pushed the lever to put his side of the love seat recliner back to rights, and stretched once he was on his feet.

"Anytime," she said.

He picked up her hand, opened it up, and kissed her palm. "Happy Monday, Annie Rose."

And then he strolled out of her sitting room, leaving the warmth of his lips on her hand. She folded her fingers over her palm and held it tightly to her chest for a few minutes before she started the brand-new week.

Chapter 11

ANNIE ROSE PUSHED THE BIG POLY CART OUT OF THE pool area toward the gate and heard a commotion out near the goat pens. If those damn goats had found a way out of the pen again, she just might take them to the auction, or maybe she'd bypass that and cook them for dinner.

She opened the gate and peeked out around the corner. Lily and Gabby were both swearing as they held the goats down.

"What's going on out here?" Mason said right behind her. "I forgot the keys to my truck."

She turned quickly and his strong arms went around her. Her hands flattened out on his hard chest and their eyes locked. They stood for a few seconds then Annie Rose raised a finger to her lips and turned around in his embrace.

"Shhh, I'm not sure. Be quiet and let's watch."

"Looks like they're trying to saddle break those goats. Let's film it," he said, his breath warm on that soft spot where her shoulder met her neck. Her pulse raced as he slipped back into the house for a video camera. He was back in a flash.

"I'll enhance the audio so we'll be able to hear what they are saying," he whispered in a deep drawl. Much more of that, and he'd be filming her as she pushed him backwards into the box elder hedge and jumped on top of him.

The sound came through as well as the picture, and she focused on the pens to keep the blush from her wicked thoughts at bay.

"Shit! Gabby, this damn goat is strong as Superman," Lily said.

"Well, you're bigger than he is, so hold him down tighter. You said you was going to be a roper last week. Djali ain't nearly as big as a calf, and you don't even have to sling the lasso to bring him down. I done got him on the ground. All you got to do is hold him still," Gabby said.

"Do you think Daddy kissed Mama-Nanny when they were in the swimming pool?" Lily grabbed Djali around the neck and held his forehead with her hand. He kicked and squirmed, but the rope around his legs kept him from doing too much damage.

"I hope he did. We did our best, leavin' them alone for a whole afternoon. It ain't fair that they got to float down the river and we had to listen to Kenna's singin'. That girl sounds like O'Malley with his tail caught in the door." Gabby picked up a bottle of rubbing alcohol, poured it on Djali's ear, and quickly jabbed a big darning needle through the bottom.

"Smart little devils, even at nine years old." Mason's words were audible enough that there was no doubt the recorder picked them up. "We might want to edit this part out before we make discs to share with their grandparents."

"Oh, my God! You wouldn't share that with your folks, would you? They'll think I'm a hussy and not fit to be a nanny," she gasped.

"Yes, I will, but I'll edit that part out," he said.

"Yes, please, Mason. I'd be mortified," Annie Rose whispered. "Omigod! They're trying to pierce those goats' ears."

Lily's voice rose above the din. "Would've been easier if we could have found the tag applicator in the barn, but Daddy must've hid it from us."

"Yes, her Daddy did hide it," Mason said. "That's because he said they cannot have pierced ears until they were older and he is afraid they'll use the tag applicator to pierce each other's ears."

Annie Rose looked over her shoulder to find him staring at her, the camera pointed at the ground. Several seconds passed before Gabby's worried voice jerked their attention away from each other and back to the filming business.

"I was watching your expression instead of filming," he said as he whipped the camera back up to catch Gabby's words and actions.

"There was blood, Lily. Do you think he'll be all right?"

"Don't you get all crazy over a teaspoon of blood. We still got to do Jeb's ear. He'd be jealous if Djali got a gold hoop and he didn't get one," Lily said sternly.

Gabby's face skewed up in a frown. "What if he gets infected and dies?"

"Then we get another goat or else we don't and we don't have to feed them and train them to be good at the stock show next fall," Lily said.

"I guess Gabby isn't going to be a nurse," Mason said.

Annie Rose glanced over her shoulder again, and the camera was still held at the right position to film the girls, but his eyes were on her. She could feel the kiss about to happen right there in the bushes and moistened her lips with the tip of her tongue. But suddenly his focus shifted and he was staring at the screen. She felt so cheated that she wanted to pitch a fit and cuss like Lily.

"Hey, there's O'Malley, sittin' on the fence post. You reckon he wants an earring too?" Lily's voice came through loud and clear.

"Let's get Jeb done and then we'll see about the cat, but I do have a diamond if we can catch him," Gabby told her.

Mason's breath smelled like coffee and maple syrup from the morning pancakes when he looked at Annie Rose and breathed out, "Let's see if they're mean enough to pierce a tomcat's ear."

Lily sat down on the edge of the hay bale and started talking to the goat. "Jeb, darlin', it's like this. I'm putting a gold hoop in your ear, and you can like it or not. I don't give a damn which one you choose." She made a dive and grabbed him by the legs. "I got him, Gabby. Bring the rope and tie him up."

Jeb fought them like a drunk on drugs, but when they untied him, he had a gold hoop in his ear. He joined Djali in the far corner of the pen, and the bawling duet they did was enough to break a grown man's heart.

Annie Rose had an almost overwhelming urge right then to turn around and make Mason put the camera down and talk to her about this thing that was between them and decide what they were going to do about it before her thumping heart jumped right out of her chest. It's a wonder the noise of it didn't come through the audio on the film.

Gabby grabbed the tomcat off the fence post and said, "Okay, O'Malley. It's your turn." She reached into the pocket of her cutoff jean shorts and brought out a sparkling diamond stud.

Lily grinned. "O'Malley will be the biggest, meanest-assed tomcat in the whole state of Texas with a diamond in his ear. You think we ought to put it in the top or the bottom of his ear?"

"In the bottom. If we put it in the top, it'll make his ear sag, and he'll look like a sissy. If we put it in the bottom, he'll be real cool, like them guys on television," Gabby said.

The camera wiggled again and Mason laughed out loud. "This is fun, but I wish I had two cameras. I can hardly keep this one trained on them because I keep wanting to watch you, Annie Rose. Your expressions are priceless."

"Well, you're getting a big kick out of it too," she said, glad that a camera couldn't record thoughts and visions or she'd be in big trouble.

"You bet I am. Here we go again. Now it's time for the tomcat." He whipped the camera back around to the girls.

O'Malley came alive when he smelled alcohol, but Gabby held him tightly even when he tried to climb over Lily's frame. Then quick as a wink, the tomcat had a diamond flashing in the morning sun as he tore out in a streak toward the barn.

"Shit! Shit! Shit!" Gabby yelled.

"What?" Lily held on tighter.

"That sorry little shit done scratched me."

"And that, folks, including you, Damian, is the reason you do not try to win a fight with my girls," Mason said. "Any kid who can pierce a tomcat's ear is not someone you want to cross. Way to go, Lily Harper."

Anyone crazy enough to have visions of sleeping with a cowboy they've only known a short while has less sense than those silly little girls, that niggling voice said inside Annie Rose's head.

"Oh, hush," she whispered.

"What did you say?" Mason asked.

"I was arguing with myself, not you," she answered honestly.

"There you have it, folks, another day in the lives of Gabby and Lily Harper, with short clips of what Annie Rose now realizes she's let herself in for. They have horns and little spiky tails, not halos and wings." He laughed.

"They are coming this way, and I didn't think they were angels, not for one minute," Annie Rose whispered.

Mason turned off the recorder and they hurried back into his office, where Annie Rose pulled the drapes back and peeked out. The girls fell into two lounge chairs.

"I guess that was hard work," she said.

Mason's arms went around her waist and he buried his face in her hair. She turned slowly and wrapped her arms around his neck. "It was harder work for me, Annie Rose. I couldn't keep my eyes off you."

His fingertip traced her jawline and then her lips before his mouth covered hers in a solid, hard kiss that weakened her knees. That was followed by a quick, sweet kiss and then he said hoarsely, "I'll see you at noon."

She barely had enough sense to nod and then he was gone, leaving her hanging onto the drapes for support.

Mason pulled up a chair to the supper table and bowed his head. "Gabby, will you say grace tonight?"

"I will, Daddy. Gabby got to say it last time, and it's my turn," Lily said.

Lily quickly bowed her head and said in a loud voice. "Dear God, we are glad for this day and we're glad that Mama-Nanny is here to cook our food and be our mama. And if Daddy kissed Mama-Nanny yesterday, then we ask your blessin' on that too."

Mason's eyes popped open so fast that it took a minute for the spinning room to right itself.

"Fried chicken?" Annie Rose handed him the platter filled with crisp home-fried chicken.

Gabby snagged a biscuit from a bowl and passed them to her sister. "We put earrings in our goats' ears today and in O'Malley's. It's all right, Daddy. We used alcohol."

"And we borrowed our real mama's earrings from your room. We had some that we got for our birthday, but they are for our ears when we get them pierced. They aren't for goats' ears," Lily said.

"Oh, my God!" Mason said through clenched teeth.

Annie Rose wished she had the camera when she saw the look on Mason's face. She would never have believed he could go from suppressing laughter to curtailing pure rage in the blink of an eye.

"You took those earrings without even asking me?" Mason didn't raise his voice, but the tone said that the whole goat episode wasn't nearly as funny as it had been when he was filming. "I gave the hoops to your mother the last Christmas she was alive. And the diamond stud was one of a pair I gave her for our first anniversary. She lost the other one, and it upset her really badly."

Gabby tucked her chin down to her chest. "We're

sorry, Daddy, but our real mama wouldn't care. I just know she wouldn't."

Lily inhaled deeply. "We'll ask next time. I promise. We didn't know that the earrings would make you all mad."

"Not mad," Annie Rose said. "It makes him sad."

"Then we're real, real sorry, Daddy." Gabby jumped up and hugged Mason.

"I've got a poker game tonight," he blurted out. "We'll talk about this later, but it will involve a punishment."

"Don't make me weed the flowerbed. I hate to pull weeds," Lily groaned.

"Or straighten the tack room. Last time we did that, I saw a mouse and I hate mice," Gabby said.

"I'll think about it," he said.

"Okay. Mama-Nanny, after we take a bath and you put more of that anti-whatever stuff on Gabby's arm, can we please watch *The Hunchback of Notre Dame* in your room?" Lily asked without a worry on her face. "O'Malley didn't take too kindly to us piercing his ears and we got scratched up pretty good."

The little pewter jewelry box on his chest of drawers was open and empty. He'd bought it the day after they buried Holly and put the three earrings in there. Hardly a week went by that he didn't look inside and remember her. Beside it was a picture of her on their wedding day, wearing her white dress and smiling into the camera.

He started to shut the jewelry box and accidentally knocked the picture to the floor. The frame hit the baseboard and broke into two pieces. The glass covering the picture shattered and the picture fell out on the carpet.

He opened his bottom dresser drawer and took out a Texas Longhorns T-shirt. At least those ornery girls hadn't decided they needed his lucky poker shirt for the goats.

He was on his way down the stairs when O'Malley passed him. The diamond looked downright ridiculous in the big tomcat's ear, and the girls would be pulling weeds and cleaning the tack room tomorrow for their stunt. And they couldn't help each other, either. They'd spend the day apart, each one doing a chore she hated. They needed a real good lesson this time.

Chapter 12

PIERCING EARS MUST HAVE BEEN SOME REALLY HARD work, because the girls were yawning by the end of the movie. Annie Rose expected their showers to energize them right back to full power, but for the first time since she'd been in the house, they didn't even want to read. Their little eyes were shut before she closed their bedroom doors.

She sat down on the top step of the staircase and O'Malley rubbed against her hip and she instinctively scratched his head. "Holy shit! That thing has to be a full carat. There is no way you are losing something that valuable." She kept petting the big old tomcat and eased the stud out of his ear. He shook his head as if he was glad to be rid of the weight and stretched out beside her. When she stopped stroking his fur, he opened his eyes, stood up, and ambled toward Mason's bedroom.

Diamond in her hand, Annie Rose tiptoed inside the room right behind O'Malley. In one leap the big cat jumped up on the bed, smashed the pillow into the right amount of softness with his big paws, turned around a couple of times, and wound himself into a ball. She turned on the light, but it didn't bother him at all.

Something glimmered in the moonlight on the floor, and she flipped the light switch. Glass cluttered the floor, and there was an empty pewter jewelry box on the chest of drawers. The satin lining inside showed where the edges of the diamond stud had rested, and two small circles gave testimony to having been home for a couple of hoops.

"I expect they were real gold," she whispered. "I shudder to think what Nicky would have done to me for not stopping them. I'm not comparing two men. I'm just being thankful that all men aren't evil."

She carefully laid the diamond back in its place and pulled a small trash can over to the mess on the floor, fussing at Mason the whole time she cleaned it up. "I swear if you'd come home and stepped on a piece of this in your bare feet, your boots would have hurt your feet for weeks."

That brought on a picture of him stretched out beside her on the love seat, his body so close that she could see every feature, softened by the light of the moon coming through the window. She was crazy as hell to let herself get caught up in the moment when his heart still belonged to his dead wife, and yet there she was, thinking about his hard body sleeping beside her, his hand covering hers, and his thick eyelashes resting on his cheeks.

She made sure every sliver of glass was in the trash before she picked up the picture and carried it down to the living room. A frame the same size as the broken one waited on the mantel to hold the girls' birthday picture. She removed that glass and put it into the one in her hand, and held it up to get a better look at the luckiest woman on earth.

"You were beautiful," she whispered as she ran a finger over Holly's gorgeous red hair. "Your daughters have your smile and the same twinkle in their eyes as you do here. You would have thought today was funny too. I just know you would."

When the picture was back on the chest of drawers beside the jewelry box, Annie Rose checked the girls one more time. They were sleeping soundly. Hopefully those pesky goats were doing the same.

The hot night breezes must have carried her scent to the goats, because they were backed up into the corner of the pen and eyeing her like she'd come to butcher them.

"You'd do well to hear me when I say this isn't my first rodeo, boys. I've done some calf roping, and believe me, I did not come unprepared," she told them in a soft tone. "You *will* be giving me those hoops, and you *will* be happy with the cheap ones I'm replacing them with. And you *will* be still while I make the change."

Djali's eyes rolled when she grabbed him around the neck. He screeched and carried on like a hoot owl when she wrapped the rope around his front legs and tied them to his hind ones. He thrashed his head and flopped his ears, but she was fast and determined. The earring was changed out in seconds and she turned him loose to hide behind the hay bale in the middle of the pen.

She and Jeb had a very different experience. The goat ran laps around the outer edge of the pen with her right behind him for three rounds. Then she abruptly turned and ran right at him. Poor old Jeb didn't even know what hit him until he was on the ground, trussed up like a Thanksgiving turkey.

"There now. Be still and this will be over in a split second," she said.

Jeb didn't obey. He bit at her and tossed his head back.

"It can be easy or hard. Your choice," she said as

she wrapped her arms around his neck. She managed to get the earring out and safely into the pocket of her jeans, but then that damned goat hopped up on his four tied-together legs and tried to run. She grabbed him, but in the dark, she couldn't find the hole that Gabby had put in his ear.

"Dammit!" She ran her fingers over his ear twice and couldn't locate it before she realized she had the wrong ear. When she moved to the other side, Jeb took advantage of the situation and bit at her arm. His teeth grazed her skin, leaving a red streak but no blood.

"You remember that you asked for this." She sat down and felt a soft squish under her butt as she grabbed his beard. "Now be still and let me get on with this. I'm only changing one earring for another. There's no way in hell I'm letting you lose that much real gold."

The smell of fresh manure wafted up to her nose, but she couldn't rub it, not when she needed both hands to get the new hoop into Jeb's ear. "I got to hand it to you. You're the meaner goat and the most devious. I bet you even cuss in goat language like Lily does."

She stood up and untied Jeb. He took off like a streak to butt Djali off the hay bale. They were still playing king of the mountain when she let herself out of the pen and headed back toward the house. Without thinking, she brushed her butt when she stepped up on the back porch, and brought back a hand smeared with fresh goat manure.

"Jeb, you win that round," she said as she opened the door into the utility room with her other hand. She kicked off her boots and carefully removed her jeans, tossed them in the washer and washed her hand in the warm water as it ran into the machinery.

"Well, shit!" she yelped when she realized the good hoops were still in her pocket. "And I mean that in every sense of the word."

The hoops weren't even wet, but her hands were slippery, so she carefully carried them to the kitchen and laid them on the cabinet. When she'd washed up with soap and dried completely, she picked up the first earring and carefully cleaned it with a bit of alcohol on a paper towel.

That's when she saw the inscription on the inside.

I love you was engraved on one; *Forever and ever* on the other one.

Wearing only her underpants and a dirty shirt, she carried them up to Mason's room and gently laid them back in their place.

—◦◦◦—

Poker night usually involved five to eight guys, but that night only Colton, Lucas, Greg, and Mason were around the table in the kitchen at Greg's house. Mason had a decent hand, but he couldn't concentrate. He had had a moment of anger and he stood by his decision about the chores the girls had to do to atone. But the guilt about feeling something for another woman was gone. And he found himself on a guilt trip because he didn't feel guilty. Add that to the picture of Annie Rose embedded in his mind, of that cute little rounded butt bending over to take something from the oven, her flashing blue eyes when she was happy, and even the way her hand fit so well in his... well, it damn sure made for a mixed-up set of complicated emotions.

Greg poked him on the arm. "You're as nervous as a cat in heat. What's going on?"

"Nothing. The girls pierced two goats' and a tomcat's ears today," he said.

Lucas slapped his leg. "I'd let you win if I could see that."

"I videoed the whole episode. I'll bring it to the next poker game if you really want to see it," Mason said. "And don't laugh. You've got twin girls on the way and they'll even have an older brother to help them get into mischief."

Lucas's expression changed instantly. "Damn. I hadn't thought about having a set of twins like yours. I figured little girls would be all sugar and spice and hair bows and sweetness."

"Think again," Mason said.

"So is the new nanny still in good graces?" Colton asked.

"You didn't tell us much at the picnic. Doc Emerson said she had a case of amnesia. Is she remembering anything?" Greg asked.

"Most everything. She was running from an abusive boyfriend. Nicky Trahan."

Greg tossed in a few chips. "The one that got killed in that plane crash? The oil well Trahans that think they're the Louisiana mob or something like that?"

"That's the one. Anyway, it's all over now and she's safe."

"And the girls haven't run her off in what? Ten days?"

"Nine," Mason said.

"That's almost a record, isn't it?" Greg asked.

"We went fourteen once when they were real little." Mason grinned. "They think she's their new mother and they mind her better than they did the other nannies. Besides, she's damn good with them."

"She looks like she could have birthed them," Colton said.

"They are spittin' images of my mother," Mason said.

"So?" Lucas wiggled his eyebrows.

"What?" Mason raised one dark eyebrow.

Greg pushed back his chair and went to get four more beers from the refrigerator. "It's way past time for you to move on, Mason. It's been eight years. That's long enough to mourn."

"This is supposed to be a poker game, not a therapy session." Mason chuckled.

"Then get your head in the game and stop giving us your money. We want to feel like we won something, not stole it from you," Lucas said.

It was past eleven when he drove away from Greg's place and headed back south to Bois D'Arc Bend. He crawled out of the truck and stumbled over a pair of rubber boots inside the door. O'Malley strutted down the steps and weaved around his legs as he set boots, sandals, and shoes against the far wall. When he reached down to rub the cat's ears, he realized that the diamond earring was gone.

"Well, that didn't last long. So now there is a high-dollar diamond out there in the hay barn or shining out in the pasture for a crow to eat?" Mason grumbled.

The cat ran into the den and Mason followed, figuring that he was on his way to the back door, but O'Malley jumped up on the back of the sofa and began to give his long, fluffy tail a good washing.

Mason started to pet him again, and there was Annie Rose asleep on the sofa. Blond hair fanned out on a throw pillow. Lashes resting on her delicate cheeks.

Nightshirt with a faded Betty Boop on the front. She sighed and shifted positions, rolled over on her side, put a hand under the pillow, and drew her knees up. The nightshirt shifted, flashing bright red lacy underpants.

Annie Rose was surely a contradiction. Faded nightshirt and sexy panties. Just thinking about touching those full, ripe lips made his breath come in short gasps and put him into instant semiarousal. Common sense said that he should cover her with one of the throws from the rack over beside the fireplace and go directly to his bedroom. Desire said to wake her with a kiss. She looked uncomfortable in that position. If he didn't move her to the bedroom, she'd have a sore neck the next morning. If he was gentle, she wouldn't even wake up when he laid her on her bed and covered her with the edge of the bedspread.

She didn't fight him or even stiffen up when he picked her up, but snuggled down into his chest and wrapped one arm around his neck. She mumbled something when he kicked the door open with his foot and O'Malley ran in ahead of him, hopped up on the rocking chair, and curled up in a ball.

"Damn cat!" she mumbled.

Her eyes were still shut.

"Damn goats!" she said clearly.

Her eyes moved rapidly behind her eyelids. She was dreaming about the tomcat and the goats. Mason tried to put her on the bed, but she held on tightly and said, "Don't go."

He checked and she was still sleeping. He stretched out beside her and she rolled toward him, throwing a leg over his body. He kissed her on the forehead and her eyes flew wide open.

"Mason?"

"Well, it ain't Superman." He chuckled.

Her arms went around his neck and she tangled her fingers into his dark hair, pulling his lips to hers. "I missed you sitting on the swing with me," she whispered.

His hands slipped under her shirt and her skin was every bit as soft as he'd imagined. She groaned softly when he massaged the muscles between her shoulders and almost purred when he moved one hand around to cup a breast. It didn't fill his big hand, but touching her hardened him until the pressure ached behind the zipper of his jeans.

She arched against him and that gesture assured him that she wanted him as badly as he did her. He slipped the nightshirt up over her head and she pressed her body against him as he strung kisses from forehead, down to her lips, where he followed one steamy kiss with another until they were both panting.

"Daddy, are you home?" Lily's voice floated down the stairs.

"Shit!" he muttered.

Annie Rose pushed away from him and grabbed her nightshirt. "That squeaky step rattled. They're coming downstairs. Go to the kitchen and I'll meet you there."

He rolled off the bed, and when the girls reached the kitchen, he had his head inside the refrigerator. That didn't help a damn bit, but he had remembered to jerk his shirt out to cover the bulge in his jeans. "You should be asleep," he said.

"Gabby woke up and she woke me up and we're sorry about Mama's earrings," Lily said.

"You are still going to be punished because you took

something without asking. Gabby is going to straighten the tack room and Lily is going to weed the flowerbeds. All of them, not just the ones in the front yard," he said.

Annie Rose's hair was all messy and her lips were bee-stung when she wandered into the kitchen. He couldn't take his eyes off her legs or stop imagining them wrapped around his naked body.

"Mama-Nanny, did you hear what we have to do because we took things without asking?" Lily asked.

"Yes, I did and you are getting off easy."

"Tell him not to make us do chores. We said we were sorry," Gabby whined.

"Sorry, darlings. I'd make you do more than that. Now get on back to bed where you belong. You'll need your rest so you'll have the energy to do your chores in the morning," Annie Rose said.

"All right," they said at the same time.

Chapter 13

STATIC ELECTRICITY BOUNCED AROUND IN THE ROOM when Annie Rose and Mason locked gazes, but neither one made a move. O'Malley darted across the kitchen floor and meowed at the kitchen door.

"Hey, you want something to eat? How about a bowl of ice cream?" Annie Rose asked.

"You talking to me or that pesky cat that has already lost his high-dollar earring?" Mason asked.

"He's not getting ice cream if he can't take care of an earring. And I thought maybe ice cream would cool us both down," she said.

"I'd rather have a cold beer," Mason said.

"You're right. That does sound a hell of a lot better than ice cream," she said.

He took two from the refrigerator and motioned for her to follow him out to the porch. They both sat down on the swing and Mason used the heel of his boot to kick-start it into motion.

"Nicky hated to kiss me after I drank a beer."

Mason leaned over and kissed her hard on the lips. "He was a fool. You taste like a bit of heaven."

"He's gone. Door closed and I don't want to think about him anymore, but I do, and when I do, it makes me angry. Does Holly do that to you?"

"Tonight she did. I broke her picture."

"We've both got a lot of baggage, don't we?"

"You ready to throw yours into the pond?" he answered her question with another one.

"I am, but will that keep the memories from popping up?"

"Probably not, but it will keep us from letting them control either one of us. I'm ready to move forward with my life. I figured it out tonight at the poker game."

"Reckon the bad memories for me and the good ones for you will get fainter and come around to haunt us less and less?"

"Oh, yeah. And I think that we are helping each other with that issue more than we realize right now. We should go back to bed now," he said softly.

"I'd like that, but there's two little girls who aren't asleep yet, and if we got interrupted again, darlin', I'm afraid their chore list would last a whole week." She kissed him on the cheek and started toward the door.

"Annie Rose?" he said.

She turned.

"I wanted to see your face one more time tonight. The moonlight dancing off your hair is beautiful," he said.

She smiled. "Thank you. I'll take that and the feel of your hands on my body with me into my dreams."

"If you can sleep, that's a hell of a lot more than I'll be able to do," he said.

———

Mason flipped the light switch on in his bedroom and the lucky shirt went to the laundry basket. His jeans and socks joined it, and he adjusted the water for a quick shower. A towel wrapped around his hips hung like a low-slung loincloth and his hair was still wet when he

realized that the picture was back on the chest of drawers
and there was no glass on the floor. He peeked inside the
jewelry box, and there were the hoops and the diamond
stud in their right places.

He dropped the towel, pulled on a pair of lounge
pants, and curled up on his big, empty king-sized bed
alone. Sleep was a long time coming, and when it did, it
brought such vivid dreams of Annie Rose that he awoke
the next morning with a painful erection that took fifteen
minutes in a cold shower to ease.

Chapter 14

ANNIE ROSE WAS ALREADY DRESSED AND BREAKFAST was cooking when he made it to the kitchen. He caught her at the kitchen sink and slipped his arms around her waist from behind, drawing her back to his chest and breathing in the fragrance of her shampoo on her hair and the first morning coffee on her breath.

"Thank you," he said.

"For what?" she asked.

"Thank you for putting the jewelry back. How did you get the girls to agree to it?"

"I didn't ask them. I did a swap on the goats with some junk jewelry I had in my suitcase. They can think that O'Malley lost the stud. You might need to put the little box in another place though, so they won't know," she answered.

"Why?"

"Because that is some very valuable jewelry."

He kissed her on the ear. "No, why did you do it?"

"Because goats don't need expensive hoops and the cat would have lost that diamond and that was just plain crazy, and"—she inhaled deeply—"you were upset about not having them as a reminder of Holly."

"How did you manage it?" he asked, wanting to stay in that position all day, wanting to listen to her voice until daylight softened into dusk.

"Roping a goat isn't a lot different than roping a calf.

You get the loop around them, tie their legs together, and then change out the earring. Let me tell you something, Mason. Those goats put up a worse fight than a calf. Jeb is a strong old boy. He gave me a run for my money. My jeans are on a second washing to get the goat crap off the rear end, and he tried to bite me. He must've been attached to that hoop," she said.

"In the dark? You managed all that in the pitch-black night?"

"The moon was shining, but I can tell you that the old tomcat wasn't any trouble at all compared to the goats. He seemed grateful to be rid of his jewelry. They didn't want to give theirs up."

He heard the girls coming down the stairs and took a step back. "Well, thank you again."

The third stair step squeaked and he quickly kissed her, tasting the coffee on her lips before he crossed the kitchen in a couple of long strides and poured a cup for himself.

"Daddy, did you change your mind?" Lily asked. "We really are sorry."

Gabby was right behind her. "We promise to never, ever do it again."

"I didn't change my mind, so eat a good breakfast. I expect the jobs will take most of the morning, and you'll need lots of energy," he said.

"Mama-Nanny, help us out," Lily begged.

"I love you both, but growing up means that you are accountable for your actions," Annie Rose said.

"But, Daddy, you never punish us," Gabby wailed.

"It looks like maybe I was amiss if you think you can take things without asking. Punishment stands. After breakfast put on old clothes and get after it. Annie Rose and I will inspect the jobs, and if they aren't done right, then you'll have to do them over," Mason said.

"Well, shit! Damian was right. Mamas are meaner than nannies, and they make Daddies mean too," Lily grumbled.

Mason pointed at her. "Be careful with that language, young lady, or you'll be doing another job this afternoon."

O'Malley meowed at the back door and Mason opened it for him. The tomcat weaved in and out of his legs.

Lily slapped both hands on her cheeks. "Oh no, O'Malley has done lost his earring. You aren't going to make me do more work because he lost it, are you?"

"No, that's his fault, not yours," Mason said.

"Well praise the Lord," Gabby whispered.

"Thank you for backing me up. It's not been easy to punish them all these years," Mason whispered when the girls headed toward the kitchen table.

"You did the same for me with the playpens, remember?" She smiled.

—⁓—

"Can we have waffles for breakfast?" Gabby asked from the table.

"Not this morning. I've already made omelets and sausage gravy. Waffles wouldn't give you enough energy for this morning," Annie Rose said. "The biscuits will be done in five minutes, so rush upstairs and put on your work clothes. That way you can get right at your jobs when you are done eating."

They sighed and stomped up the steps, grumbling

under their breath the whole way. When she heard the doors to their rooms slam, she sat down in Mason's lap and drew his lips down to hers for a long, lingering kiss.

"Do they really have to work all morning?" She broke the kiss and laid her cheek against his chest, listening to the rapid beat of his heart.

"Did they have to clean up the playpens before breakfast?" he asked.

"United we stand. Divided we fall. It's not easy being a mama-nanny."

Or being a woman who wants you so bad she can hardly bear it, she thought.

His lips erased any more words, and his hands found their way up under her shirt, putting an end to any more thoughts. The kisses went from soft and sweet to hard and demanding, ending abruptly when the girls started back down the stairs.

"They have to sleep sometime," he whispered.

She jumped up from his lap and was taking the biscuits from the oven when the twins plopped down at the table for the second time that morning.

———— ∿∿∿ ————

Mason whistled as he rolled up his sleeves and got ready to haul small bales of hay to the barn closest to the house. He and his foreman, Skip, had unloaded and stacked two truckloads by midmorning, and the summer help was on their way back to the field to load up again. He propped a boot on the side of the barn and watched the girls hauling water from the house to the goat pens.

"I'm damn sure worried about you." Skip lit a cigarette and chose a spot downwind from Mason. "That

new nanny has got your head in a spin. I can tell, and
it scares me. She might be good with the girls, but she
could be up to something, Mason. A woman does not
show up on the porch for no reason. She could be working a scam on you."

"You haven't even met her, so don't judge her,"
Mason said.

"Well, we can damn sure fix that. I'll be having dinner with you today at noon in the house. You can call
her and tell her or surprise her. Your choice," Skip said.

Mason shook his head. "Come right on but, Skip,
you're wrong. She's not got a fake bone in her body."

"Time to get to work." Skip snuffed out his cigarette
on the heel of his boot. "And I'll save any more com-
ments until I meet her. Wish I could take her down to
Nash's place. Ain't nobody in the world can fool that
old fart. He's the best judge of people I ever knew."

"That's fine by me," Mason said. "And any day you
want to take her to meet your grandpa, all you have to
do is ask her. I bet Nash likes her."

On the way to the barn, Mason pulled out his cell
phone and called Annie to tell her that he was bringing
his foreman, Skip, home for dinner, and that the other
hired hands wanted to meet her. "So after dinner, could
you plan a trip with me down to the bunkhouse?"

"I can do that," she said.

―◇―

She'd only planned on throwing together a Mexican
casserole for dinner, but with a three-hour notice, she
quickly changed the menu plans. She'd make steaks,
baked potatoes, and a cucumber, tomato, and onion

salad with her mother's special dressing. And cupcakes would be a fine thing to take to the bunkhouse for the guys when she met them. Four dozen should be enough. Too bad the girls had chores and couldn't help her decorate them.

When it was almost time for Mason and Skip to stop for noon, she took a few minutes to take her blond hair down from the ponytail and put on fresh makeup, change into a sundress and sandals, and spray a little perfume on her wrists. She should be a person that Mason was pleased to introduce to his foreman, not a harried woman who'd chased after little girls and cleaned all day.

A tall, lanky cowboy with a mop of gray hair, a gray mustache, and a long, lean face arrived right at twelve o'clock and went straight for the sink to wash up. The girls wasted no time in starting a constant chatter.

"Uncle Skip, we haven't seen you in more than a week. Where have you been? Have you seen your grandpa Nash? When can we go see him? I bet he's got new kittens and he's always got cookies and we get to ride the four-wheelers when we go to see him. And I know he misses us something horrible. Tell Daddy to take us today. Did you know that Daddy punished us for taking Mama's jewelry today, and I had to pull weeds? I broke a fingernail too, and Mama-Nanny didn't even feel sorry for me. I told Granny about it when she called me this morning," Lily said.

"Well, ain't that just so sad," Gabby smarted off. "I broke three fingernails cleaning that dirty old tack room and Mama-Nanny didn't feel sorry for me, neither. And Granny said that we had to mind Daddy and he was right. I thought she'd feel sorry for us."

"I checked their work and it's good," Annie Rose told Mason.

He smiled at her, but there was a veil over his eyes, as if he was worried or angry. She knew that look well, and although she didn't fear for her life, she wondered what had happened that morning.

Skip answered their questions while he dried his hands and then said, "In all the melee, no one has introduced us."

"Annie Rose, this is Skip. He's been foreman on the ranch since before I was born. I'm not sure it could run without him. He's third generation in his family to be the foreman of Bois D'Arc Bend. Skip, this is Annie Rose. She's..." Mason stopped.

Annie Rose stuck out her hand and smiled up at Skip. "I'm the new nanny."

"I heard that you showed up on the porch on the twins' birthday. I missed the party. I raise some rodeo stock and had to take them down south of Dallas that weekend. Couldn't make it back in time for the party."

His shake was firm, but Annie Rose could see the doubt in his body language. He was as stiff and formal with her as he was happy and carefree with the girls.

"Dinner smells good," he said.

"You guys best get after these steaks before they get cold. I hope you like yours medium well, Skip," she said.

"Only way to eat a good steak," he said.

"We could have helped cook dinner if we didn't have to do chores." Lily shot a look across the table toward her father.

"And many more of those eye rolls and looks, and you'll be doing more," Mason said.

Gabby changed the subject. "When are we going to see Nash, Uncle Skip?"

"Anytime your daddy wants to get the four-wheelers out. Mason tells me that you were raised up on a ranch, Annie Rose."

His tone said that he doubted her story, not that she could blame him. It was a damn crazy tale and sounded like a scam in the making. "Yes, I was. It wasn't nearly this big, but a ranch is a ranch and you run them about the same way. Raise cattle, make hay. Put in a vegetable garden in the spring. Do some cannin' and freezin' to get ready for winter."

"Can we have a garden next spring?" Lily asked.

"Only if you want to work even harder than you do now," Annie Rose said.

Mason's hand slipped under the tablecloth and rested on her knee and then it moved higher and higher, inch by fiery hot inch, until she thought she'd either have to drag him to the bedroom right that minute or shoot him. The decision was leaning toward the latter when his hand stopped short of the elastic in the legs of her underpants and started back down to her knee, this time barely half an inch at a time.

"I'll work," Gabby said. "Can we grow yellow squash? I like it real good with cheese on it."

"That grows very well, so we could plant it for sure," Annie Rose said, but her mind was on the heat growing rapidly in her body.

Looking at his face, no one would guess that he was driving her right up the kitchen walls. When both his hands were back on the table and he was busy cutting another bite of steak, she returned the favor, only she started a lot higher than his knee and didn't stop until she could feel a bulge behind his zipper.

"So are we putting in a garden?" Skip asked Mason.

"If Annie Rose wants to mess with it," he said hoarsely.

"Please, Mama-Nanny," Lily begged.

"It's a long time until spring. We'll see." She moved her hand back down to his knee and gave a gentle squeeze before she pushed back.

"Don't rush with your dinner. I'm going to put this on the table so it will be ready when you are," she said.

She had to put some space between her and Mason so she could catch her breath. Skip already didn't believe that she was genuine. If he caught the vibes flowing from her right then, he'd for sure think she was up to no good.

"I thought we were having cupcakes," Lily said. "I saw them in a box out on the washing machine."

"No, those are for the guys in the bunkhouse," Annie Rose said.

<hr />

Skip laid a hand on Mason's shoulder when they were outside. "Son, I'm still not convinced she's real, but she puts on a real fine dinner. I reckon if she's pulling the wool over your eyes, that you ain't the first cowboy to fall for them blue eyes. Just promise me you'll be real careful and take things slow."

"I'm not rushing into anything," Mason said.

Gabby skipped across the lawn and threw her arms around Mason's waist. "Mama-Nanny says that we can pass the cupcakes out since we didn't get to help decorate them. Can we ride in the back of the truck, Daddy? You can drive real slow."

Lily made it a three-way hug. "Please, Daddy."

"Only if me and Mama-Nanny can ride back there with you and Uncle Skip will drive," he answered.

"I haven't ridden in the back of a truck in years. Can I sit with you girls?" Annie Rose said.

"Yes!" Both girls yelled at the same time as they climbed up over the fender and sat down with their backs to the cab.

Mason put his hands on Annie Rose's small waist and lifted her into the bed of the truck in one fluid movement, then put a hand on the fender and hopped inside to sit beside her.

"This is like the old wagon train days," Gabby said.

"Wagons-ho!" Skip yelled from the open window and drove at five miles an hour all the way down the path to the bunkhouse.

"And now it's time to meet the rest of the bunkhouse crew," Mason said.

"I'm ready, but don't expect me to remember all their names," Annie Rose told him.

"We'll help you, Mama-Nanny. We remember them every one, and you can always use your *How to Remember* book. It worked last time," Lily said.

Mason introduced her to cowboys with names like Ryder, Johnny, Jack, Laramie, and Paul. She shook hands with each of them, knowing full well that even the booklet the girls made her wouldn't help that much.

"I'm pleased to meet you all, and maybe in a few weeks I'll have names and faces all sorted out," she apologized.

"Hey, there's one of you and twenty of us. You'll get

us straightened out by the end of summer," Ryder—or
was it Paul—said "And, honey, you can call me anything if you'll bring these cupcakes down here every
so often."

"Deal," Annie Rose said. "Now I reckon us girls can
walk back to the house, and you guys can get on back
to your work. It's after one and I know you are making
hay today."

That evening when Mason came home, she handed
him a cold beer and led him outside to the patio.
"Tempers were a little warm this afternoon. Arguments
followed the chores they had to do. Water is cool, and
we're eating out here. Want to take a dip with them before you eat?"

"No, ma'am, but if you offered to skinny-dip with
me, I might change my mind." His eyes roved down
over her body so seductively that she envisioned shuck-
ing her clothing and romping in the water, both of them
buck naked.

"Right now?" she teased.

He stretched out on a lounge and kicked off his dusty
boots. "I could find a sitter real quick. Natalie is always
offering to keep them. They love Josh."

"Hi, Daddy. You ready to eat?" Lily crawled out of
the pool and tugged the top of her bathing suit up to its
rightful place.

Gabby followed her sister. "Daddy, I did a swan dive
off the board. You should have seen it."

Annie Rose slung her legs over the side of the lounge.
"Who's hungry?"

All three of them raised their hands. The girls rushed
over to the table, with Annie Rose right behind them.

Brown paper bags and a Crock-Pot sat on the table. She pulled a canned soda pop out of a cooler for each of them and then ladled soup into four disposable bowls before removing the top of a plastic container containing cheese slices, crackers, and pickles.

"I love paper bag picnics." Lily dug into her bag to find a chicken salad sandwich and a bag of chips.

"Me, too. Mama-Nanny is the best mama in the whole world. Daddy, you should marry her tomorrow if y'all didn't really get married when she wore the wedding dress," Lily said before biting into her sandwich.

"Yes, only this time we get to sing at the wedding," Gabby said.

"Well, you're not singing RaeLynn's song," Lily declared.

"Nope, I'm singing 'I Cross My Heart.'"

"That's a boy's song."

"Well, I'll make it a girl's song, because it says what I want Mama-Nanny and Daddy to say when they get married."

"You were right." Mason winked at Annie Rose.

He was back to his old self and that worried Annie Rose, even it if was the reverse of what Nicky had been. He'd been all sweet and honey-pie lovely in public and then treated her like shit when they got home. What in the hell was going on anyway?

Chapter 15

ANNIE ROSE SET THE FROSTING BOWL TO THE SIDE OF the double-layer chocolate cake she'd iced when she heard the squeak of the front door. Lily and Gabby had gone to their rooms to play and Mason wasn't due to come home for the noon meal for another hour. Strange female voices floated from the front door and the tone was coated with icicles right there in the hot Texas summertime.

"If he didn't pay so damn well, I wouldn't even do this job. Those two little heathens…"

"I know, but he does pay well, and it's only half a day once a week. Just think of what the nanny must face when she has to deal with them every day."

"Hello. Can I help you?" Annie Rose poked her head into the foyer to see two women wearing jeans and knit shirts.

"Oh, my! You must be the new nanny. How long have you been working? I'm Janie, and this is my daughter, Martha. We're the housekeepers who usually clean once a week, but we weren't here last week," the older of the two said.

"Mason didn't tell me there were housekeepers. I've been cleaning the house, but y'all do whatever you are accustomed to doing," Annie Rose answered.

Janie was a tall, lanky woman with gray streaks in her light brown ponytail. Martha was a younger version of the same but without the gray hair.

Martha crossed the kitchen in a few long strides and went straight to the utility room. "We'll get on with our work. Some nannies clean. Some don't. One thing for sure, they never last too long around here."

"Mama-Nanny, can I have some milk? I don't feel so good," Lily said on the way into the kitchen.

"Hello, Lily. Where's Gabby?" Martha asked. "You've got a sunburn, child."

"I want ice water," Gabby said right behind her sister.

Annie Rose motioned for the girls to come closer and touched their foreheads. "That's not sunburn. That's a fever."

"Don't call Doc Emerson, please. We'll get well without shots. Promise, Mama-Nanny, please promise. And don't tell Daddy or he'll make you call Doc and he'll say we need a shot," Gabby whined.

"Mama-Nanny?" Janie's eyebrows shot up.

"She's our new mama. Daddy got her for our birthday present and left her on the porch swing for us to find," Lily said. "Can I have some milk?"

"No, but you can have some apple juice over ice." Annie Rose opened the freezer and filled two glasses with ice.

"We'll be well by the time Daddy gets home for dinner, won't we, Lily?" Gabby declared.

Lily nodded. "I already feel better. I don't even need the juice."

"Don't try to con me, kiddo. Up to bed with both of you. You've most likely got sore throats from allergies, because you were sneezing when you came home from Kenna's on Sunday. I'll bring medicine up. You carry your juice and go slow so you don't spill it," Annie Rose said.

Gabby shook her head emphatically. "Mine ain't sore."

Lily touched her throat. "Mine ain't sore, either."

Annie Rose pointed and they obeyed.

"How long have you been here?" Janie asked.

"Little more than a week." Annie Rose found fever reducer in the cabinet above the utility-room sink, along with a coffee cup holding a digital thermometer, tongue depressors, and alcohol swaps.

"That's amazing," Janie said.

"What?" Annie Rose picked up the whole thing, along with liquid medicine.

"That they mind you," Martha answered. "You might last longer than the rest have."

"I hope so," Annie Rose said.

She found them both sitting on the side of Gabby's bed, sipping juice.

"Put on your cotton nightshirts and cover up with only a cool sheet. No blankets or fluffy throws that will make you hotter. Open your mouth, Lily, and let me look at your throat." She set the supplies on the bedside table and tore the paper from one of the tongue depressors.

"Say ahhhh," she said. "Tell me the truth, girls. How long have you had a sore throat?"

Lily glanced over at her sister and shook her head.

Gabby snapped her mouth shut.

"Truth, or I tell Doc that we're coming in to see him. You choose," Annie Rose said.

"In church Sunday," Lily spit out.

Gabby glared at her.

"You need antibiotics, but I bet Doc will call them in for us," Annie Rose said.

Gabby latched onto her hand and squeezed.

Tears welled up in Lily's eyes. "Don't let him come out here and give us shots. Please, Mama-Nanny."

"Hey, are you the same girls who pierced a tomcat's ear?" she asked.

Lily stiffened her upper lip and wiped away the tears. "But that didn't hurt like a shot in the heinie."

Fear did have its advantages. Any other time Lily would have spit out *ass*.

She drew them both close to her side. "Let's call before we panic."

———————

Mason couldn't keep the smile off his face all morning. Tonight he was breaking out a bottle of wine, thawing out a cheesecake, and if he had time after work, he was making a run into town for roses. Annie Rose was an amazing woman and she deserved to be courted properly. He whistled as he kicked off his boots at the back door and headed to the sink to wash up for dinner.

"Well, hello." Martha folded sheets in the utility room.

"Oh, I forgot this was cleaning day. How are things going?" He turned on the water and picked up the soap.

"You got sick kids. The new nanny is upstairs with them. She left a note on the countertop about your dinner," she said.

Mason quickly washed his hands, didn't even stop to read the note but took the stairs two at a time. He burst into Lily's room to find the twins propped up in bed with a tray in front of each of them and Annie Rose sitting in a rocking chair right beside the bed.

"Hi, Daddy, we're sick," Lily said.

Gabby nodded as she continued to eat chicken noodle soup. "And Doc Emerson isn't coming."

"Who says?" Mason pulled his phone from his hip pocket and started hitting buttons.

"Daddy!" Lily wailed. "Mama-Nanny done called him and the drugstore done brought us some pills. We're big girls, so we don't have to take that old nasty red medicine no more. And Mama-Nanny says that we can have ice cream if we eat all our soup."

Mason put his phone back in his pocket and motioned toward Annie Rose. "A word please."

She took her own good easy time in getting from rocking chair out to the landing. By the time he shut the bedroom door, his jaws ached from grinding his teeth.

Annie Rose sat down on the top step. "What's your problem? You look like you could eat nails."

"First rule of being a nanny is that you call me the minute, hell the second that one of my girls gets sick. And then you call Doc Emerson and get him out here as fast as he can drive," he growled.

She stood up and poked him in the chest with her forefinger. "I checked them both then I called Doc. They have allergies to whatever is probably floating around in this part of the world and the drainage has caused a sore throat, which caused a fever. He phoned in some antibiotics and agreed with me that fever reducer every six hours, lots of liquids, and rest today would be good. The fever has already broken, but I want them well by Saturday for their Pink Pistol day, so I'm being overcautious."

He slapped at her finger. "They are my kids and you will follow my rules."

"Or what?"

———

"I asked you 'or what?' Do you intend to answer or stand there in all your self-righteous mad spell and go up in red-hot flames before you answer me?" she asked again.

He brushed past her, and for the first time, his brief touch on her bare arm was like cold wind whipping across her entire body. When he reached the foyer, he leaned against the wall and made a phone call.

"Doc, I want you to come out here and examine the girls. They're running fever and…"

A long pause.

"I don't give a shit if she is or was a nurse. I want your opinion and…"

Another pause while he listened.

"I'll take them to the emergency room if you don't get in your truck and come out here."

More silence.

"Okay, okay. But I don't like it."

He pushed himself away from the wall just as Gabby yelled, "Mama-Nanny, we're ready for ice cream."

Annie Rose raised her voice. "I'll go get it and bring it right up."

Mason was putting his phone back in his pocket when she said, "You didn't answer me. Or what?"

"I've fired nannies for less."

"Then fire me. I'll get Skip to drive me to the nearest bus station. You can tell the girls that you fired me," she said.

"Their mother…" he started.

Annie Rose turned around and crowded into his

space, her nose only a few inches from his. "Their mother died from an aneurism that had nothing to do with a sore throat or a fever. I'm a nurse, for God's sake, Mason. If I thought for one minute those girls had something life threatening, I would have called you while I was on the way to the hospital with them. I wouldn't have even waited for you to make it from the fields to the house."

Lily peeked out into the landing. "Mama-Nanny, did you forget our ice cream?"

"No, darlin', I'm on my way to the kitchen right now." She spun around and left Mason on the landing, stewing in his own juices.

She set the bowls on a tray and took an extra two minutes to pull a pot roast from the oven, a salad from the fridge, and uncover a pan of yeast rolls.

"You ladies feel free to take a few minutes to eat. There's plenty cooked and Mason will never eat all of it. Dessert is the cake. Y'all know where the plates are. I'm going back up to the girls before the ice cream melts," she said.

"Get on out of here," Janie said. "I've seen those two kids when they're upset. It ain't a pretty sight. We'll enjoy a nice quiet meal right here in the kitchen."

"Dinner looks wonderful," Martha said.

Mason barely even shrugged when she passed him in the foyer. Fear plus pride made for strange bedfellows, but her mama always said that when a man was in a snit to give him some room. Crowding him would make everything worse.

Well, Mason damn-his-soul Harper could sure have all the room he wanted.

"They're arguing," Lily reported back to Gabby.

"Is he going to call Doc?" Gabby whispered.

"He's pretty mad. So is Mama-Nanny. It's not fair. I know he likes her. He's mad because she didn't call Doc, but shit, Gabby, she's a real nurse," Lily said.

"What are we going to do?" Gabby asked.

"We're going to fix it. Tonight when it's time to go to sleep, I'm going to cry and say that I'm sicker…"

Gabby slapped her sister on the shoulder. "If you say that, they'll call Doc. What are we going to do? Daddy can fire a nanny but not a mama and I love her."

"We're going to get them back together, like on *The Parent Trap*. Don't you argue with me when I say that I want Mama-Nanny to sleep in our baby room across the hall," Lily said.

Gabby's eyes twinkled as she threw a hand over her forehead. "But we can't be too sick or Daddy will call Doc and he'll give us a shot."

Lily shivered. "Okay then. We won't be sicker. I'll have a nightmare when we first go to bed. You don't get shots for bad dreams and I'll scream and throw a fit and you'll have to wake me up. Then I'll cry and say that Mama-Nanny has to sleep across the hall or else Daddy has to sleep on the floor beside my bed."

"That's better," Gabby said. "We can always lock them in their rooms if they don't be nice to each other."

"We might have to," Lily said seriously.

Annie Rose was happy to see them dig right into the ice cream. "So another movie?" she asked.

"The old *Parent Trap*," Lily said.

"But you just watched the new version and it's about the same," Annie Rose said.

"I know, but we like to watch them back-to-back to see if we spot anything different. And I like the twins' accent in that one. Lily and me are thinkin' about learnin' to do that, aren't we, love?" Gabby said in a fake British accent.

Annie Rose found the version with Brian Keith and Maureen O'Hara and slipped it into the DVD player. "While you watch it, I'll slip over into Lily's room and read. If you need me, holler."

She nodded at the argument the hero and heroine were having in her brand-new romance book on page ten. It appeared that men were the same whether they were real or characters, and she could relate to the attraction plus the anger that the heroine experienced. It was damn frustrating to want a man to touch you so bad that your skin ached from yearning and then be so mad at him that you didn't want him to even look at you.

She had turned the page to find out how the lady in the book handled the roller coaster of emotions when she heard Mason in the next room, teasing the girls. "Hey, I see you ladies ate all your ice cream. So I don't reckon you are too sick. You want to come outside and help me haul hay this afternoon?"

"Dadddeee!" Lily groaned.

"I do, but only if Mama-Nanny can help us too," Gabby said quickly.

"I'm joking." Mason's voice sounded edgy. "Where is Annie Rose?"

"In my room, reading her book while we watch the movie. She can hear us if we need her," Gabby answered.

Mason went through the connecting bathroom and cleared his throat to get her attention. The words were swimming on the pages, but she'd be damned if she forgave him.

"Annie Rose?" he said finally.

She answered without raising her gaze to meet his. "Yes?"

"I'm staying with them this afternoon. I've already called Skip, and he'll take care of things. I don't leave them when they're sick."

Annie Rose snapped her book shut with a pop. "Good. I'll call it my day off then. Can I borrow a vehicle to drive into town?"

He worked a set of keys up from his pocket and tossed them on the bed. "Take my truck. Just be sure that you bring it home by dark."

His handsome face was still etched with worry and the little lines around his eyes had deepened in the last hour. She'd like to fix everything for him, but there wasn't a damn thing in her virtual toolbox that would take care of jackassitis.

"What if I want to leave it at the bus station in Sherman?" she asked.

He rubbed a hand across his forehead and then combed back his dark hair with his fingertips. "If you do, leave the keys under the floor mat in the backseat and lock it up."

"Yes, sir, Mr. Harper. And I'll even be kind

enough to give you a phone call if I make that decision," she said.

"Don't threaten me, woman," he said gruffly.

Heart thumping, she stood up and pointed her finger up at his nose. "I don't threaten. I deliver what I promise."

She hated arguments. With her first boyfriends it usually meant breaking up. With Nicky it meant bruises. Her inner voice said to back down or she might be doing both with Mason, but she disagreed. They weren't dating, so they couldn't break up. And Mason didn't slap women around.

Just when she was about to suggest they talk this thing through, he folded his arms over his chest and said, "Call me when you make up your mind."

Evidently, he needed a hell of a lot more room to stew, so she let him have the last word and left by way of the landing instead of telling the girls good-bye.

Retail therapy.

That's what she needed. She jerked the suitcase out of the closet and fiddled with the secret compartment until it was open. She shoved two banded stacks of bills into her purse and then changed into a nicer shirt. She kicked off her sandals, donned socks, and shoved her feet into her boots. Now she was ready for a good therapy session, and Mason could bite her square on the ass if he didn't like what she bought the girls.

She might even buy presents for the tomcat and the goats, but by damn, Mason wasn't getting a damn thing. She checked the gas gauge in the truck before she put it in reverse. It read half a tankful, and she'd be bringing it home that much or more. No way was she going to be indebted to Mason for anything after the way he'd treated her. Hell's bells, she was a certified nurse, and all the girls had was a simple sore throat.

Not a single store in Whitewright called out to her to park the truck and come inside to shop, so she caught the highway up to Sherman. When she saw the signs for Walmart, Ross, and Books-A-Million, she had no doubt that she was on the right track to have some serious fun.

Right behind Walmart was a long strip mall that had far more than she could cover in one afternoon and evening. She parked at the end and went into the bookstore first, browsed around for an hour, and left with two heavy bags. One had all kinds of new authors for the girls and the other was stuffed full of fat romance books for herself. One by Joanne Kennedy had a cowboy rolling up the sleeves of a white T-shirt on the front. Another by an author she hadn't read, Julie Ann Walker, had reached out and insisted that it was coming home with her, and the dark-haired hunk on the front wore a white T-shirt too. Cowboys or bad boys, those T-shirts reminded her of Mason and the way the knit stretched over his muscles. Then she simply could not pass up the brand-spanking-new Sue Grafton novel.

She put the bags in the backseat of the truck and drove up to the next place that caught her eye. A children's clothing store that netted her four bags of cute things for the girls, from Sunday dresses to cute little summer shorts and tops to match.

By then her stomach was growling, because she'd been too angry to eat, so she drove across the highway to a little catfish place. It was one of those fast-food places where you order at the counter from a menu stuck up above. She ordered the combo platter that had half catfish and half shrimp. What she didn't eat, she'd take home to O'Malley for his snack. Poor old boy deserved something for getting his ear pierced.

When her folks passed away, when Nicky was abusive, when she lost a patient, it upset her so badly that she couldn't swallow. But she had no trouble eating that day as she went over every nuance of the argument she'd had with Mason. She was right, and he was wrong, and she didn't intend to back down, not even if he put on a snowy-white T-shirt, and his eyes went all dreamy and soft.

Her phone rang and there was Lily's picture, smiling up from the swimming pool with her blond hair stringing down in her face. Gabby's picture was one of her with Djali at the birthday party, her arms around his neck and the goat looking scared shitless.

"Hello," she said.

"You will come back, won't you?" Lily whispered.

"Why are you talking like that? Is your throat worse?" Annie Rose was already sliding out of the booth and on her way out the door. What if the sore throats had gone into strep before the antibiotics kicked in? What if she'd been wrong not to insist that Doc come on out to the ranch and check them out himself? What if they needed to be hospitalized?

"No, me and Gabby are okay. We miss you, and we have to whisper. Daddy is in the bathroom, and we don't want him to hear us callin' you."

Annie Rose sat back down with a thud. "Why?"

"Because y'all were fighting."

She could hear Gabby fighting with Lily. "Give me that phone. It's my turn. Tell her that if she leaves, we're going to be awful, and tell her that nannies can leave but mamas can't…"

"I hear the water running, so Daddy is coming back. Just come home, Mama-Nanny," Lily said.

Damn men! She fumed as she found a couple of plastic bowls for ice cream. She was still having an inner hissy fit when something colder than ice water flushed through her veins. She knew the feeling well. She'd lived with it for years, both while she was in a relationship with Nicky and then the two years she'd been on the run.

Fear!

That's what Mason dealt with every time Lily or Gabby sneezed. Because Holly had died so young, he was terrified of losing one or both of his girls.

⁓

Mason was bored out of his mind, more miserable than he'd been in years and ready to climb the walls if he had to watch one more kid movie. Even Janie knocking on the open door to tell him that they were through cleaning and ready for payment was a good distraction.

"I'll be right back," he told the girls.

"Can you bring us some frozen pops? I want a red one and Gabby wants a yellow one," Lily said.

"No, I don't. I want purple. You don't know what I want," Gabby argued.

They were definitely getting tired of being cooped up and every bit as tired of movies as he was. He missed Annie Rose even more than the twins did. The whole house was empty without her, and every time he blinked he got another picture of her. There she was in the kitchen with the girls helping her cook. And there she was stretched out on one of the lounges by the pool. But the ones that stayed the longest was when she was curled up in his arms on the swing or when their lips met in a fiery kiss that rocked his world.

Janie poked her head out from the utility room where she'd been moping. "Had a little spat with the new nanny, did you? That's a different twist. Usually it's the twins who hate the nanny, but they really like this one. And she cooks like a dream. What's the matter with you?"

Mason wrote a check from the big black business book and tore it out with a flourish. "I don't have many rules, but when it comes to the girls being sick, I want to be told, and I want the doctor to come out here immediately."

Janie put the check in her pocket. "Well, shit! Did you tell her that when you hired her?"

"Now I know where Lily gets her nasty mouth," he said.

Janie leaned across the desk until she was looking right into his eyes. "I been cleanin' this house since long before she was born, and you knew I cussed when you hired me to stay on after your mama moved out. Hell, boy, I helped raise *you*, so don't be givin' me no lip. And you'd better listen up. That woman loves those girls, so you'd best make things right with her."

Mason managed a tight smile. "She is pretty amazing."

"Amazing don't even begin to cover it. I'd swear she was those girls' real mama the way she is with them…"

Mason held up a hand. "Okay, I was a jackass. You don't have to keep reminding me, but it worries me when they're sick."

"A sore throat is just a sore throat and Annie Rose had it all under control. I've sent my kids to school when they were worse off than those girls."

Mason sighed. "I guess I owe her an apology."

"Honey, you owe her more than that. I ain't never seen no one control them girls like she does. Martha is in shock. And Lily said that Annie Rose is a nurse, to boot? Man, you ain't never had it so good or shit in your nest so bad, either. We're leavin' now. We got another place to clean this afternoon. Tell the girls I hope they're all better by next week." Janie waved over her shoulder as she left.

Mason dragged his phone from his hip pocket and hit speed dial for Annie Rose. It rang five times before she picked up.

"Are they running fever? It's time for their next dose of medicine. I forgot to tell you what time to give it and I was fixin' to call you," she said.

"I'm sorry, and I don't want you to leave," he said.

A long pregnant pause made him hold the phone out from his ear to see if it had gone dark.

"Well?" he said.

"Good, because I'm on my way back, and I'm too damned tired to pack or go anywhere tonight."

"Then we'll see you in time for supper?"

"Yes, and I'm bringing a bucket of chicken with me, so don't let the girls eat until I get there," she said.

"Are we good, then?" he asked.

"Not really, but we'll talk about it later."

Chapter 16

WHAT IN THE HELL WAS SHE THINKING? SHE COULD not give the girls everything she'd purchased. It would completely spoil their Saturday trip to The Pink Pistol. That day should be special and a hundred dollars should feel like a lot of money, not a ho-hum, piddling amount after what Annie Rose bought on Tuesday.

She stared at the bags covering her bed and groaned. She'd broken the first and foremost rule she'd made when she disappeared two years before. Never buy anything you don't want to leave behind.

She'd also blown the hell out of rule number two: never have more things of importance than you can put in the ready-to-go suitcase.

"Mama-Nanny. Mama-Nanny!" Voices and footsteps said they were running across the foyer, through the dining room, and toward her quarters. She quickly grabbed the bags containing supper and hurried to the kitchen.

"I'm in here," she called out.

"We're hungry and we're tired of our room and we want to go see our goats and get in the pool and is that chicken?" Lily stuck her nose in the air and sniffed.

"Yes, it is chicken, and no pool until after Saturday. You don't want to get water in those ears and get a worse infection. Then you'd miss your trip to The Pink Pistol."

That familiar little tingle up the back of her neck said that Mason was right behind the girls. Blue eyes met green ones in a long gaze that told her he'd had enough time to get over his snit. And be damned if he hadn't showered and changed into faded jeans and a white T-shirt. One strand of dark hair hung down on his forehead, and she had to fight the urge to brush it back with her fingertips.

"Ask your dad about checking on the goats." She turned away and busied herself pouring the chicken into a bowl. From the second bag she removed slaw, hot rolls, and potato salad. She took four glasses from the cabinet, filled them with ice and sweet tea, and lined them up.

"We aren't going to take the food to the table?" Lily asked.

"It's the bar or back to your room on a tray," Annie Rose answered.

Lily hopped up on a bar stool. Gabby followed her lead and Mason moved from the doorway to the far end to take his seat.

"You didn't answer me, Daddy. Can we go outside for a little bit to see the goats? They'll forget all about us if we don't go see them," Gabby begged.

"We'll see after you eat supper," he answered. "Lily, it's your turn to say grace."

Annie Rose took her place on the bar stool beside Gabby. Mason on one end. Girls in the middle. Annie Rose on the other end. Was that the story of what their lives would always be? Girls between them, because in reality she was just the nanny?

Lily bowed her head and said in a loud voice, "Dear Lord, thank you for Mama-Nanny. Thank you for this food that she brought home for us, and thank you for bringing her back and not letting her run away. We love her, Lord, and we don't want her to leave, so make her stay. And, Lord, please make Daddy let us go outside before we climb up the walls. Amen."

"Amen," Annie Rose whispered.

"Amen," Mason said loudly.

"Pass the coleslaw," Gabby said.

"You was gone a long, long time when all you bought was chicken. We thought you'd run away forever," Lily said.

"Where did you go?" Gabby asked.

"I did some shopping. I have a little surprise for you for tonight at bedtime," Annie Rose said.

"Really!" Gabby's eyes lit up.

"Yes, really." She laid the back of her hand on Gabby's forehead. Cool as a cucumber. The girls would be wild again by morning, running and romping through the house like puppies let loose from a pen.

"Did you buy something for Daddy?" Lily asked.

"Of course. He's eating it right now." Annie Rose smiled sweetly.

"Well, thank you for bringing me something that I love," Mason said.

She was determined not to look at him, but her eyes went to his mouth. Those lips had kissed her, had sent shivers down her backbone when he nuzzled the curve of her neck. It had teased and flirted with her. How could she stay mad at him?

"We're sleeping in your room tonight," Gabby said bluntly.

"Why?" Annie Rose asked.

"Because we are sick, and what if we die?" Lily said.

Annie Rose felt the solid wall of fear that shot up on Mason's end of the bar. If the girls had any idea of how that word affected him, they'd never use it again.

"Anyone who can eat fried chicken and slaw like you two are not in any danger of dying," Annie Rose said.

"Okay then, but we'd sure feel better if you slept in the little room across the landing from us," Gabby said. "That way if we don't feel good, you'd be right there. Or we could sleep together in my bed and you can have Lily's room."

The little urchins were not sleeping in her quarters. Her bed was covered with stuff they couldn't see. She was not sleeping in Lily's room, because there was no telling what they'd cooked up.

"Okay, okay! If it will make you feel better, I'll sleep in the little room. Now finish your supper," Annie Rose said.

"Or you won't get to go see those rascal goats," Mason told them.

"Djali probably thinks I ran away with Mama-Nanny. If goats ate chicken, I'd take him a piece," Gabby said.

O'Malley let out a wailing meow as he wove his way around the bar-stool legs. Annie Rose pinched off a dime-sized chunk of chicken thigh and dropped it. The tomcat grabbed it midair, chomped a few times and swallowed, then put his front paws on her stool and begged for more.

"Djali is my goat. Jeb is Lily's goat. I guess we can loan you O'Malley until you can get your own pet. Daddy, we should get Mama-Nanny a puppy," Gabby said.

"Thank you for loaning me O'Malley. He is

enough pet for me," Annie Rose said quickly. Rule number three: never, ever bring home a stray. You'll get attached to it, and when you run, you'll have to leave it behind.

That reminded her of her last apartment. It had come furnished, so all she'd left behind was a few clothes in the closet, a couple of books in the living room, and some food in the pantry. It would take more to drive out there or to hire someone to clean out the apartment than losing the deposit would amount to.

But the wedding dress that she'd run away in was another story. The price tag that she'd carefully unpinned and left lying on the table in the conference room at the library had $1045.99 written on it. That could easily be a felony if she didn't pay for the thing. Merciful heavens, she'd been so careful, and now she could have a price on her own head for stealing a wedding dress.

"Excuse me for a minute," she said.

She hurried to her quarters, shut the door, and hunted up the name of the bridal shop that had loaned the dresses for the style show, hoping the whole time that they were still open.

"Betsy's Bridal." The voice said it was an older woman.

"Is this Betsy?"

"Yes, it is. You just caught me. I was on my way out the door."

"This is… Rose. I was one of the models at the library show a couple of weeks ago. The one who disappeared."

"Oh, my, are you all right? We were afraid you'd been kidnapped. The authorities are looking for you and your coworkers are very worried," Betsy said.

"I'm fine. It's a long story, but I had to run away from

someone, and I messed up the dress. I'll send a check or a money order tomorrow morning if you'll figure the tax. The dress was $1045.99. I remember the price tag very well."

"That's very kind of you. Let me see. That would be…" Betsy rattled off a number.

"Thank you. Your check will be there in a couple of days."

"Now take a minute and call the police in Odessa and your coworkers to put their minds at ease."

"Yes, ma'am," Annie Rose said.

The first phone call to the police station took a few minutes. They asked a dozen questions and were finally satisfied when she told them about Nicky Trahan. The one to the library took a little longer. They begged her to come back, offered to give her a raise, and said they'd hold the job until the middle of June.

She wrote the check for the dress before she ever left the room and signed her name to the bottom. That would be the first activity in the account in two years, so she took a minute to call the bank and tell them that she would be using the account more often.

When she finally got back to the kitchen, Mason had cleaned the counter, put away the leftovers, and done the dishes. A dish towel was thrown over Lily's shoulder and Gabby was drying the last of the silverware.

Lily ran to her side and wrapped her arms around Annie Rose's waist. "Thank God! We thought you crawled out the window and run away."

"I knew you didn't run off. I watched out the window. If you'd have run, I was going to chase you down," Gabby said. "Daddy said we can go play with the goats soon as we help clean up. Will you go with us?"

"Of course, and both of you listen up to what I'm about to say. I'm not planning on leaving the ranch, but if I do, I won't sneak out the window. It might make us sad, but I will tell you good-bye," Annie Rose promised.

"I'm glad. Now let's go see our goats. Daddy says we can play for thirty minutes and then we have to come back inside," Lily said.

Mason dragged two lawn chairs across the backyard, through the gate, and to the edge of the goat pen. He placed them side by side and motioned for her to have a seat beside him. As she eased into a chair, she was still thinking of all the phone calls she'd made, the opportunity to go back to her librarian job, and making a mental note to put the check in the mail to Betsy's Bridal shop the next day.

"Crazy goats. If someone had held me down and stuck needles in my ears, I'd be damned if I ran up to that human being and treated them like a friend." Mason chuckled.

The sound of his laughter and the girls playing with the goats was music in her ears. "You going to sit in this chair or did you drag it out here so I could prop my aching feet in it?"

"Prop away. I've spent the day sitting in a rocking chair and I'll gladly stand a while. We need to talk," he answered.

She stuck her boots in the extra chair and sucked in a lungful of air. "I'll go first. To begin with, first and foremost, I am their nanny. I will take care of those girls as if they were my own. I'm a nurse and I know medicine. I deserve some trust if I'm going to take care of them."

"You are right," Mason said. "I overreacted."

"And now about us. We need to go a hell of a lot slower until we get to know each other better," she said.

Rule number four: Don't trust anyone. And if you do, then you really need to give it lots and lots of time. No rushing. No moving in together. No engagement ring.

"Daddy, can we show our goats at the stock show next year? We're both in 4-H already and I bet Djali could win the champion trophy," Gabby yelled from the hay bale in the middle of the pen.

"No, he would not. He'd be reserve champion and Jeb would be the champion," Lily protested.

"Just because you got the champion trophy for your steer don't mean you would for your stupid old goat," Gabby argued.

Gabby and Lily suddenly put their heads together and whispered for a long time.

"You are right about all of that, Annie Rose. I worry too much. I wonder what they're cooking up now?" Mason nodded toward them.

Annie Rose waved at them. "You can bet it's something that involves us, because they keep looking this way."

The girls did a fancy handshake and then ran from the far side of the pen to where Annie Rose and Mason were watching.

"Looks like they've got their plans made," he said. "We'll talk more after they go to sleep tonight."

"We've decided that we are ready to get a shower and play a game. Y'all want Scrabble or Monopoly?" Lily asked.

"Why do we get to choose?" Mason asked.

"Because Mama-Nanny came back home and because we get a prize at bedtime and because we've got four people to play and four is better than three and besides you always win when we play and…" Gabby stopped for a breath.

Lily threw up both hands in exasperation. "And because we are *trying* to be nice."

"Annie Rose can choose," Mason said.

"Scrabble," she said quickly. Monopoly was as boring as watching grass grow, and if the girls argued over whose goat would win at the stock show, then they'd be rascals over who bought Park Place. Lord, help the whole ranch if one of them put a hotel on it and wound up winning the game.

"I got to warn you, I won the spelling bee last year," Gabby said seriously. "You sure you don't want to go with Monopoly?"

"I'll take my chances," Annie Rose said.

"We're going to get our showers, and Daddy can set up the game in the kitchen. That way we can have chocolate cake if we get hungry while we're playing. Does one of us need to stay with you two to keep you from fightin'?" Lily asked.

"I think we've got it settled," Mason said.

Lily shook her finger at Annie Rose and narrowed her eyes at Mason. "If you get into it again, we're going to make you stay in the same room until you are nice to each other."

"Bet I can beat you to the house," Gabby said.

"I can run faster than you." Lily was gone in a flash. "Whoever gets to the bathroom first gets first shower."

Gabby was right behind her. "You cheated. You didn't count."

Mason laid a hand on Annie Rose's shoulder. "The joys of parenting."

"Think they'd really put us in the same room if we had an argument?"

"It's what I do with them, and they hate it, so yes, ma'am, they probably would try to be that bossy." He laughed.

"Kind of hard to stay mad when there's two imps running around on the ranch, isn't it?"

"You got that right. Ornery kids, tomcat, and goats. Never a dull moment around here."

A warm glow started in the pit of her heart and radiated out to her fingertips. So this was the way normal adults settled arguments. They didn't run away, at least not forever, and they didn't use fists or belts.

A wide smile spread across his face. "You are blushing, Annie Rose. I like that you can do that. Not many women do anymore."

"I've always hated it, but it's part of me," she said.

He wrapped his arms around her in a hug, and with the sun setting behind them and two goats romping across the pen, they walked arms around each other back to the house.

Mason fought to the finish but lost the Scrabble game to Lily, who drew the *Q* and a *U* and held on to them until the end, played it on a triple letter with the word *quit*, and then managed on her final play to get in the word *quite* by using her last letter.

"I won. I beat Daddy for the first time ever." She danced around the room with both arms in the air.

"I do believe she is well, but since I said I'd sleep in the little room across the hall, I will. However, this is a one-night deal, girls," Annie Rose said. "I'm going to get my things and your little surprise and bring them up. I expect you to be in your beds when I get there."

The girls were both in Gabby's room, sitting on her bed, when Annie Rose brought out a journal and a set of fancy pens that wrote in bright neon colors for each of them. "If you start now, you can fill that journal up by Christmas and ask for another one from Santa Claus. When you are an adult, you can read them and see what was important to you when you were nine years old."

"Wow!" Gabby held the bright purple book to her chest. "I'm going to write in it right now. What is today, Daddy?"

"Today is May 26," he answered.

She wrote that down and said, "And no one can read it unless I say so, right?"

"That's right," Annie Rose answered. "A personal journal is very private. You can put your thoughts in it that you wouldn't tell anyone, not even Lily."

"She tells me everything, and I tell her everything," Lily said quickly.

Gabby's chin shot up. "But you aren't going to read my journal."

"Why would I even want to? We'll write the same things. I'm glad I got the pink one. It's my favorite color. Now y'all go on across the hall. Me and Gabby have to do our journals before we read ourselves to sleep." Lily bounced off Gabby's bed and headed toward her own room.

"Call if you need me," Annie Rose told her.

Mason kissed Gabby on the forehead. "When you finish logging in your entry for today, you can read for thirty minutes. Then it's lights-out."

"Okay, Daddy." She was already choosing another pen to write about her day.

"You, too," he told Lily when he kissed her.

"Okay. What color are you using, Gabby?" she yelled through the bathroom doors at her sister.

"Pink. You?"

"Green. Put in there what we did today and don't forget the good parts," Lily said.

"Good parts?" Mason asked.

"Poetry license," Lily said.

"You mean poetic?" Mason smiled.

"Yes, that's it. We are authors, and you can't see our finished work until it is published when we are old and write our memories," Lily said.

"Memoirs," Mason corrected her.

"That, too. Good night, Daddy."

The door into the old nursery was shut already when he crossed the landing and went to his room. He picked up the remote and flipped on the television. Reruns of *NCIS* were on, so he left it on that station. He kicked off his boots, removed his shirt, and was on the way to take a shower, when Annie Rose appeared in the bathroom doorway.

She had a pair of cute little pink bikini underpants in her hand, along with the well-worn, oversized nightshirt. Her blond hair had been freed from the ponytail and floated on her shoulders, and the harsh bathroom lighting made her eyes even bluer than normal. He wanted to take her in his arms and hold her tightly, to tell her to forget the nightshirt and underpants after her shower and come to his bed buck naked.

"Mind if I have a shower first? I could go down to my quarters and use my own bathroom. But if the girls hear me, they'll fake sudden nigh-unto-death symptoms," she said.

"Sure, I'll get one when you are done."

—᠁—

Annie Rose left her jeans and shirt in the old nursery and padded barefoot and naked into the bathroom after Mason had shut the door into his bedroom. Two sinks, two mirrors, made for two people. Did Mason remember Holly every time he looked at them?

She adjusted the water and flipped the switch to route it from faucet to shower head, pulled back the shower door, and stepped into the extra-deep tub. Jets in the sides meant that it doubled as a Jacuzzi. Leaning back, she let the water flow through her hair and then applied shampoo.

Mason swung the door back. "Mind if I join you?"

He was totally naked, ripped abs, bulging pecs, thighs made to fill out jeans, but oh, so sexy without anything covering them, and oh, my Lord! Her eyes stopped a few inches south of his belly button and refused to move up or down. Those hunks on the fronts of the romance books in their snowy white T-shirts could never compare to Mason.

"Here, let me work that shampoo into your hair, darlin'," he said.

Her knees went weak when his hands tangled into her long blond hair and started a deep massage. His hands were magic and the rest of his body touching hers seductively as they moved in the small confines of the shower was almost more than she could bear.

"You have lovely hair," he whispered. "The color of light honey right out of the comb."

"What if the girls…"

"I made sure both our doors are locked and their lights are out now." He moved her hair to one side and kissed the soft spot where shoulder meets neck, and she forgot everything, including her name and all the rules she'd made about relationships. When he'd rinsed the conditioner from her hair, she turned around to face him, gave a little hop, and wrapped her legs around his waist. He cupped her butt with both hands and groaned when she nipped his lower lip in a scorching kiss.

His tongue found hers and did a mating dance that produced a low growl from Mason. Annie Rose could scarcely breathe for panting. She moved one hand from around his neck and snaked it down between their slick bodies until she could circle his erection pressing against her belly. She shifted her weight and guided him into her in one swift motion, and he backed her up against the far wall.

The steady shower stream felt like warm rain. The bottom of the tub was cold and his hands were fiery hot. He took her right up to the edge of satisfaction before he slowed the pace, then he built up the speed again until she couldn't stand it anymore. She tensed her thighs and locked her feet together, pressed her body tighter against his. The kisses deepened more and more until she whispered his name in a throaty Southern growl, begging him to take the plunge with her.

Then he said something that sounded faintly like her name and they exploded together. He turned around, slid down the tile wall into the tub, leaned his head back, and she stretched out on top of him, the water spraying over her back as if they were behind a waterfall.

"My God!" she said.

"I know," he said as he ran his hands down the length of her wet body. "I like the way you feel on me… oh, my God!"

She propped an elbow on the side of the tub. "What?"

"Birth control. I had a condom. It's on the vanity," he said.

"Guess we'd best do some powerful praying." She giggled.

"It's not funny, Annie Rose."

She laid her head on his chest. "It kind of is funny. We're grown adults acting like a couple of sex-starved kids. I don't know about you, but I guess I am sex starved. It's been two damn years and birth control didn't cross my mind in all that heat."

"It's been over a year for me if that's an excuse and then there is the fact that you are sexy as hell."

She shut her eyes and found his lips for another kiss, as sweet as the afterglow turning the bathtub/shower into a rainbow of beautiful colors.

"Ready for round two?"

"Yes, but not in the shower. Let's take it to the bedroom," she said.

"Yours or mine?"

She kissed him on the chin and shifted her weight until she was beside him, one hand on his chest, the other snaked around his back. "You have a bed. All I've got is a futon."

He flipped the shower switch with his foot and then turned the water off with his toes. "Give me another minute so my legs can grow bones back in them."

"This ain't your first shower sex, is it?" She giggled.

"Matter of fact, it is. You've taken my shower virginity. I learned to turn off the water a long time ago when I was reading a book in the tub," he explained.

"Me, too," she whispered.

He sat up then stood up, slung the door open and motioned for her to go before him. When he stepped out, he dried himself quickly, then wrapped her in an oversized fluffy towel and put another one around her wet hair, scooped her up in his arms, and carried her out into his bedroom. He sat down in a wooden rocking chair with her on his lap and dried her body from neck to toes and then towel dried her hair. Then he picked up a hairbrush and carefully worked all the tangles from her long hair.

Afterglow hadn't ended in the bathroom. It had followed them into the bedroom, and now the whole room had fuzzy edges. His naked, hard body holding her, the sensation of a man brushing her hair, the kisses that were growing hotter and hotter with every one all blurred together into a hot puddle of lusty hunger.

He moved from chair to bed with his lips still on hers, but the towels had been left behind. She wasn't sure when they were finally sated and fell asleep, but the last time she checked the clock it was after two in the morning.

Chapter 17

MASON'S SINGING IN THE SHOWER AND GIGGLES OUTside the bedroom door woke her as the sun rays drifted through his window and made pretty patterns on the dark brown comforter. She sat straight up and wondered where in the hell she was for a split second, before the whole previous night played out in her mind in fast speed. She jumped out of bed, made a mad dash through the bathroom, and was jerking on her underpants when the girls knocked on her door.

"Just a minute," she called out.

"For what?" Mason asked from the open bathroom door.

He didn't have blond hair or she would have thought he was a Greek god. Instead he was a bad-boy cowboy with a body of steel and tough hands that all made her feel like a wanton hussy.

"Shhh." She nodded toward the door.

He crossed the tiny room, slid his arms under hers, and picked her straight up, planted a hot kiss on her lips, then set her back down. "Good morning, beautiful. I'll see you in the kitchen in a few minutes."

"Mama-Nanny, we're all well and we're going to go out to feed the goats. We'll be back real soon to help you fix breakfast," Lily yelled through the door.

"Okay," she said.

Mason picked up her bra from the futon and

held it out. She walked into it and he brushed a soft kiss across each breast before he covered them. He reached around and fastened it as he moved upward to the hollow of her neck and made sweet love to her body with nothing but his mouth. When he slipped her arms through the straps, she was ready to forget breakfast, her job as a nanny, and turn into the wanton hussy again.

"I wouldn't mind a bit if you moved up here into this room permanently," he whispered.

"It's tempting," she answered. "But many more nights like last one, and there'll be nothing left of us but ashes."

"It was hot, wasn't it?" He chuckled as he slipped a shirt down over her head. "There now. You are a nanny."

"I like being a nanny, but I really liked…"

"Being a lover?" His green eyes sparkled.

"Yes," she said honestly.

"Me, too."

———

That evening after the girls were asleep, Mason and Annie Rose watched the edited video of the ear-piercing on the television screen. She was cuddled up in the curve of his arm with her head resting on his hard chest and her leg slung over his.

"It was funnier at the time, but my folks will get a kick out of it," he said.

"It would be funnier now if I could get my mind off the hot sex we had last night." She snuggled even closer. "Listen. That's rain."

"Texans can't ever complain about rain or hot sex."

He made lazy circles on her upper arm with his thumb. "Both are pretty important in our world."

"You mean ranchin' or bedroom?" she asked.

"Both. You ever wish you hadn't left the ranchin' business?"

"I cried all the way home after I signed the papers to sell it."

He laced his fingers in hers and squeezed gently. "Would you buy it back?"

"At one time I might have."

"But that road is closed. You chose another path that led you to today, right?"

She shifted positions until her lips reached his for a long, sweet kiss and then whispered, "Experience is what you get when you didn't get what you wanted."

"Another bit of wisdom from your mama?" Mason asked.

"No, I saw it on a T-shirt. Wished afterwards that I'd bought the shirt."

"We've all been there. Tonight I'm getting the experience of sitting here with you and wishing that I could have broken away from work long enough to go to town to buy you roses and candy," he said.

She leaned far enough back that she could see his face. "I'm not a roses-and-candy woman. I would far rather have a bouquet of wildflowers stuffed down into a Mason jar, and the type of man that goes with that kind of life."

"I have to admit I was also thinking about something called sex. We pushed our luck last night and we can't be taking chances with the birth-control issue anymore. I should have gone into town for condoms," he said.

She kissed him on the cheek. "You mean you don't buy them by the case and keep them in a safe in your room?"

"Why would I do that?"

"You're pretty damn sexy, Mason Harper. You've got a good-sized ranch, two girls that are adorable, and you aren't too shabby between the sheets. I'd figure you for a cowboy who would get lucky real often," she teased.

"One out of three isn't too bad."

She frowned.

"I do have a big ranch, thanks to my ancestors who built it up for me. But, honey, you might be the only person in the great state of Texas who thinks my girls are adorable. I've had a couple of relationships that could have possibly gotten serious since Holly died, but they couldn't stand the girls. And I haven't gotten lucky in more than a year, because word spread like wildfire that the whole package here comes with a set of twins that would scare the horns off of Lucifer. And rule number one, that I've never broken one time until now, is that I do not have women in the house," he said.

She settled back into his shoulder. "Their loss."

"Reckon we could stay here all evening like this? Or maybe sleep together without sex? I love the way you fit in my arms, like it was meant to be."

"No, sir. The air around me is already cracklin' with sexual energy and all you are doing is holding me. If you were beside me in bed, I wouldn't sleep a wink for wanting you," she answered.

A grin split his face, showing even, white teeth. "Honest, aren't you?"

She remembered the way those teeth felt when they raked across her lips or nipped gently at her breasts, and shivered. "The girls will be antsy about The Pink Pistol on Saturday, so I intend to keep them real busy tomorrow. We will do errands all morning and have lunch out, so you can eat in the bunkhouse with the guys. Got anything you need done in town other than for me to pick up a big box of condoms at the drugstore?"

"You'd buy condoms?" he asked.

"Darlin', I'd steal them if that's what it took to take care of this yearning in my body," she answered.

His chuckle was deep and sensual. "Take the truck and have a good day. I'm going up to bed, and since you asked, there are a few things you could take care of while you are in town."

She pulled his face down to hers for one more lingering kiss. That's all she allowed herself to have though, because one more, and she'd throw caution out in the goat pen.

She broke away and said hoarsely, "Make a list."

"After that kiss, I'm not sure my brain can function well enough to write my own name." He blew a kiss over his shoulder on his way out of the den.

The lights were out in the girls' rooms, but when he made it to the top of the stairs, he heard whispering, so he put his ear to the door and listened.

"They're still not fightin'. We did a good job," Lily said.

"I wish we'd thought to get our walkie-talkies out

and hide them so we could have heard the fight they had when they got in their rooms. So you think they got it settled?" Gabby asked.

"I don't know. On *The Parent Trap* those parents fought for a long time before they learned a damned thing. Don't look at me like that. I can cuss and Daddy didn't hear me, so that one don't count," Lily said.

"Do you wish we hadn't asked for them goats for our birthday?"

Lily's voice came through loud and clear. "I thought they'd be like O'Malley. We'd let them in the house and play with them and then they'd go on out in the yard. That's the way it worked in the cartoons. But now that we got them, I intend to whip Damian's ass at the stock show next spring with Jeb. His mama was mean to Mama-Nanny."

Mason pressed his ear harder so he wouldn't miss anything.

Gabby's voice was next. "Damian said that next year was going to be a good one in school because his mama was going to teach fifth grade."

"Well, shit! I'm not going to be in her class. Are you?"

"Hell, no!" Gabby said. "If they put me in there, I'll give Damian two black eyes the first day and they'll put me somewhere else."

"She don't like us, so she won't let us be in her class anyway. We ain't got nothing to worry about," Lily said.

"But what if they don't give her a choice and we get her?"

"You think we could get Mama-Nanny to home-school us?" Lily asked.

"We've got all summer to plan it so that she has to,

don't we? Maybe we need to make her another how-to book."

"What does she need to know how to do? She started rememberin' right after we made her the first book, and now since she read the second one, she's doin' a good job of bein' a ranchin' woman," Lily said.

"We need to make her a *How to Be a Mommy Book*," Gabby said.

That put an idea in Mason's head and he smiled all the way to his bedroom.

—∿∿—

Both of the girls' booklets were on Annie Rose's nightstand and she read them at least once a day. When she found another one lying on the coffee table the next morning, she smiled and picked it up. Would it tell her how to pierce a goat's ear, or better yet, how to hold a tomcat down and put an earring in his ear?

The title on the front of the third booklet said *How to Be a Mommy*. She sat down in her recliner and smiled as she opened it.

Number 1: *First you got to get kids. You can't be a mommy without kids. It just ain't possible.*
Number 2: *Twins are the best kind of kids, because only kids like Damian are little shits. Lily said that, Mama-Nanny, so if anyone gets in trouble for bad words, it's got to be her.*
Number 3: *Girl twins are better than boy twins. Two of Damian would make the angels and even God shudder.*
Number 4: *You got to love the kids to be a*

good mommy. We think that you love us almost
as much as we love you, so you will make a
good mommy.

Number 5: *A good mommy would never put*
her girls in a schoolroom where Damian was or
where his mommy was a teacher, neither one.
We love you, Mama-Nanny.

They'd both signed their names using the bright-colored ink pens that she'd bought them. She traced the letters with her fingers. There was no way they loved her as much as she did them. It simply wasn't possible.

There was a soft rap on her door, and Mason opened it before she could. She walked into his open arms, and he said, "Good morning, beautiful."

"I love the way you say that," she murmured.

"What do you have there?" he asked.

She put it in his hands and took a step back. "It's the third *New York Times* bestseller, entitled *How to Be a Mommy*. I have two more in the bedroom: *How to Remember* and *How to Be a Rancher*. They're all full of important information written by a set of twin girls who are experts in the field."

He smiled all the way through the reading and handed it back to her. "Do you think they'll buy a jet with all the money they'll make from selling those books?"

"Probably a tour bus for their country band." She giggled. "I love the books and hope that by the time the twins are grown, I have a dozen or more."

He pulled her toward him, she laced her arms around his neck, and her lips found his. Two giggling girls were evidently having a race to the kitchen, but she didn't want the kisses to end. She wanted to melt right into his body and become one with him and to find her way into the depths of his sexy green eyes before she faced the day.

"I don't know how to explain it, but this sure feels right," he whispered.

"Me, too," she said. "But we'd better do some racing of our own if we're going to beat them into the kitchen."

Chapter 18

THE GIRLS HAD BOOKS TO RETURN TO THE LIBRARY, SO that was the first stop they made that morning. The librarian's expression looked like she'd sucked all the juice out of a lemon when she saw Lily and Gabby, but she did manage a weak smile when she noticed Annie Rose.

"Hello, are you the new nanny out at the Harper place?"

"Yes, I'm Annie Rose. We've got some books that are due back in the next couple of days, and I understand that it's story hour this morning."

The librarian nodded. "It's starting in five minutes. Are Lily and Gabby staying?"

"Please, Mama-Nanny. Please," Lily begged.

"Of course, you can stay. I've got a couple of errands to run right here close, and I'll be back in an hour," Annie Rose said.

"We require a cell phone number for emergencies," the librarian said.

Annie Rose wrote her number on the sticky note that the librarian handed her and then stooped down so that she was on eye level with the girls. "Be on your best behavior or you won't get to come next week."

"Yes, ma'am," Lily said.

"If we are good, then we get to come every time?" Gabby asked.

"One week at a time. If you are nice, then you come

back the next week. I was the story-hour lady at my last job, and it's hard if there's child who doesn't behave. Do you understand me?" Annie Rose asked softly. "A bad apple can ruin the whole barrel."

"Damian is a bad apple, right?" Gabby asked.

Annie Rose asked, "Is Damian Miller here?"

"No, ma'am. He is staying with his grandparents in Bells this week, thank goodness." The last two words were barely audible and the woman blushed after she'd uttered them.

"Thank you. I'll be back in an hour," Annie Rose said.

"Bye, Mama-Nanny," the girls said in unison.

"Mama-Nanny?" she heard the librarian ask as she showed the girls to the story-hour area.

"She's our new mama. Daddy gave her to us for our birthday. She was wearing a wedding dress and sleeping on our porch swing," Lily said.

Hopefully, the librarian would chalk that story up to an overactive imagination, like Dinah had done.

She walked from the library to the drugstore to buy condoms, a bottle of alcohol, since the one in the cabinet was almost empty, nonaspirin fever reducer, and maybe one of the thermometers that read the temperature from the ear. She'd always found them to be a lot more accurate, and since the girls had allergies, she wanted to be absolutely sure what she was dealing with when they got sick.

"Well, hello. I'm surprised to see you still in the area." Dinah Miller was behind the counter. "What can I help you with today?"

Well, you can bet your bitchy ass it's not condoms, Annie Rose thought, but she smiled brightly and said, "I've got a list, so I'll gather it all up."

Dinah rounded the end of the cash counter and followed her. "I guess Lily and Gabby are waiting in the truck. I have to thank you for not bringing them in the store. We do have breakable items in our gift section."

"They are at story hour," Annie Rose seethed. She'd gladly pay for whatever they wanted to throw at Dinah. Hell, she'd pay double if they hit her every time they hurled an item across the store.

"Well, thank God Damian is at his grandma's for the week. Poor little thing doesn't stand a chance when those two heathens gang up on him," Dinah said.

"I thought you taught school," Annie Rose said through clenched teeth.

"I do, but in the summers I work here part-time. I'd go crazy if I had to sit at home all day with nothing to do," she said.

"I don't see what I need and I'm sure the prices are better at Walmart, so I'll buy what I need there," Annie Rose said.

"You don't need to get pissy," Dinah hissed. "You might fool the whole town, but I know you're out to fleece Mason. I'd be willing to bet that within a month after you get Mason to marry you without a prenup, that you ship those horrible kids off to boarding school. Not that I'd blame you for that, but Mason deserves better."

Annie Rose knotted both hands into fists but remembered the lecture she'd given the girls about being good. "I'm not going to ship them anywhere. I'm going to request that they both be put into your classroom next year."

"You wouldn't dare!" Dinah gasped.

"Don't test me. A nice big donation to the school

library would probably get the principal to do what I asked, don't you think? Now you have a nice day and a wonderful summer." Annie Rose walked outside with her head held high and drove straight to the Dairy Queen. She ate a banana split, but it didn't cool her raging temper one bit

Story hour was just ending when she arrived at the library. The librarian gave Annie Rose a thumbs-up sign as they left, so evidently the girls behaved much better than they had in previous trips.

"Dinner or Walmart first?" Annie Rose asked when they were buckled into the backseat of the truck.

"Walmart. We had cookies and milk at story hour. Next week we get to bring our favorite book and read two pages out of it," Gabby said. "The lady said that nine years old was kind of old for her to read to us and that she wanted to know what kind of books we like. And what about Daddy and his dinner?"

"That sounds like a wonderful idea. Your daddy is eating at the bunkhouse today with Uncle Skip. Which book are you taking to read next week?" Annie Rose asked.

"Well, it damn sure won't be my journal." Lily clamped her hand over her mouth. "Sorry, Mama-Nanny. I try not to cuss but it comes out like it does when Janie talks."

"Try harder," Annie Rose said.

After the X-rated language that had run through her mind in the drugstore, she sure didn't have the right to condemn Lily for one little naughty word.

Walmart was off Highway 82 and only fifteen minutes from Whitewright. The girls talked nonstop about what book they were going to read from the next week, while Annie Rose swore that she would indeed home-school the girls if the principal said they had to go into that bitch's classroom. Or she really would try to buy them a place in another room. Surely to goodness the elementary school in Whitewright had more than one fifth grade.

She found a parking spot not far from the store entrance, and watching the girls skip along in front of her came close to putting her in a good mood. She grabbed a cart right inside the doors and pulled out the ranch credit card and the list Mason had made. His handwriting was bold and masculine, like the man behind the pen. That made her think of his hands working the tangles from her hair.

"I need shampoo," she said aloud.

"So do we but not that baby stuff, Mama-Nanny. We're grown-up enough to read in story hour, so we can have big-girl shampoo, right? The kind that smells like green apples or coconut like you use," Lily begged.

Gabby put in her two cents. "And she didn't even say a bad word, so that ought to count for something."

"Okay, but if you throw a fit and cry when soap gets in your eyes, I won't feel sorry for you," Annie Rose said.

They squealed and hurried ahead of her to the cosmetics department. They had to check out every bottle in the whole section before they agreed on one that smelled like green apples. The next item was toothpaste, and Annie Rose almost shouted when they tossed it in the cart without a five-minute discussion. She was rounding the corner, searching for alcohol, when she spied the condoms, but how in the hell was she going to get them out of the store?

"Condoms." Lily giggled.

"We don't want any of those," Gabby said loudly.

"You know what those are?" Annie Rose asked.

"Kenna told us when we went to a sleepover at her house. She lives in Savoy and her daddy had some of those in his medicine cabinet and when she asked her mama what they were for, she found out that they keep babies from happening, so we don't want any of them in our house," Gabby said.

"Why's that?" Annie Rose prodded further.

Lily gave her an adults-are-sure-stupid look, sighed loudly, and shrugged. "We wanted a mama real bad because we need a mama. But if we don't have a mama then we can't have a baby brother, and that's what we really want. Kenna is getting one and it's not fair that we can't have one too."

Annie Rose couldn't get a box of condoms in the cart under their all-seeing eyes, but she did sigh when she passed them by.

"Babies are noisy and messy and they sure take a lot of time and attention. You can't put them in a pen and water and feed them twice a day, like you do the goats," she said.

"We know, and we know that we'd have to share Daddy, but Kenna is always braggin' and sayin' how she's goin' to teach her baby brother how to ride a pony and how to swim, and all we got is O'Malley and goats. It's not fair," Lily complained.

"What if you got a baby sister instead?" Annie Rose put three loaves of bread in the cart.

Gabby clapped her hands. "We'd like that even better. Kenna can have her old brother baby if we can have a sister. She can be in our band and sing with us and we'll dress her up and put those big bows on her head."

Lily smiled like the old proverbial cat who'd found the canary out of the cage. "And if you are our mama, she'll have blue eyes and hair like ours, right?"

Annie Rose had been shoved so tightly into a corner that she was speechless. Never in her life had she been so grateful to see someone as she was Natalie Allen pushing her cart right toward her.

"Well, hello! Y'all out doing the week's errands?" Natalie asked.

"We're talking about getting us a baby sister. Maybe we'll even get two, like you are getting. I bet you don't have condoms in your house, do you?" Lily asked.

"Lily, there are some things that ladies don't discuss in public," Annie Rose said.

"See, that's why we need a mama, so we'll know them things," Gabby declared.

"Why don't you girls go find me a bottle of vanilla extract over in the spices aisle? Stay together and make sure you get the pure vanilla," Annie Rose said.

Gabby grabbed Lily's hand and off they went.

"Sounds like you're having fun today." Natalie laughed.

"Oh, yes, ma'am. We passed the condoms aisle, and they found out this past week that they prevent babies from happening. They aren't sure how, but now all they want to talk about is that." She laughed. "It won't be long until you've got a couple just like them."

"I hope so. I know they can be a handful, but I don't want a couple of wimpy, whiny girls. I want them to be like Lily and Gabby." Natalie put a hand on her round belly.

"Be careful. You might get what you wish for," Annie Rose told her.

And I wish I was carrying Mason's child, Annie Rose thought.

Sweet Jesus! Where did that thought come from? she questioned the crazy voice that had thought such a ridiculous thing.

"We're ranchin' women, not city gals, so we have to be able to do everything the boys do and then shuck our boots and turn into divas when it's necessary. That's what Mama told me," Natalie was saying when Annie Rose jerked her mind back to listening mode.

"Mine, too." Annie Rose nodded.

"Y'all going to the Resistol Rodeo next weekend?" Natalie asked.

"Have no idea. Mason did mention it."

Lily and Gabby returned, vanilla in hand, and Lily said, "Not this weekend. We're going to Miranda Lambert's store in Oklahoma."

"The Pink Pistol?" Natalie smiled.

"Yes, yes, yes." Gabby said. "I can't wait."

"Well, y'all have a good time. Maybe I'll see you at the rodeo this summer. It was good to see you again, Annie Rose. Y'all need to come out to the ranch for the afternoon. Or maybe we could go to dinner. I bet these girls could help Henry babysit Josh," Natalie said.

"Yes, we could," Lily said.

—∾∾—

Errands were run.

McDonald's had provided a fine meal of chicken strips, fries, and chocolate malts.

The truck bed was loaded with bags of cattle feed and the other supplies Mason needed for the ranch, and there were no more stops to be made. It was four o'clock and in amongst the bags was everything from toothpaste to air freshener but not a single condom.

She could always go to another pharmacy, out of town, of course, since Dinah worked at the one in Whitewright, and get a morning-after pill. That might seem extreme, but desperate times called for desperate measures and Annie Rose wanted to have sex with Mason that night. Everything she touched or saw that day brought up a mental picture of him, and she couldn't wait to get home.

"I'm thirsty. Can we stop at the Mini-Mart for a Dr Pepper?" Lily asked.

"We are five minutes from home, and there's soda pop of every kind in the refrigerator," Annie Rose said.

"But I'm thirsty now, and I might die from dehibration before we get home," Lily said.

"Dehydration is the word."

"It won't matter if I'm graveyard dead, and that will make Daddy so sad," she said.

"Then I expect we'd better have a Dr Pepper. We sure don't want your daddy to be sad." Annie Rose put on the blinker and pulled into the parking lot of the little convenience store on the outskirts of town.

"Besides, we haven't seen Miz Edith all summer," Gabby said.

"You've only been out of school two weeks," Annie Rose said.

Lily quickly undid the seat belt and slung open the truck door. "That's all summer."

"Well, look who has come to give me hugs." A little, short woman who was as wide as she was tall, came around the end of the counter and swept the girls into an embrace. "How's your summer going? I heard you had a new nanny. You girls want to introduce me to her?"

Lily nodded. 'Miz Edith, this is Annie Rose Boudreau. Only she's not our nanny. She's our new mama. We got her for our birthday and she's going to have us a baby sister."

Annie Rose shook her head. "These girls are wishing for the moon."

Edith smiled. "And stars, I'd say. You girls better get on back there to the cooler and find you a Dr Pepper and then I expect since you haven't been here in almost a month, you better pick out a candy bar to go with it. My treat today, since you give such good hugs."

Lily grabbed Gabby's hand and they chased off toward the back of the store to the coolers and then came back halfway to ponder over which candy bar they wanted.

"They've wanted a mama for a long time," Edith whispered. "And bless their hearts, they need one desperately, so don't get on to them for speaking what's on their minds."

"Wouldn't think of it." Annie Rose smiled. "While they're picking out a candy bar, could you point me toward the restroom?"

She was sitting on the potty when she saw the condom machine in the ladies' room and had to bite her lip to keep from giggling. Thank you, God, for a bathroom with a door that locks, she thought as she pulled up her jeans and fished in her purse for money. She found several quarters in the bottom of her purse and used all of them, not even caring that the condoms were neon pink, yellow, and green when they fell out of the vending machine. She stuffed all three into the side pocket of her purse and made sure the zipper was closed all the way before she left the restroom.

—◦—

"Damn woman! You smell like roses, vanilla, and something else exotic." Mason gathered her into his arms and sank his face into her hair that evening. The door to her apartment was closed and locked firmly.

"I'd almost given up on you," she said.

She'd taken a long bath after she kissed the girls good night and helped them choose the book for next week's story hour. Candles were lit in the sitting room and in the bedroom. Both were rose-scented, so the tiny apartment smelled like a garden. Everything was ready, even Annie Rose. If he had a notion that he wanted to play for an hour, then he could pick something up and knock it out of his brain. She wanted raw sex and instant satisfaction, at least the first time around. The second and third, she might be ready for slow, lingering lovemaking.

"Oh, honey, I've waited for this all day. You did find the protection?" Mason said.

She wrapped her arms round his neck and rolled up on her toes. He bent slightly and their lips met in a scorching kiss that left her with boneless legs and no air in her lungs. "I have protection and I'll tell you the whole story later. Right now I want you to hold me and make wild, passionate love to me."

He picked her up and carried her to the queen-sized bed in her room. "I'm glad you aren't naked. I like unwrapping presents."

She hadn't thought when she bought the sexy little teddy in Victoria's Secret that she'd ever be wearing it for Mason. Not that day, not after the argument, but she hadn't bought pretty lingerie in two years, and she wanted it. So it had come home with her.

"Looking at you in jeans and boots turns me on. Looking at you in this... there are no words." He untied the strings holding it together and carefully kissed the hollow of her neck and her breasts.

He tossed it to one side, removed his own pajama bottoms in one swift motion, and stood beside the bed like a god from another world—tall, sexy, lean, strong, and sinewy. She reached out and ran a hand up his thigh to his erection.

"Foreplay or play?" he asked hoarsely.

She tumbled into the bed and propped up on an elbow. "Play this time. Foreplay next time. I've waited all day for this and thinking about it was enough foreplay. Protection is on the nightstand. Take your pick of colors."

"Oh, we got inventive, did we? We really should have a little preseason show with all this bright color." He picked up the yellow one and chuckled. "I haven't used something like this since I was in high school."

"I don't want to hear about you and other women," she said.

"Annie Rose, there's never been a woman other than

you that I've had in this house. It was my number one rule." He pulled her close to his body as he stretched out on the bed beside her and massaged her back with one hand as he traced the outline of her lips with the forefinger of the other one. "I love the shape of your mouth. Just thinking about it all day turned me on."

"Mmmmm!"

"Feel good?" he whispered.

"Don't wake me if I'm dreaming." She put a hand on each of his cheeks and brought his lips to hers. She rolled over on top of him and tried to wedge a hand between their bodies, but it was impossible, so she shifted her weight slightly so she could touch all of him. His pulsing body said it was time and she started to straddle his waist.

But Mason wasn't finished playing. He flipped her to one side and started at her toes, kissing each one slowly, stringing more kisses up her inner thighs, stopping to taste long enough that it made her arch her back and beg for him to make love to her.

"Now?" He kissed her hard and rolled on top of her at the same time, covers going every which way on the bed.

She wrapped her legs around him. "I thought we were having fast sex. I want you."

With a firm thrust he started a rocking rhythm that shot her straight upwards toward the twinkling stars outside her bedroom window. He made love to her with open eyes, and she did the same. When the end came, everything in the room sparkled and the afterglow was absolutely brilliant.

"Oh. My," she mumbled.

His mouth covered hers and her body went completely limp.

Mason rolled to one side, and space, even though it was only a few inches, separated them. She quickly plastered herself next to his body.

"Now I'm hungry," he said.

"For what?"

"I'd say seconds, but, darlin', after that it'll take me a while to build up the strength for another go at it."

"I've never, ever…" she gasped.

"Intense?" he asked.

"Doesn't begin to cover it."

He drew her closer to his body. "You are…"

"What?" she asked.

"Absolutely amazing. Every time is spectacular. Long, short, yellow protection, no protection. I swear, Annie Rose, it's fantastic with you," he said.

"That is the best after-sex line I've ever heard," she gasped.

He rolled to one side but kept her in his arms. "It's not a line, darlin'. It's the God's honest truth."

She made a mental note that, tomorrow morning, she'd take care of the trash. She damn sure didn't want to explain to Lily or Gabby why she had a yellow balloon in her trash can. But right then Annie Rose made plans to take the girls to the convenience store for soda pop, and she planned to have a whole roll of quarters in her purse.

Chapter 19

BLAKE SHELTON'S "HONEY BEE" PLAYED ON THE truck radio. The girls whispered in the backseat about what they might buy at Miranda Lambert's Pink Pistol store. Mason kept time with the music on the steering wheel with his thumbs.

Crossing the bridge over the Red River, Annie Rose could see the big "Welcome to Oklahoma" sign. It reminded her of all the bridges she'd burned or crossed in the past two weeks.

Thank God, it seemed like months since she'd jumped when the phone rang or avoided surveillance cameras in service stations and grocery stores. "Daddy, do they have condoms at The Pink Pistol?" Lily leaned up and yelled over the top of Blake's song.

His thumbs went completely still. "What did you say?"

"She wants to know if they have condoms at The Pink Pistol," Gabby hollered even louder.

"Where did you even hear such a word?" Mason asked.

"Kenna told us about them. We don't want any in our house, because Kenna says that they keep babies from being born. And we want a baby sister. We did want a brother like Kenna is getting, but we changed our mind," Lily said.

"You got us a mama for our ninth birthday. We want a sister for our tenth," Gabby said.

Mason turned off the radio and glanced over at Annie Rose.

She smiled. "Your turn. I had mine yesterday right in the middle of the Walmart store."

Mason took a deep breath. "That is not something we are going to discuss today. It's only been two weeks since your ninth birthday, so it's too early to talk about the next one."

"Can we discuss it when we are older?" Lily asked.

Mason looked into the rearview mirror. "Much older."

"O… kay!" Lily stretched the word out to six syllables.

"Like ten years old," Gabby pressed.

"Like maybe twelve years old," Mason said.

"But, Daddy, that's three whole years. We'd be grown-ups before our baby sister could even walk," Lily moaned.

"Well, if they have those things we aren't supposed to talk about at The Pink Pistol, then I'm not even going to look at them," Gabby said. "I'm using my money to buy stuff for my room. I want a poster of Blake and one of Miranda and I want a T-shirt to wear the first day of school to show everyone that we got to go there and I want to sit up on them bar stools and have a Dr Pepper before we leave because I'm sure that Miranda has set on them bar stools. It's going to be a wonderful day and when our baby sister is nine years old we'll take her to The Pink Pistol."

"By then we'll be famous enough to open for Miranda on her concert tours," Lily said.

Annie Rose poked Mason on the shoulder. "Dodged a bullet there, didn't you?"

He gave her a long sidling look and shook his head. "So how did you fare in Walmart?"

"Not much better," she admitted.

"So that's why you bought vending machine items?"

"That and the fact that Dinah Miller works at the drugstore in Whitewright," she said. Mason had kissed her. Mason had made love to her. Mason had had wild sex with her. And still just sitting close to him turned on hot chemistry that she couldn't begin to understand or explain. Maybe it had to do with the topic of conversation and the visual of him wearing those neon colors the past few nights.

Lily stopped whispering and exclaimed, "Dinah Miller! Did I hear you say her name? Please, please don't let them put us in her room next year. Can't Mama-Nanny homeschool us, Daddy? We'll be good and do our lessons without fussin' about it."

"How do you know about homeschooling?" Mason asked.

"Kenna says her mama might homeschool her next year. If her mama and daddy decide to go do missionary work all the time, then she'll be homeschooled and she told us all about it. She says that she will get to go to school in her pajamas if the school is right there in her house and her mama is the teacher," Gabby answered.

"Kenna again," Mason said out the corner of his mouth.

"Don't blame her. This is the age of curiosity," Annie Rose told him.

"You are not going to be homeschooled. If you were, you couldn't be in 4-H and show your animals. You couldn't play basketball or be cheerleaders. Do you want that?" Mason asked.

"We'd be damn nuns rather than go to Mrs. Miller's class. And I'm not saying I'm sorry for cussin' neither. She's a..."

"Lily Diane Harper," Mason said in a low voice.

Gabby took up for her sister. "Well, she is, Daddy. I bet she even has condoms in her house because she wouldn't want another baby like Damian. He might even be the reason she is so… crazy."

"The next girl that says that word is going to be grounded to the house for a week. No swimming, no television. I might not even let her have dessert or play with the goats all week either."

"Whew! It must be worse than cussin'," Lily said.

Gabby made the gesture for zipping her mouth. "We didn't know it was a bad word, Daddy."

"The next person who talks about that word is going to do dishes for a week too," he said.

Lily abruptly changed the subject. "Gabby, do you think they have petticoats at The Pink Pistol? I need one for my lace skirt so I'll look like RaeLynn when I sing 'I Want Your Boyfriend.' Someday I'm going to be on *The Voice* and I'm choosing Blake Shelton for my coach."

"Smart daddy," Annie Rose said.

"I'll be a crazy daddy by the time I get them raised."

They passed the Choctaw Casino on their way to Durant and the flashing billboard out front said that Carrie Underwood would be appearing there in four weeks. Squeals rattled around in the truck like high-pitched echoes in a canyon.

"Daddy, can we go see her? Please. We'll give up our trip to Six Flags this summer if you'll take us to see Carrie," Gabby begged.

"And if we can get a backstage pass to get an auto-graph, I won't even burn down the school if they make me be in Mrs. Miller's room," Lily declared.

"It's air-conditioned. Six Flags isn't," Annie Rose reminded him.

"That is six weeks away. We'll see what happens between now and then," Mason said.

"That means we have to be good for six weeks plus give up our trip to Six Flags, but I guess it's worth it," Lily said.

"Hell, yes, it's worth it! It's Carrie, baby!" Gabby high-fived with her sister.

"Win one. Lose one." Annie Rose giggled.

Miranda renovated an old drugstore to make The Pink Pistol. She kept the soda fountain and the bar stools, and that's where Mason and Annie Rose headed while Lily and Gabby touched every single item in the store at least a dozen times.

"What can I get for y'all?" the dark-haired girl behind the counter asked.

"Coffee," Mason said.

"Vanilla Dr Pepper," Annie Rose told her.

"You were going to tell me the whole story, but we were busy last night," Mason said.

"If I say that word, will I have to wash dishes for a week?"

"I've got a better idea. Every time you say it, we have to use one in the coming week. I wonder if Miranda has pink ones in this store." He made a show of looking around the place.

"Here you go. You want to wait to see if you buy something else before I run the tab?" the girl asked.

"Yes, please," Mason said.

"Were you looking around for something particular?" she asked.

"No, ma'am, just checking on my daughters, who intend to spend some serious cash in here." He smiled.

"Well, let me know if you need anything else," the girl said and went to the far end of the counter to wait on another customer.

"You blushed!" Annie Rose popped him.

"Is it as sexy as when you blush? Don't answer that. Nothing is that sexy. Now tell me the story about the things they must not sell in here," he said.

She told him the whole thing as she sipped the vanilla Dr Pepper.

"You really need to go to the doctor so we don't have to worry about those things." He motioned for the girl behind the counter to refill his coffee cup and bring Annie Rose another soda pop.

"I'm making an appointment with a gynecologist in Sherman on Monday. Are you trying to force me to have to use the ladies' room by buying all these sodas for me?" she asked.

"Yes, ma'am, but it will all be up to you about what you buy from the vending machine, since you avoided saying the word through the whole story. However, you did talk about the forbidden word, so I suppose by rights we should buy at least one today. Since the girls want a baby sister, maybe it should be neon pink."

She leaned in close and said softly, "That's not even funny after the way we got carried away a few times."

Mason leaned over, kissed her on the cheek, and said, "I think I'm falling in love with you, Miz Annie Rose."

"Daddy, Daddy, look! We found petticoats and

there's two of them so we can each have one and look like twin RaeLynns. Can you hold them for us, Mama-Nanny, so no one else will get them? We're going to look at some more stuff. And guess what, I found a sign for my room but I want to make sure that's what I really want." Lily shoved two fluffy petticoats at Annie Rose and disappeared around the end of an aisle that had round racks offering all kinds of Miranda T-shirts.

"I can take those for you and hold them back here until the kids are done," the girl from behind the counter said.

Annie Rose passed them over to her. "Thank you so much. Now where were we?" She turned back to Mason.

"I said that it would be easy to fall in love with you," he repeated.

"But would it be wise?"

He cocked his head to one side and their eyes locked in the short space between them. Slowly his chin went up and down in a nod. "I believe it might be the wisest thing I could do in this lifetime."

"Then you have my permission," she said.

Gabby ran from the shirt rack over to the soda fountain. "Mama-Nanny, which one do you like better?"

One was pink and the words on the front said, "You gonna pull them pistols or whistle Dixie?" The other one was brown and said "Pink Pistol... for the wild at heart."

"I'm buying whichever one she doesn't buy," Lily said.

"They both look too big for you," Annie Rose said.

"Not with these," they said together and whipped blinged-out cowgirl belts from behind their backs.

"We're goin' to wear them like dresses with leggin's

under them and our boots and with new belts. We wanted to buy boots, but all they sell is big-girl boots and we don't have enough money. So we decided on the petticoats, a T-shirt and a belt, and a sign for the door into our rooms," Lily explained.

"Well, then in that case, I think Lily should have the pink one and Gabby should buy the brown one and you can share," Annie Rose said.

"What sign?" Mason asked.

Gabby pointed. "That one right there. They've got two of them. That one has hot-pink letters and the other one at the back of the store has baby-pink letters. Lily is getting the hot-pink."

The sign was nothing more than an old piece of barn wood with a big metal Texas star in the middle. "Dang" was written above the star and below it was "Cowgirl."

"It's not really cussin', Daddy," Lily said.

"And it will remind Lily to say dang instead of damn," Gabby said.

Annie Rose smiled at Mason. "Sounds like a good deal to me."

Mason narrowed his eyes at the purchases and said, "It looks like you've put a lot of thought into your birthday presents. So if you are sure, we'll pay the lady and go up to the Dairy Queen for lunch."

"Well, we did want a Blake calendar, but we ran out of money," Lily said.

"It's almost June. The year is more than halfway done," Annie Rose reminded them.

"But we'd have the pictures forever." Gabby sighed.

"They're goin' on for half price tomorrow and there's only two left," the girl behind the counter said.

"So you'd sell them to me for half price?" Annie Rose asked.

She nodded. "Yes, ma'am."

"Okay, then that will be my present to you girls today," Annie Rose agreed.

Lily hugged Gabby. "Wow. We got it all. We are going to be stars."

"You spoil them as bad as I do," Mason whispered.

She brushed a quick kiss across his lips as the girls ran to the cash register with their purchases. "I know, and I love it."

You could never walk away from them now. Not them or their father, her inner voice said as she pulled a bill from her purse to pay for the two calendars.

I don't intend to. I'm falling in love with him, too, she said silently.

Chapter 20

ANNIE ROSE AWOKE TO THE AROMA OF BACON AND coffee. She slipped on a pair of lounge pants and an oversized sleep shirt. The scent was even stronger when she started down the short hallway to the foyer. Near the kitchen she heard the girls' giggles and Mason's deep drawl.

When she peeked into the kitchen, Mason shook his head at her and held up his palm before he said loudly, "Now, it's time to run out to the backyard and pick the biggest, prettiest rose for the tray. You want your mama-nanny to be surprised and happy when we take her breakfast… in… bed."

When the back door slammed, he crossed the room in a few long strides and turned her around by the shoulders. "Go back to bed and pretend to be asleep. This is a big surprise they cooked up all on their own for you."

As she ran back to her quarters, she heard Lily saying, "We got two roses right by the porch. A red one and a yellow one. We don't know which color our mama-nanny likes best."

High-pitched giggles preceded footsteps as Mason carried in breakfast on a tray, with the two flowers taking center stage. Annie Rose cracked one eye open in time to see both girls jump right in the middle of the bed and squeal.

"Wake up, Mama-Nanny. It's Sunday and we brought

you breakfast in bed because we had such a good time yesterday and we wanted to do something nice for you," Gabby said.

Annie Rose grabbed them both and pulled them down into the pillows with her, showering kisses all over their cute little faces. "What a lovely surprise. I feel just like a queen."

"Well, Queen Mama-Nanny, if you will sit up, we'll put this over your lap and you can have breakfast in bed this morning."

She'd never get tired of seeing the glimmer in Mason's green eyes or the crow's-feet around them when he grinned.

"Daddy helped us. When we make bacon, it burns, but we stirred the waffle mix all by ourselves and we put the strawberries and whipped cream on the top. Did we get enough strawberries? We got more in the kitchen if you want more," Lily fretted.

"They look perfect." Annie Rose put a forkful in her mouth and rolled her eyes toward the ceiling. "You girls didn't make this. Angels did."

"No, Mama-Nanny, we made them. Now taste Daddy's bacon," Gabby said.

She bit off a piece of crispy bacon and chewed. "Wonderful! Is this a dream? If it is, don't wake me, because I'm sure enjoying it."

"It's not a dream. It's for honest-to-God real," Lily declared.

Annie Rose wiped a hand across her forehead and stole a glance at Mason standing beside the bed. Damn, that man stirred her juices when all he did was look down into her eyes with a smile on his face.

She turned back to the girls. "I thought for sure I was dreaming. This is the most wonderful thing anyone's done for me in a long, long time. And would you look at those beautiful roses. Did you order them special?"

"No." Gabby giggled. "But we picked them special from our own rosebushes just for you. We're going to get ready for church now. Daddy says we can wear our new shirts and our belts with our boots. I'm wearing my pink lacy leggings and Lily is wearing her black ones. Will you use your curling iron on our hair and put a flower on one side like RaeLynn wears?" Gabby asked.

"I sure will, but I'm not rushing with this wonderful breakfast so take your time," she said.

Their bare feet slapped against the hard wood floor as they raced to their rooms. Mason sat down on the side of the bed, picked up the fork, cut a piece of waffle, and fed it to her. "No wonder they love you so much. You really are a great mama-nanny."

He kissed the tip of her nose and then both eyelids. "I've completely fallen in love with you these past two weeks, Annie Rose. I'm wondering if fate brought you to me for a lifetime, instead of the girls for their birthday. Please don't ever, ever leave us."

She started to speak, but words wouldn't come out past the lump in her throat.

He laid a finger across her lips. "I don't want you to say the words right now. First I want you to think about what I said. And if you ever do feel the same way, then tell me, but don't say anything right now. The moment is perfect, and if you don't feel the same, I can't bear to spoil it."

"Daddy, Daddy, shut your eyes," Gabby bellowed from the top of the steps.

"Why?"

"We want to surprise you." Lily's voice was even louder.

"Trash!"

"Why would you say that?" he asked.

"Trash! Put it in my bathroom under the sink. Hurry!" High color filled her cheeks at what must have been going through his mind when he realized what was right there on the top of the trash can. There they were two grown, consenting adults, having to hide the evidence of a night of wild sex. Not from their parents but from a couple of little girls.

He'd picked up the can and shoved it under the bed and had barely sat down in the rocking chair close to her bed when Gabby and Lily rushed into the room. They were a cross between rockers and country stars in their outfits, but the smiles on their faces were pure little girl.

"Open your eyes, Daddy," Gabby said.

He pretended to study them, rubbing his chin, cocking his head to the left and then to the right, pursing his lips, and drawing his dark brows down. "What do you think, Annie Rose?"

"I think they look almost like country music stars," Annie Rose said.

"Almost," Gabby wailed.

"Well, your hair is a mess of tangles and you don't have your flowers on one side. When we get that done, then you'll be guaranteed, bona fide country stars for sure," she said.

Mason clicked his fingers. "It's the flower. That's what was missing. Ask me again when you get your hair all fixed and then I'll pass judgment. I really think it's going to make you look too old, though. What happened to my little girls?"

"We're growing up. We are country music stars in the making," Gabby said.

Mason grabbed a hairbrush from the nightstand and used it like a microphone. "Move over, RaeLynn and Miranda. The Harper sisters are taking center stage."

"Yes, we are," Lily said. "Now go shave. Mama-Nanny is going to finish eating and then we have to get our hair fixed all up and our flower in it."

Annie Rose chose a white eyelet sundress trimmed in baby blue for church that morning. She'd bought it on her therapy trip, along with pale blue sandals made of soft kid leather and decorated with white pearls. Her hair was pulled to one side in a loose braid that hung over her shoulder.

Mason sat at the end, Lily and then Annie Rose with Gabby at the other end. He wore creased jeans and a plaid shirt, but she undressed him with her eyes and relived bedroom hours right through the first hymn, the Sunday school report, and until the preacher cleared his throat.

"This morning it has been laid upon my heart to preach about the value of friendship," he said in a booming voice.

That reminded her of Gina Lou, her best friend in South Texas. She and Gina Lou had grown up on adjoining ranches, rode the bus to school together, went to college and got their nursing degrees at the same time, and then worked together at the same hospital. It had been two years since Gina Lou had convinced her that if she didn't get away from Nicky that he'd kill her in a fit of rage someday.

"Run away and don't look back. Don't even call me, not until the time comes that you know for a certainty that you are really safe," Gina Lou had said. "That way if he has connections and checks my phone, he won't find a call from you."

Annie Rose was safe now, and as soon as church was over she planned to call Gina Lou. If her cell phone number had changed, surely the hospital would know how to reach her. Then an antsy feeling that someone was staring at her jerked her right back to the church. She glanced over to see Mason's eyes go from amused to dreamy soft, and Gina Lou took a backseat to her previous visions of Mason's hard, trim body lying next to hers.

"And now," the preacher said, "I'll ask Everett Bradshaw to give the benediction, but instead of standing at the door, I'll be in the fellowship hall to greet all y'all. This is our church's seventy-fifth anniversary and we are having our annual potluck today. Don't worry if you forgot. I checked the tables, and there's enough food in there to serve a whole army. Just join us for good visiting, good food, and a good time. Now, Everett, if you'll say a blessing for the service and the food of which we are about to partake, I would be grateful."

"I didn't bring anything," Annie Rose whispered.

Everett's loud voice sounded across the sanctuary. "Our father in heaven."

Mason leaned behind Lily and whispered, "I gave the church half a beef for the party."

Evidently Everett was hungry, because his prayer was short and to the point. He thanked God for the church to worship in, for the food, and for the hands that prepared it, amen. And immediately the noise level went from a one on the Richter scale to a ten plus.

Lily grabbed Gabby by the hand and raced to the other side of the church, where Doc and his wife were sitting with Kenna, and guessing from the pregnant lady with them, Kenna's mother.

"Sorry I didn't tell you sooner, but when we get a few minutes alone, I'm damn sure not thinking about things like church parties and Angus picnics." He grinned.

"I would have brought something, like a cake or even one of those cheesecakes you keep in the freezer," she fussed.

He ran a finger down her bare arm and asked, "Are we fighting? Does that mean makeup sex later?"

She poked him in the chest. "Next time, tell me when there's something going on. I hate going to a party empty-handed."

"I told you that I brought the meat for the party."

She folded her hands across her chest, right under her breasts. "How many people know that bit of news? They'll all think I'm shirking my duties."

"Lovely shelf you made there for some lovely items."

His eyes settled on her breasts sitting so pertly on top of her hands, which turned into a blur when she jerked them down and popped them on her hip bones.

"Dinah will think I didn't bring anything, won't she?" Annie Rose asked.

"Who gives a rat's ass what she thinks?"

Annie Rose put a finger over his mouth. "You are in

church. If Lily said that, she'd have to wash dishes for a week."

He smiled and kissed her forefinger. "The word we aren't going to discuss has nothing to do with a rat's posterior."

"So, are you two having a lover's spat?" Greg Adams asked from the end of the pew.

Annie Rose's cheeks immediately burned with high color. She'd completely forgotten that they were in a packed church and there were other people around.

"We know what those are like, so don't deny it," his wife, Emily, chimed in.

"Did y'all ever have one?" Annie Rose asked.

"Oh, honey, you come on with me to the fellowship hall, and we'll discuss how many we've had. There's one good thing about a real good fight."

"Makeup sex," Greg said under his breath.

"You got it, darlin'." Emily kissed him on the cheek and looped an arm through Annie Rose's, dragging her away from Mason. "Let me tell you our story. I'm a mail-order bride."

Mason couldn't remember the last time his world had been so right. "How did you know that Emily was the one?"

"I didn't. My heart did. Took me a while, but I finally listened to it. Is Annie Rose the one? Have you told your mama?"

"Not yet. I want to be sure."

"Well, my friend, I got news for you. She's going to know the minute she sees y'all together."

Mason patted Greg on the shoulder. "I'll tell her before she sees us together."

Greg motioned toward the church doors. "Guess you'd best get a speech ready in a hurry then."

Sure enough, there was his mother and father, Lorraine and Sam Harper, in the flesh, coming right at him.

"Surprise!" Sam waved.

"We decided at the last minute to come home for the church anniversary and see y'all," Lorraine said when they were closer.

"Where are my granddaughters?" Sam asked in a deep, booming voice as he hugged Mason.

"Already in the fellowship hall," Mason answered.

Lorraine pushed Sam to one side and tiptoed to hug her tall son. "Seems like a year since we've seen them, instead of three months. There's something different about you."

"I wouldn't know what," Mason said.

"I think he's speechless. You've really surprised him," Greg said.

Lorraine turned slightly and patted Greg on the shoulder. "Greg Adams. I'm glad to see you. Once I had my baby boy in sight, I couldn't see anyone else. Is your grandmother here?"

"Already in the fellowship hall. It's good to see you, too."

"I understand you got married recently. Congratulations!" Lorraine said.

"Thank you, Miz Lorraine. I can feel Emily willing me to get my butt in there with her." Greg reached out a hand and shook with Sam. "Good to see you, sir. You're lookin' fit."

"Lots of sunshine and good food, son. And that business about willing you to come to her… it don't never end." Sam smiled. "Well, Son, what are we waiting for? When we talk on the phone, my granddaughters tell me that you have bought them a new mama. There was a big story about finding her in a white dress on the front porch swing. Was Gabby pulling my leg or was she telling the truth?"

"It's a long story, Dad," Mason said as he led the way to the fellowship hall.

"Is she here?" Lorraine asked.

"Yes, she is, and the girls love her, Mother," Mason answered.

"They seem to. How about you?"

"That's another long story," he said.

The minute they were in the fellowship hall, Annie Rose left a group of women and joined him. "The girls want to know if they can sit with Kenna and her mama. I told them I'd come ask you. I don't know what the protocol is at a church function here. Do families sit together at this thing?"

"Annie Rose, I'd like you to meet my mother, Lorraine, and my dad, Sam," he said.

"You are Annie Rose, the new nanny?" Sam asked.

She extended her hand. "Yes, sir."

His handshake was firm and his face an older version of Mason's. His eyes weren't as soft or as deep green, but they were kind. "We had a couple of free days, so we decided to surprise Mason and the girls with a visit."

"The girls will be so tickled to see y'all. And I'm pleased to meet you, too, ma'am." She turned and held out her hand to Lorraine.

"We talk to the girls at least once a week, and they seem to like you better than those damn goats they got for their birthday." Lorraine did a no-nonsense quick shake and then drop.

"Lorraine," Sam scolded.

"God knows I cuss," she said. "Let's go eat. I'm hungry. And, Mason, we will be here for two days. Our flight to London is booked for Tuesday night, so if Annie Rose would like some time off, this would be a great opportunity."

"Whatever Annie Rose wants to do is fine with me." Mason held his arm out, but Annie Rose shook her head.

Lorraine waved across the room and grabbed Sam by the arm. "Oh, there is Clarice. Come on, darlin', we've got to go talk to her. And I see all the old crowd with her. I can't wait to hear the newest gossip in the area."

"Now we are fighting. That was mean, springing your parents on me like that, and now you are sending me away for two days?" she whispered.

"Hey, darlin'. I had no idea they were coming until they walked through the church doors, so we can't fight over that. Not unless you really want an excuse for makeup sex. And what am I supposed to say? That a grown woman who's worked her ass off can't have two days to do something she'd like to do?" he said out the side of his mouth.

"I'm not going anywhere, and there will be no makeup sex with your folks in the house," she declared.

Chapter 21

ANNIE ROSE PUSHED THE SWING WITH HER BARE FOOT and drew her knees up, propped her arms on them, and watched the black storm clouds brewing in the southwest. Mason had gone with Sam to tour the ranch and talk about bulls, steers, heifers, and the fall sale. Lorraine was in the girls' rooms, spending quality time with her granddaughters. Lorraine had taken over the kitchen and the girls, leaving Annie Rose feeling like nothing more than a nanny. She probably should have taken a couple of days off and driven out to West Texas to see her friends at the library.

Supper had been beef stew and corn bread with ice cream and frozen strawberries for dessert. The girls had been so excited they barely touched their food, so they'd need a snack before bedtime. She remembered times when Gina Lou had come to her house for a sleepover and her mother had made peanut butter and marshmallow cream sandwiches for a bedtime snack. She'd cut the crust off, quartered the sandwiches, and had served them on her fanciest platter.

Annie Rose instinctively reached for her cell phone in the hip pocket of her jeans, but she was still wearing the white sundress she'd worn to church that morning. The phone was in her purse, and that was in her bedroom. The swing had come to a stop, so she padded across the porch and into the house.

Lorraine's giggles mixed in with the girls' floated down from upstairs and a streak of jealousy made its way into Annie Rose's heart. Their grandmother needed time with them, Annie Rose understood that, but she couldn't help wishing that she'd been invited to join in. Truth was she was totally alone for the first time in two weeks and she hated it. Two years ago, she'd been happy in her solitude after living in tense abuse for so long, but now she loved the noise of a family around her.

She'd planned on curling up in the recliner in her sitting room, but when she had the phone in her hands, the walls closed in on her, so she stomped her feet down into cowboy boots and headed out the back door. The chairs that Mason had pulled up beside the goat pens were still there, so she claimed one and poked in Gina Lou's telephone number by memory.

It rang five times before Gina Lou answered. "Hello, who is this?"

"Gina Lou, is that you?"

"Yes, it is, and it's in the middle of the night. Who is... my God... Annie, is that you?"

"Yes only I'm Annie Rose these days. Where are you?"

"South Africa," Gina Lou said.

"What in the hell are you doing in Africa?"

"I married a doctor and we're here working for the Doctors Without Borders program," she said. "Where are you, and the service is horrible here, so if I lose you I can reach you at this number, right? Is it safe?"

"Nicky is dead."

"Then I guess you are safe unless you killed him."

"I didn't. It was a plane crash that got him and his new girlfriend."

"And where are you?"

"In a little bitty town in North Texas. It's a long story. Go back to sleep and we'll talk another time. I just wanted to hear your voice," Annie Rose said.

"We'll be home for a few days in a couple of weeks. We have to see each other while I'm home, since it's safe now."

"I agree, and I can't wait to catch up. Call me when y'all get home and we'll make plans."

"God, it's good to hear from you. I'll call you when we get back to Texas. Bye now," Gina Lou said.

Annie Rose barely had time to say good-bye when she heard the screen door slam, making enough noise that the goats hid in a the far corner of the pen.

"Mama-Nanny, Mama-Nanny," Lily yelled as she and Gabby ran across the backyard toward her. "We couldn't find you and we were scared."

"Scared of what?" Annie Rose smiled.

Gabby plopped down in her lap and hugged her tightly. "That you'd run away."

Annie Rose brushed Gabby's hair back behind her ear. "I'm not going anywhere. I was talking to my friend, who is working in Africa."

"Wow! Africa. Granny, remember when you went to Africa and brought home all those pictures of all those lions?" Lily asked.

Lorraine sat down in the chair beside Annie Rose. "Yes, Grandpa and I took a safari trip there a couple of years ago and we saw zebras and rhinos and giraffes too."

"Well, I bet they don't have goats like Djali and Jeb in Africa, so you have to stay in Texas, Mama-Nanny," Lily said.

"I don't imagine they have goats like Djali and Jeb anywhere." Annie Rose smiled.

Gabby hopped off Annie Rose's lap. "Especially goats with gold hoops. Come on, Lily, let's show Granny how they like to play."

Lorraine had changed from a flowing skirt and matching cotton sweater to a pair of faded jeans and a knit shirt with a picture of Big Ben on the front. Her blond hair was streaked with silver and her blue eyes said that she was as open and honest as her son.

"They like you," Lorraine said.

"I love them," Annie Rose said.

"That's why they like you. You've done wonders with them in such a short time. You are a good nanny, but I'm not sure I like them calling you mama-nanny."

"That was their idea, not mine," Annie Rose said.

"Hey, Granny, look at Jeb's earring. It was Mama's, and guess what, O'Malley lost Mama's diamond stud. We pierced his ear, too, but he must've scratched it out," Lily yelled from inside the pen.

"Oh, my God! Does Mason know?" Lorraine asked Annie Rose.

"I took the diamond out of the tomcat's ear and switched the hoops with some similar but inexpensive ones that I had. Mason knows, and the real ones are hidden safely now," Annie Rose explained.

"God bless your heart," Lorraine gasped.

Annie Rose waved at the parade when it passed by her. "Mason filmed it and put a copy of the video in a stick drive so you can take one with you."

Lorraine nodded stiffly. "I'd like that. They grow up so fast."

Jeb did something Lily didn't like before Annie Rose could think of anything else to say. Lily chased him down, held his ears with her hands and made him look her in the eye. "You do that again and I'll send you to the slaughterhouse. I won't even take you to the damned old livestock show, and Djali will win it. Are you going to behave?"

"She's just like me. They both have my hair and eyes, but Gabby acts more like her mother. Holly had a temper, but she didn't cuss like a sailor. She let things simmer until she'd had enough and then she exploded. Me and Lily, we take it head-on, like grabbin' a bull by the horns the minute he charges us. Not much simmers with us," Lorraine said.

Annie Rose got the message loud and clear. It was going to be a long, long two days until Tuesday when they drove away in the rental Cadillac sitting out in front of the house.

Mason parked his truck beside the house and Sam bailed out like he was in a hurry, yelling across the yard as he semi-jogged toward the goat pen. "Don't let the girls leave before I get there. I want to see if they are training those goats good enough so that they'll win a trophy next spring."

—◇◇◇—

Annie Rose had taken her shower and was curled up in her recliner with a book when she heard the gentle knock on the door. She grabbed a cotton kimono-type robe and belted it around her waist. Mason had a hand on each side of the doorjamb and she barely had time to snap her eyelids shut before his lips had claimed hers.

Nothing else touched: bodies, hands, not even eyelashes. But everything from her toenails to her hair follicles purred like a happy kitten.

"Not with your mother in the house," she whispered.

"How do you think she got me?" He grinned.

Her resolve melted. "After a marriage had taken place, and believe me, I'm the nanny in her eyes."

He picked her up and carried her to the recliner, where he sat down with her in his lap. "Is that a proposal?"

She blushed.

"It is not," she said.

"Well, damn! I was hoping it was," he teased.

"Maybe after two years. Certainly not after two weeks."

He tipped up her chin. "Time is nothing but numbers on a clock that marks the sun coming up and going down."

A strange noise like static on a cell phone caused them to look toward the bedroom at the same time. Annie Rose cocked her ear to one side and shut her eyes. There it was again, and that time it was more like white noise.

"What is that? Did you leave something plugged in, like a hair dryer?" Mason asked.

She put a finger over his lips and said, "Shhhh."

She got down on her hands and knees and followed the faint noise to the love seat. The green light on a walkie-talkie shone like an alien Cyclops eye in the darkness.

"What is it?" Mason asked.

"Thank you for stopping by my apartment. I called you in here because I want to talk to you about the girls," she said loudly. "And I need it to be private."

"What?" Mason dropped to his knees and stared at her.

She pulled his face to hers and whispered in his ear, "Walkie-talkie under the love seat."

He nodded. "Have they broken any rules? Are you going to resign from being their nanny?"

She sat up with her back against the love seat. "Oh, no! They've been very good, especially with their grandparents here. You know how kids can get when their granny and granddad come to visit. That's not the problem."

Mason drew her into his arms. "You smell wonderful," he whispered softly in her ear.

His warm breath was like a blowtorch, sending flashes of pure fire through her veins and making her ache with desire, but damn it, everything they did would be picked up on the walkie-talkie.

"Oh, no!" she mumbled.

"What?" he mouthed.

She cupped a hand over his ear and whispered, "I don't know if the girls put them there or your mother."

"Girls, I can understand. If Mother did this, we're going to fight," he said as he reached under the love seat and brought out the walkie-talkie. He left her door wide open and she made it to the bedroom window in time to see him set it on a fence post beside the goat pen.

She'd flat-out fallen in love with Mason in only a few short weeks.

In love! Her inner voice screamed so loud that she covered her ears.

"Sorry, but it's the truth. I don't intend to broadcast

it on the radio, but I will tell him when the time is right. But I bet it causes a war between him and his mother," she muttered.

Chapter 22

ANNIE ROSE AWOKE IN A FETAL POSITION FROM A nightmare, sweat pouring from her forehead and whimpering. She felt the presence in the room with her but was afraid to open her eyes. Nicky's death had been staged, so she'd let her guard down. The girlfriend had been a ruse, and he was right beside her bed. In a few seconds she would be a dead woman and she hadn't even told Mason that she'd fallen in love with him.

"Good mornin'," Mason said.

She slid one eye open and carefully scanned the room. It wasn't real. It had been a very bad dream and she was safe. The air conditioner kicked on and cool air against her wet skin made her shiver.

Mason pulled back the curtains and bright sunlight chased away the shadows hiding in the corners and the fears hiding deep in her soul. "Today is ours. We'll start by going out to breakfast."

"Where is everyone? Why didn't you wake me earlier? Lord, your mama is going to think I'm horrible," she said.

He was dressed in good jeans, the ones with creases, and a starched shirt, and he smelled like heaven. She blinked to get everything in focus and realized that he'd shaved and even shined his boots.

"Mother says that you are to have the day off, and you won't take it unless they kidnap the girls and leave.

The rest is my idea, so hop up, madam, and let's have a day and night just for us." He laughed.

She pushed back the covers. "What are you talkin' about?"

"Today and tomorrow is ours. Mama and Daddy made plans to take the girls to see their cousins and didn't tell them until they woke them up this morning real early. It's all mapped out. They are having breakfast this morning at the Dallas airport and flying to Houston. It's only an hour flight, so they'll be there midmorning. This afternoon they're touring NASA, because Dad says they need something cultural. Then this evening they'll have supper at my brother's place and swim in their pool. Tomorrow they'll fly back to Dallas, and I'm to pick up the kids at the airport. My folks won't come back here. They are leaving from the Dallas airport to fly to Germany to see my brother who is in the service. They're doing a stopover in London on the way, and on the flight back, they're going to come through California and see my other brother before they go back to Florida," he explained.

"And when was all this planned?"

He held up his palm. "Right hand to God. I did not know a thing about it until about five o'clock this morning when Dad woke me up to tell me that he was kidnapping his granddaughters. So where are we having breakfast?"

She stretched and yawned. "In the kitchen. Naked."

He leaned forward and kissed her. "Sounds tempting, but it ain't happenin', darlin'. Now if you'll hold that thought until tonight, we will definitely revisit that naked idea. We will wind up in a hotel tonight somewhere near Dallas, but the rest of the time, we will do whatever you want."

She wasted no time getting out of bed. "Give me ten minutes and I'll be ready to go."

Mason hummed Brad Paisley's "Waitin' on a Woman," as he sat down in the recliner. The last time he'd waited, there had been three ladies who came out of her quarters and they'd been headed for a ranch picnic. Would it take as long for one as it had for three? He smiled and checked the clock. Ten minutes went by and then another ten.

It was worth every minute at the end of half an hour when she walked out of the bedroom, suitcase in hand. She wore a pale blue dress that brushed the top of her knees, a pair of brown cowboy boots with cutouts of baby-blue roses. Her hair floated on her shoulders like a blond halo and her perfume made him want to gather her close and never let go.

"Annie Rose, you take my breath away," he said.

"That's a damn fine pickup line but, darlin', I'd rather spend two days in bed with you right here on the ranch than go to a fancy hotel," she said.

"And when Mother asks where you went on your days off, are you going to give her those details?" he said.

"I could lie."

He took the suitcase from her hands and laced his fingers in hers. "Not to her. She's raised four boys, remember."

When he turned the key to start the truck engine, the radio was on a country station and Trent Tomlinson was singing, "One Wing in the Fire." He reached to turn it down and she covered his hand with hers and shook her head.

"You like that one?" he asked as he put the truck in gear and left the ranch behind.

Her blue eyes floated in a bed of tears. "I could have written that song about my daddy. Mama said she'd never liked the bad-boy type before she met him. That song came out right after he died and she'd play it over and over again. Sometimes I thought they hated each other, but they had a love that ran deeper than the surface."

He laid a hand on her thigh and squeezed gently. "So was he an angel with no halo and one wing in the fire, like the lyrics say?"

Her chin quivered slightly, but she kept the tears at bay. "He was sure enough a back-row Baptist and front-row sinner like the words say. But I thought his halo was perfect and I never smelled the smoke on his wings, let me tell you."

"I can't say that about my dad. We locked up horns a lot and still do," Mason said.

The song ended and she dabbed away one lonesome tear that dripped down her cheek. "I'm sorry. I guess I'm missing them today. So where to for breakfast?"

Mason ran the back of his hand down her neck and traced her jawline with his finger. "It's your day and you get to choose where we eat breakfast this morning."

"McDonald's."

"Are you kidding?"

She shook her head. "Not in the least. I want a sausage biscuit and a cup of their black coffee."

Miranda Lambert kicked up the music with "The Fastest Girl in Town." He kept time with his thumb on the steering wheel. "So were you the fastest girl in

Beaumont? Tell me about your past. Did you ever turn on the charm when you got pulled over, like she's singing about?"

Annie Rose turned off the radio and giggled. "I'm not an angel, but I was only in jail one time. That was when I was a sophomore in high school. My girlfriends and I were running up and down Main Street in our little town, honking at the boys and yelling at our friends, like kids do in small towns. Cop pulled us over because her mama's car didn't have a current license plate. He asked for registration and her license, and when she opened the glove compartment, there was the biggest damn pistol I'd ever seen, and believe me, I grew up around guns. He hauled us to the jail and put us in a cell block until her mama could come down to the station and show that she had a permit to carry a weapon and that she'd bought her car tag but hadn't put it on the car that day."

Mason was glad to hear her voice go from sad to happy. "What'd your mama say about that?"

"Daddy was on the porch when I got home. He said that it was a lesson in small-town livin', that I couldn't do one thing that wouldn't get back to him before I could get home. And that's the extent of my jail time. I wasn't the fastest girl in town, but I wasn't the slowest either. I fell somewhere in between. Does that disappoint you?"

He parked on the side of McDonald's, unfastened his seat belt, and leaned over the console to kiss her on the cheek. "The past is just that. Here we are at the golden arches breakfast palace."

They sat in a back booth across from each other, knees touching under the table and sparks dancing all around them. Mason hadn't thought it possible to give his whole heart away twice in a lifetime, but it had happened, and in such a short time that it completely blew his mind.

Annie Rose reached across the table and touched his hand. "The gears in your mind are working overtime. I can see it in your eyes."

Mason grinned. "I'm in love with you, Annie Rose. I don't just love you. I'm in love with you. There's a big difference and adding them together makes it right."

Tears welled up in her eyes again. It reminded him of a rainbow arching across the sky while the last few drops of rain still fell upon the earth.

"You make me happy," she said. "And I didn't think I'd ever find that feeling again."

"Me, neither," he whispered as he leaned over the table to kiss her on the cheek. "It's kind of heady, having it all, isn't it?"

"There are no words. Now, tell me, how far is it from the ranch to the airport and what time do we need to be there tomorrow?"

"It's one hour to the airport if there's no traffic problems. I usually allow an hour and a half," he said.

"And where are we right now?"

"Van Alstyne."

"Which is about thirty minutes from the ranch, right?"

"Where are you going with this?"

"I'd rather have a tour of the ranch on the back of a four-wheeler than do anything else today. Can this date please, please take us home?"

Home.

She had said that she wanted to go home.

"We can leave the ranch tomorrow in time to get the girls and maybe have supper with them somewhere.

I'm not interested in malls or shopping or anything but spending time with you at home," Annie said, and Mason's heart flipped over.

He reached for her hand. "Not only are you beautiful, you are the best thing that Bois D'Arc Bend has ever found asleep on the front porch."

"Now that's one smooth line, Mr. Harper. Let's go home and you can show me the rest of Bois D'Arc Bend. I've only seen the goat pens, the bunkhouse, the house, and a barn off in the distance. Wow me with a tour. Take me back to where Skip's granddad lives."

"You got it, darlin'."

—⁓—

Mason was backing out of the parking lot when Annie Rose's phone rang. She fished it out of the side pocket of her purse and answered it. "Hello, Gabby, have you gotten to the airport yet?"

"Mama-Nanny, where are you? I called the phone in the kitchen and you weren't there, so I called the number that you told me to write in my journal in case you didn't answer the one in the house. Are you outside with the goats?" Gabby sounded frantic.

"No, your dad took me out for breakfast, but we're on our way back to the ranch now. Are you all right, darlin'?"

She heard a sob and suddenly Lily was on the phone. "We can't go, Mama-Nanny. Uncle Rory called and said that he was glad we weren't already on the plane because our cousins have the damn chicken pox and we haven't had them."

"But you've had the shot for them, right?" She looked

across the console at Mason. "Have the girls had the shot to prevent chicken pox?"

"Hell, I don't know. Doc Emerson keeps up with that stuff at his office. We'd have to call him or check their records, and they're in the file cabinet at the ranch. Why are they asking?"

"He says he doesn't know if you've had the shot or not," Annie Rose told Lily.

"Granny is going to call Daddy. We're in the bathroom and we have to go back out in the airport right now. Please don't let him make us take a shot. Please, Mama-Nanny," Lily said.

Mason's phone rang. He braked, put the truck in park, and dug the phone out of his pocket. "I have no idea, Mother. I'm sorry you are missing the plane, but until I get back to the ranch and check their records, I really don't know. Doc takes care of all that and tells me when to bring them in for shots."

"Are you mad at us?" Lily asked Annie Rose on the other phone.

"Not at all, sweetheart. I'm glad you are coming home. I already miss you," Annie Rose said.

"Okay, that's all you can do, right?" Mason said to his mother.

"We got to go now," Lily whimpered. "We'll be home in a little while. And, Mama-Nanny, we won't put any more walkie-talkies in your room, we promise. We want you to be there when we get home, okay?"

Annie Rose's voice quivered slightly. "I'll be there, sweetie. Good-bye."

"For real?" Mason asked his mother. "Let me talk to Gabby."

Mason frowned through a long pause. "But Granny says that they'll take you shopping or to Six Flags for the day. Are you sure you want to come home? Okay then, we'll see you there in an hour or so."

He hung up and sighed. "I'm so sorry. This has to be the worst date in the whole world."

She undid her seat belt, crawled over the console, and straddled his lap. Taking his cheeks in her hands, she leaned in and kissed him, each kiss gaining in heat and passion until she had to back off or incinerate the inside of his fancy truck.

"I love you, Mason Harper. And this is the best date I've ever had, because there are two little girls who'd rather come home to us than go to Houston and be pampered. I miss them and I'm glad they are coming home. I love you and… well, I can't explain."

"My heart hears yours and understands completely." He enfolded her in his big arms and buried his face in her hair. "And I love you. I don't think time has much to do with it. When things are right, Annie Rose, they are right, and that's the way it is."

"Thank you. Now please take me home. I have a wonderful idea for the rest of the day." She flipped a leg over and settled back into her seat. "You'll need to stop at that roadside barbecue place we passed on the way. We're going to put out a spread on the patio for a picnic and swim in our own pool."

"And tonight?"

"Tonight when they are asleep, we're taking a blanket so far away from the house that we can't even see the place and we're making wild, passionate love under the stars."

He put the truck in gear and turned out of the parking lot. "And if it rains? It appears that our luck isn't too damn good today."

"Then we will take our blanket up to the hayloft of one of the barns and make wild love there. I will have sex tonight, darlin', and it will be with you."

He flashed a brilliant smile. "No, Miz Annie Rose, you will not have sex tonight."

"Why?"

"Sex is one thing. Making love is something deeper and more personal. We are going to make wonderful love, not have sex."

She slid a long sidling glance his way, letting her eyes travel from his boots to his eyes, only stopping at his belt buckle a few extra seconds. "You any good at that?"

"Oh, honey, just wait and anticipate."

"Do I need to bring a fire extinguisher?" she asked.

"No, ma'am. I do believe that we've proven we have all the right equipment to put out any fires that we get started."

His fingertips grazed her bare arm, traveled on up to her neck, and outlined her jaw from ear to chin. Oh, hell, yeah! He could start a fire and he could put it out... for a little while, and then the embers flashed and another one started. It could be a long, wonderful night for sure.

Chapter 23

LILY AND GABBY WERE STRETCHED OUT ON CHAISE lounges, arms behind their heads, sunglasses on, and blond pigtails dripping water onto the tile around the pool. O'Malley had found a sunny corner and had curled up for a long nap.

"I'm in Hawaii. Where are you?" Lily asked Gabby.

"On the beach at Granny's house. We've got to take Mama-Nanny down there before school starts," Gabby answered.

The big round thermometer hanging on the fence boasted one hundred degrees. But when Gabby mentioned taking her to Lorraine's place in Florida, a cold chill came across the patio right at Annie Rose in the form of a long, dirty look.

What in the hell had she done wrong? The woman was definitely ready to stake Annie Rose out on a fire ant bed and leave her to die a slow and painful death.

"Let's get back in the water. Bet I can beat you to the end of the pool and back," Lily said.

Gabby took off her sunglasses, laid them on the end of the lounge, and smiled at Annie Rose. "Count, Mama-Nanny, so she don't get a head start."

"Okay. On your mark."

Both girls hopped up and got ready to dive into the pool.

"Get set."

They bent at the waist and put their hands out like professional swimmers.

"Go!"

Water splashed all over Annie Rose's bare legs.

Maybe Lorraine didn't like the bathing suit she was wearing or maybe she didn't like the way that Mason was stealing lusty glances her way. Or maybe she didn't want anyone to ever take Holly's place at the ranch.

"We should talk," Lorraine said.

"Kitchen?" Annie Rose asked.

Lorraine tipped her head down in a terse nod.

"You guys watch the girls. We're going inside for more sunblock," Lorraine said.

Sam waved over his shoulder to let her know that he'd heard.

Mason did the same thing. A wink would have been nice. Annie Rose felt like she was entering the lion's den with nothing. A smile from him would have really helped.

"I'll be there in a minute. Bathroom," she told Lorraine when they were inside the house.

"I'll pour two glasses of tea," Lorraine said.

Annie Rose went straight into her quarters, hoping that positive energy among her things would give her confidence. She read through all three of her how-to books that were spread out on her nightstand. She stared at her reflection in the mirror above the bathroom vanity and gave herself a pep talk.

"If you can't dazzle them with brilliance, baffle them with bullshit," she whispered as she pulled a sheer cover-up over her bathing suit.

Lorraine Harper, with all her iciness, couldn't hold a

candle to Nicky Trahan. Still, a cold shiver chased down her backbone when she headed back to the kitchen.

Lorraine was sitting on a bar stool with a half-empty glass of sweet tea in front of her. Another glass had been set in front of a stool at the other end. Battle lines had been drawn with two stools between them. Annie Rose settled in her bunker and picked up her tea, took a long gulp, and got ready for the bullets to start flying.

"I do not like this," Lorraine said.

The catfight had begun.

Two little girls splashed in the pool.

Two men talked about a cattle sale and the price of feed and hay.

Neither had any idea that the house could be nothing but a pile of rubble and ashes in half an hour.

"You care to explain?" Annie Rose asked.

"My granddaughters were hellcats. Nobody really wanted to be around them and keeping a nanny was a damn nightmare. But I'll take that over this newfound fear that they have of losing you. They're terrified that they'll do something wrong or if you aren't in their sight, that you will leave and never come back. I don't like it one bit. It would break their little hearts if you left, but I'd rather you do it now than wait six months. Every day will make it that much tougher, and after all, you are just a nanny, not a mother."

"Mama-Nanny, can we have a fudge bar?" Wet feet slapping on the hardwood floor preceded two little dripping girls into the kitchen.

"Of course, you can." Annie Rose smiled.

It wasn't their battle, and their grandmother had a legitimate gripe. It wasn't that Annie Rose's bathing suit was too skimpy or that she'd slept with Mason, but an honest-to-God worry for her granddaughters' happiness.

"Are you coming back out to the pool?" Gabby asked.

"Sure we are. It's hot out there and we wanted to cool off," Annie Rose answered. "Take your daddy and grandpa a fudge bar too. I bet they'd like one."

"I like this day. I'd rather be right here than any place in the world." Lily took out four ice cream bars and handed two to Gabby. "You give one to Grandpa and I'll give one to Daddy."

"I'll race you. Whoever gets there first gets to give one to Grandpa." Gabby didn't wait for the count but made a beeline for the foyer.

"Competitive little imps." Annie Rose smiled.

Lorraine didn't

"I told you yesterday, I love the girls," Annie Rose said seriously.

"But what happens if this infatuation between you and my son bombs? You think I'm old and too blind to see that you two are flirting right here in the house with the girls underfoot?" Lorraine's tone was coated with a thick layer of frost.

"I understand your concern, but disappointments are part of life. Their lives haven't been perfect, and face it, they won't ever be. Perfect is like magic. It doesn't exist. If it did, I'd beg, borrow, buy, or steal it for Lily and Gabby. And what I feel for your son has nothing to do with infatuation and everything to do with plain old love. We can be friends or we can be enemies, Mrs. Harper. You can choose whichever one you want, but I'm going for friendship," Annie Rose said.

It did have a hell of a lot to do with infatuation, since

she'd spent the whole day lusting after his body, but she wasn't admitting that to Mason's mother. That was need-to-know, and Lorraine didn't. Granted, she was Mason's mother and the girls' grandmother, but that didn't give her rights into what went on between Mason and Annie Rose in the bedroom, or under the stars or in a hayloft.

Sam stuck his head in the back door. "Y'all want to go for a ranch tour on the four-wheelers? The girls are tired of swimming. We'll go get 'em fired up and ready. Gabby says that she's riding with me and Lily is going with you, Lorraine."

"Give me five minutes to change into jeans. Tell the girls they might want to do the same," Annie Rose said.

Thank God for bored girls.

"Mama-Nanny! Are you going in your bathing suit?" Lily almost ran into Annie Rose in the foyer.

"No, I'm going to change into old jeans and my boots. How about you?"

"Daddy says we got to change, too," Gabby said from right behind her. "Rocks and dirt flies up on four-wheelers. You ever been ridin', Mama-Nanny?"

"Many times, so I'm sure not wearing a bathing suit."

They raced, like always, up the stairs, with Lorraine behind them taking the steps a whole lot slower than they did. Annie Rose was the first one to make it to the backyard where three four-wheelers waited. Skip leaned against the yard fence with a cowboy heel hooked in the bottom rail. Sam was already seated on the red machine. Mason propped an elbow on the fence beside Skip.

"Hello, Annie Rose." Skip waved. "When are you and the girls bringing cupcakes to the bunkhouse again?"

"We'll try to get some made next weekend," Annie Rose said.

Mason shook his head. "Not next Saturday. We've got a rodeo on Saturday and we'll be taking the girls down on Friday night so they can have the whole day."

"Are they singing at the rodeo?" Skip asked.

Gabby mounted up behind her grandfather and waved. "Not this year. We won't be opening for Miranda until next year, but we're hoping that she and Blake tour together then and we can be there for both of them."

"Then I think I'll stay home this weekend," Skip teased.

"Is Mama-Nanny going with us?" Lily got seated behind her grandmother.

"I don't know. Haven't asked her yet. Maybe she'd like the weekend off to go see her friends," Mason said.

"Well, I'm damn sure not going if she's not. I'll go with her to see her friends," Lily declared.

"Daddy, I try and try to make her stop talking ugly, but does she listen to me? No, sir, she does not. Does that mean we don't get to go see Carrie Underwood?" Gabby whined.

"It means that your grandmother is not a good influence on her." Sam laughed.

"Oh, hush! Janie cusses worse than I do and she's around her every single week," Lorraine argued.

"Lily, watch out. You are on probation," Mason said.

"What does that mean?" Gabby asked.

"It means that if she doesn't watch her mouth, I'll take you and she will stay home," Mason explained.

Lily stuck out her tongue at her sister. When Mason pointed at her, she shrugged and said, "Well, I didn't cuss at her. And you sure have gotten to be tough since we got a mama-nanny."

Lorraine cut another one of those chilly looks at her, but Annie Rose settled in behind Mason and put her arms around him, instantly feeling the chemistry flowing from his chest through her hands and into her heart and soul.

The first leg of the journey took them down a two-rut path to an old trailer house sitting in a copse of mesquite trees. At one time it had been turquoise, but nowadays it had more rust than paint covering the outside. Chickens pecked in the yard and a south breeze brought the distinctive smell of a nearby hog to Annie Rose's nose.

"Want to tell me what is going on?" Mason asked out the side of his mouth when they stopped. "Lily whispered that you and my mom might be fighting."

"Nothing I can't handle," Annie Rose answered. "What is this place?"

Lily jumped off the back of the four-wheeler and ran up on the porch to knock on the door. "Uncle Nash! Where are you?"

"It's where Skip's grandfather lives. A long time ago he was the foreman on this ranch. He hasn't been off his five acres in years. Loves company but never leaves his place," Sam explained to Annie Rose.

"Is that my girls I hear?" A wizened little man stepped out on the porch. He had gray hair that curled on his head like he'd had a fresh perm, brown eyes set in a bed of wrinkles, and a wide smile.

"It's us, Uncle Nash. You got any baby chickens?" Gabby asked.

"No, but there is a litter of kittens in a bushel basket

out by the well house. I put them inside when it rains. I thought you might come see me soon, so I been pettin' them so they'd be tamed up," he said.

"Hello, Nash." Sam waved.

He leaned on the railing around the tiny porch. "Glad to see you, Sam and Missus Lorraine. Y'all ever goin' to move back to Texas?"

"No, sir! We like it in Florida," Sam answered.

Mason turned around on the four-wheeler seat and whispered, "He's a little paranoid and a lot eccentric since he moved up here."

"And you'll be Miz Annie Rose," Nash called out.

"I'm pleased to meet you." She waved. "You should come to Sunday dinner."

"We'll have to wait and see about that. Y'all want a glass of sweet tea?" Nash asked. "I can make some up."

"No, we just stopped so the girls could say hello," Mason said.

"You got some fine-lookin' kittens. One looks like O'Malley," Lily told Nash.

"I reckon there's a reason for that, like there's a reason you look like your grandma," Nash said. "Thank you for comin' by to see me. Y'all come back anytime." He disappeared into the house and shut the door.

Annie Rose settled in behind Mason again and whispered, "That was weird."

"He's grown to be an old hermit. You'll get used to him. We try to come back here once a month when the weather lets us. In the winter, he doesn't come out on the porch and invites us into the trailer," Mason said.

Annie Rose patted his muscular chest. "Well, I'm going to invite him to dinner every time I see him, and one day he'll say yes to keep from turning me down again."

"I like the way you hug up next to my back," Mason said.

"I don't think your mama does."

"She'll come around. Give her time," Mason said.

The next stop was to what was left of an old house foundation with a chimney still standing.

"That's the first house that my great-grandparents built on the place. It was horse-and-buggy days, and their nearest neighbor was about five miles away. They lived here until they died and never saw the new house up closer to the road," Sam explained.

"Those neighbors were my ancestors," Lorraine said. "We knew each other our whole lives, just like Holly and Mason did."

Annie Rose flashed her most brilliant smile. "That is so sweet."

"Granny!" Lily rolled her eyes. "We've heard that story. Let's go home and you can listen to us practice reading our books for story hour next week. Mama-Nanny said we can go back and she even lets us stay all by ourselves while she runs errands."

"Is that right? I thought you didn't want to be away from her," Lorraine said.

Lily sighed loudly. "It's only an hour, and we're big girls."

"But you didn't want to go to Houston this morning."

Gabby clapped her hands over her cheeks. "Do you know what chicken pox does to a girl's face? We're going to be country music stars. We can't have nasty scars on our faces. Mama-Nanny understands that."

"But…" Lorraine started.

"And if we went, you might make us get a shot just in case," Lily said.

"What is going on here?" Mason asked.

"A mother who overthinks things, evidently," Lorraine said.

"I don't know what that means," Lily said. "But I'm ready to go home and eat supper. I'm hungry enough to eat a bear."

"Would you eat O'Malley?" Gabby asked.

"Hell… heck, no! He's a cat, not a bear."

"Would you eat Jeb?"

Lily narrowed her eyes at her sister. "No, I would not, but if you don't be quiet, I will barbecue Djali, earring and all, and eat him."

"Daddy, we should leave her at home when we go see Carrie Underwood. She's too mean to go. She said she'd eat Djali."

"Looks like you two aren't as nice as I thought you were," Lorraine said.

"Ah, Granny, we're nice. We just ain't nice all the time. That would be boring. Remember? That's what Grandpa told you this morning on the way home from the airport when he told you not to start a ruckus. What is a ruckus anyway?" Lily asked. "Is it something like a hissy fit?"

"No, silly! A hissy fit is what Janie throws when we leave cow shit on our boots and she has to clean it off," Gabby smarted off.

Lily pointed at her sister and tattled. "She cussed, Daddy. She don't get to go with us."

"Nice just ended," Mason groaned.

Chapter 24

ANNIE ROSE LEFT THE DOOR CRACKED INTO HER APART-
ment but didn't turn on a single light or even light a
candle. She heard every sound, from the buzz of the
refrigerator motor to the crickets outside and one lonesome old coyote howling at the moon. An antsy feeling put an extra skip in her pulse and she knew he was
close. Her ears strained as they tried to pick up the sound
of Mason's footfalls, but she didn't hear the third step
squeak or boots coming down the stairs. It wasn't until
she felt his presence in the dark room that she realized
he was there.

Before she could say a word, he brushed a soft kiss
across her lips and scooped her up into his arms. His
warm breath tickled her ear and sent shivers down her
whole body when he whispered in a soft Texas drawl,
"Shhh! I'm kidnapping you."

When they reached the back porch, he sat down on
the top step and shifted her over beside him while he
shoved his feet down into the boots sitting beside the
door. "Now hand me a foot and I'll put your boots on
you. We'll be walking a ways."

"Why?"

"Noise."

She suppressed a giggle and controlled the blush, but
sneaking out was as exciting as it had been when she
was a teenager. More so, because she'd never snuck out

with someone like Mason Harper. She wondered where they were going as she laced her fingers in his and let him lead the way, but she really didn't care where it was as long as they were together.

"Are we going to the hayloft?" she asked when he started walking down the rutted four-wheeler path.

"No, somewhere prettier. The truck is parked right over there under that big pecan tree. We'll drive from there. You are gorgeous with the moonlight dancing on your blond hair. May I have this dance?" He pulled her close to his chest, picked up her hands, and looped them around his neck.

"Music?" she asked.

"The tree frogs and crickets are doing a good job of providing that." He started humming an old love song that she recognized immediately. The vibrations from his body to hers were so sensual that her chest tightened and her knees went crazy weak.

The song ended and he stepped back, picked up her hand, and kissed the palm. "Thank you, ma'am. Save the last dance of the evening for me, please."

"Why?" she asked.

"Because your last partner is the one you go home with, and I want you to go home with me, Annie Rose."

"Then I'll put your name on every page of my dance card for this evening," she said.

He picked her up again and carried her to the truck. "Do you trust me, Annie Rose?"

"More than you'll ever know," she said.

"Do you love me, Annie Rose?"

"More than words can say," she answered.

"I feel the same about you." His lips met hers in a

hungry kiss, pregnant with the promise of something even better later on. Then he set her down and opened the pickup door.

"Where are we going?"

"Somewhere quiet and secluded." He chuckled.

After several curves, he parked beside a bubbling, clear creek and she crawled out of the truck. Crickets and frogs joined voices for a nighttime, country music concert. A sweet little summer breeze ruffled the mesquite and willow branches and a hoot owl added his tone to the music.

She kicked off her boots and socks, rolled up the legs of her jeans, and plopped down close enough to the cold water that she could stick her feet in it. "That feels so good."

"You sit right there and don't even turn around until I get the surprise ready." He dropped another kiss on her forehead.

She could hear the noise of a quilt snapping out over the grass and the soft sigh as it floated down to rest. Then a glass rattled, and the faint smell of sulfur was in the air. Wine and candles and a quilt under the willow tree, with stars glistening in a perfect sky—far better than a fancy hotel.

Mason slipped a hand under her knees and one around her shoulder and carried her a few feet back from the water to a quilt under a weeping willow tree. Rose petals were scattered all over it and two jar candles cast a dim light at the top where two pillows rested.

He laid her down gently, making sure her head was resting on a soft pillow. The willow branches held the sweet, soft smell of roses close, as if they were walls. It wasn't until he stretched out beside her that she realized he had kicked off his boots and socks. He reached across the space separating them and took her hand in his, lacing her small fingers into his and just holding it there, as if that was enough.

"I want to touch you, to undress you, and kiss you, but for five minutes we are going to hold hands and look at the stars. If we say a word, it has to be about each other, not family, not past, not future, not kids. Just us. I'll go first. I love having you in the house. I love the way you look at me with those big blue eyes. I love eating breakfast with you," he said.

She grazed the edge of his forefinger and thumb. "Do you believe in fate?"

"Tonight I believe in magic."

"I never believed in fate until now. I thought we chose our own paths, faced the consequences of our decisions, and fate was a myth that showed up in romance books and fortune tellers' tents. But I think fate brought me to the ranch and made me sleep longer than I'd planned to on the porch," she said.

"Then thank you, fate," he said. "See that star up there? The bright one hanging right below the moon? That is the fate star. It led you to the ranch and to me."

She rolled up on an elbow and said, "Whether five minutes are up or not, I'm going to kiss you, Mason." She threw a leg over him and straddled his waist, leaned forward and pressed her lips to his. The first kiss was painfully sweet, but the second deepened, and the third was hungry, eager, and wanting more than that moment, aching for a future together with Mason.

When she broke away to catch her breath, he sat up

slowly, eyes never leaving hers, and unbuttoned her shirt, one button at a time. It took forever and was deliciously sexy. His fingertips barely touched the tops of her aching breasts, then her abdomen, and finally her belly button. Everywhere he touched created a little fire that grew into one big blaze.

"My turn," she said.

She unfastened his shirt, laid it open, and started a string of soft butterfly kisses from his chin, down his neck, across his chest, and to the big silver belt buckle.

"I want you," he said with so much sweetness that her eyes misted.

"They will find nothing but a belt buckle and ashes in a pile of wilted rose petals when they come looking for us, if we don't put out this fire that burns within us," she whispered.

He peeled off her shirt and unhooked her bra, tossed both of them toward the bottom of the quilt and added his shirt to the mix. "Now I will unwrap the rest of the present."

"Just remember I get to unwrap after you do," she said.

He pulled off her boots, undid her jeans, and pulled them all the way to her toes. His kisses on the tips of her toes made her wiggle and moan. By the time he reached her knees, she was arching against him and tugging at his belt buckle.

Forget foreplay. Forget making love. She wanted satisfaction. Would it always be like that with him?

Well, it has been ever since the first time in the shower, hasn't it?

She pulled him on top of her and wrapped her legs around him. He took care of the condom and slid into her with a long, hard thrust, and she rocked with him. He was right, though. They were making love, not having sex, and it was more intense, sweeter, and more satisfying than ever before.

"I. Love. You," she said in a hoarse whisper.

His lips found hers, and without words, she knew that he was telling her the same thing. Mason did love her. Where their relationship went next or how it progressed didn't matter. Annie Rose had found the right cowboy, the right place, her soul was at home, and she was not leaving.

"Ready?" he asked.

"Oh, yeah," she said.

"I love you, Annie Rose."

And the whole world around her softened into colors that blended together. Light willow tree green, fuzzy stars, and a moon that didn't have distinct edges. Satisfaction, pure and simple, was hers, and she truly felt as if she'd been made love to for the very first time.

"That was beyond amazing," she said.

"Yes, ma'am." He shifted his position, picked her up, and carried her to the creek.

"Skinny-dipping?" she asked.

"No, just washing up and then we're going to roll that quilt up around us and sleep for a while. Even though we'll have to leave before daylight, I want to wake up with you in my arms."

The cool water felt wonderful on her feverishly hot skin, but words could not describe the feeling when she was wrapped in the quilt with Mason. His arm around her was security. The night breezes coming off the cool creek water and feathering her hair back was magical.

The stars and moon hung there especially for them, and the sweet smell of roses permeated through the night air.

Everything was absolutely perfect. This was going to be *their place* forever. Instead of Paris or London or even Dallas, this was where they were going when they fought, when they had a few minutes of alone time or when they needed to get away and reconnect.

———

"Looks like your truck has some creek sand in the tires," Skip said the next morning.

Mason shrugged.

"Thought y'all took four-wheelers on the tour yesterday."

"I don't kiss and tell."

"You just did. By the way, Nash says to tell you when you get ready to marry that girl, he'd like an invitation to the wedding." Skip smiled.

"You're kiddin' me. Nash hasn't left that piece of ground in years."

"I know, but that's what he said. He told me he needed a couple of days' notice to get his black suit cleaned and his hair cut."

"I'll be damned. He only met her the one time," Mason said.

"He said to tell you that he's almost a hundred, not to drag your feet. I spent some time with him last night and he told me I was wrong about Annie Rose. I respect his opinion, Mason. He's the best judge of character that I've ever known."

Mason chuckled.

"I'd say that we'd best get this feeding done so you can spend some time with your folks. Ain't they leavin' today? Unless you intend to keep them here a couple of extra days, so Nash can get his suit cleaned and they won't have to come back real soon," Skip said.

Mason nodded. "He can get it cleaned, but there won't be a wedding this week. And for your information, Mother's got a burr in her underbritches about Annie Rose. She got in a worse snit over not getting to take the girls to Houston, and the crazy thing is that Doc says they have had the shots. But if they hadn't, I'd have had to drape the mirrors to save my sanity and their vanity."

"Lorraine told me that she's afraid Annie Rose will leave and break their hearts," Skip said.

"Not if I have anything to do with it," Mason said.

Skip smiled. "I'll tell Nash to at least get the suit out of the mothballs. Now let's get this feeding done with."

Mason was amazed that Nash even considered coming out of his hermit state to go to a wedding. What was it about Annie Rose that he liked? The old guy had never liked Holly, and she hadn't liked him. It wasn't long after they'd married that he went into hibernation and refused to step foot off the five acres that he'd fenced in and called his retirement estate.

Life sure had gotten stirred up since Annie Rose showed up on his porch. Could it really have been less than a month ago? It seemed like he and Annie Rose had been together for years—like they'd been soul mates since they were babies.

Mason headed for the driver's side of the truck. "It's strange, isn't it? You think you got a plan all figured out for the next five or ten or fifty years, and then fate steps in and tosses a wrench into the mix."

Skip got into the passenger's side. "Don't make plans. That's my theory. When something feels right, do it and don't make a big deal out of it."

Chapter 25

WHEN ANNIE ROSE HEARD SOMETHING IN THE BACK-yard, she figured the goats had gotten loose that early Friday morning. The sun was barely peeking through the limbs of the mesquite trees when she rushed out to herd the two pesky critters back into their pen, but the goats were in their pen. A movement caught her eye and there was no mistaking Nash riding a horse bareback down the rutted lane.

Mason said Nash hadn't left his place in years and yet there he was on a paint horse, gray hair shining in the first light of morning. Something brushed against her leg and right there on the porch was a small red rosebush with the roots wrapped in a wet burlap bag. The early morning breeze picked up the soft scent and reminded her of the night she and Mason had spent on the banks of the creek.

Mason slipped up behind her and wrapped his arms around her waist. "What's going on?"

"Nash came to visit and left me a present. Can we plant it in the front yard right beside the porch, so I can see it when I'm sitting on the porch swing?" she asked.

"I'll be damned," he said.

"Does that mean yes or no?"

"It means we can put it anywhere you want. I'll take it around there for you right now and after breakfast we can plant it. This is the first time I've known him to leave his place since he moved out there. Are you sure it was him and he didn't send it with Skip?"

"Does he ride a paint horse bareback?"

"That's Nash, all right. He must like you a lot."

―⁓―

They'd planned to take the girls to the rodeo on Saturday, but when the girls found out that Blake Shelton was playing the rodeo the following weekend, they set up a howl to put it off for a week.

On Saturday morning, Annie Rose awoke when Mason slipped out of her bed and headed for his room. She pulled on jeans and a shirt, made a cup of tea in the microwave, and carried it to the front porch. She caught a whiff of her new rosebush beside the porch and inhaled deeply.

Something smelled different than roses. It took a minute for her to locate the quart-sized jar stuffed full of gorgeous wildflowers in a profusion of colors. They were arranged around a weeping willow branch. She had no doubt that Nash had left them.

Mason joined her on the swing and slipped an arm around her shoulders. "Good morning, darlin'. Did I wake you when I left?"

"I feel empty when you aren't beside me," she said.

He pulled her closer. "Me, too, Annie Rose. It's going to be a beautiful day."

She pointed at the flowers. "It's starting off right."

Mason chuckled. "Evidently he approves of where you put the rosebush."

"Evidently he found rose petals beside the creek," she said.

"I'll be damned!" Mason said.

"That's what you said yesterday morning." She laughed.

"I know, but I still can't believe it."

"He's a sweet old cowboy."

"He and Holly didn't get along," Mason said.

"Well, I don't really know him, but I like him. When I'm almost a hundred, I'm going to put a trailer right beside the creek and become a hermit like him."

Mason pulled her closer to his side. "So you're planning to be around when you are a hundred?"

"I guess I am," she said. "Do you think he'd mind if I took them inside?"

"They are your flowers, honey, but remember, those pretty red ones house chiggers. When we brought Mama wildflowers, she always left them on the porch. She put a saucer of water under them so the chiggers couldn't crawl out of the flowers and get on us," he answered.

"Then I'll enjoy them right there. You got a problem with me putting a trailer out beside the creek when I'm a hundred?"

Mason stood up and held out a hand to help her. "No, ma'am. I'll even transplant your rosebush out there beside it and we'll watch the sunrises and sunsets together."

"Why didn't they get along? Nash and Holly?"

"He told her that she should stay on the ranch and help me run it, that she shouldn't have a job in town."

"That's the old way of thinking. He might not like me if he finds out I'm a nurse and a former librarian." She sighed.

"Are you plannin' to leave the girls with a nanny and get a job in town?"

"No, sir! The girls need me here and I like what I'm doin' just fine."

"That's why Nash loves you."

"Think he'll come to Sunday dinner if I invite him?"

"You never know about Nash. He told Skip that he wouldn't leave his place until he saw that I'd finally gotten some sense. Evidently he thinks I got smart when I hired you, so feel free to invite him."

———————

Wednesday morning, Annie Rose found an old boot box sitting on her swing. The holes poked in the sides said something that needed air was inside. She carefully took the lid off to find a yellow kitten curled up on the remnant of an old blanket.

Tears broke through the dam, flowed down her cheeks, and dripped on to her work shirt. The kitten meowed and stretched. Nash had left her a kitten, the first pet she'd had since she lived on the ranch in South Texas.

"What have we got today?" Mason asked. "I looked out the window and saw him riding back down the path on that old horse of his."

She held up the kitten. "Meet Tennessee Moses."

"That's a big name for such a little fellow."

She snuggled the yellow fur ball against her cheek. "It's Tennessee because Nash reminds me of Nashville. We'll call him Moses."

"Why?"

"Moses parted the sea so the children could go across. This little fellow brought Nash out into civilization. Could you take some extra time at noon today?

I'm going visiting and I want to go alone. So the girls will need someone close by to keep an eye on them," she said.

"Sure thing, but it won't take a whole hour. He'll come out on the porch and talk five minutes, like he always does, and then go back inside. You want to drive the truck or take a four-wheeler?"

"I'd better take the truck if I'm going without the girls. You know how they love to get on four-wheelers," she said.

"Not with a new kitten in the house. You are going to share, right?"

She tiptoed and kissed him on the cheek. "Oh, yes. We might need a babysitter occasionally, especially if we want to go back to the creek and the willow tree."

Nash was sitting on the porch when she arrived. He wore overalls, a starched shirt, and his hair had been slicked back. That old coot was expecting company. She wondered if he'd gotten dressed up every day since Saturday, and a pang of guilt washed over her for not coming to see him sooner.

He pointed at the folding lawn chair on the other side of a small round table holding sweet tea, two jelly glasses, and a tin of store-bought cookies. "Come on up here and sit a spell with me. I made a pitcher of sweet tea and the ice ain't melted in it yet."

"Can I pour for both of us?" she asked.

"Yes, ma'am, and you can take the lid off them cookies, too. I didn't eat none after I had my dinner, in case you come by." He smiled.

front of his eyes, that I'll come courtin' you, because I know a good woman when I see one." Nash walked her to the truck and opened the door for her. "You take good care of Moses. His mama is the best mouser I ever had, so he's got good blood in his veins."

"Yes, sir, and thank you for the tea and cookies."

"Come back to see me."

"You come see me," she said.

"After the wedding." He nodded.

Lily met her on the porch with a finger over her lips. "Take off your boots and walk easy. Moses is asleep and we don't want him to wake up."

Annie Rose sat on the swing and removed her boots. She tiptoed into the house to find Gabby sitting on the bottom step, staring into the boot box. And there was Moses, wrapped up in a yellow ball and tucked into O'Malley's tummy. She could have sworn she saw pride in the old tomcat's eyes.

"I'll be damned," she said.

"That's my line." Mason chuckled.

"It's mine now," she said. Lord, would she ever get to the place in her life when looking at Mason didn't set her heart into a flutter? If they ever did stand before a preacher and get married, would they act like an old married couple or would there still be fire and embers burning when they reached their last breath?

"How did the visit go? And what are you thinking about?" he asked. "There's a question in your eyes and an impish smile on your face."

"Shhhh." Gabby frowned.

"Kitchen?" Annie Rose whispered.

He followed her to the kitchen, and the minute they were alone, the hot kisses and roaming hands began. He sat her up on the cabinet and she wrapped her legs around him, let her hands wander all over his strong back, while his tongue teased her mouth open and then dived inside.

When they were both breathless, he asked again, "What were you thinking about?"

"I was wondering if we'd ever act like old married people," she answered.

"I'm not real sure we could put out this burning fire that we share in a lifetime, so the answer is no," he said.

Chapter 26

ANNIE ROSE AWOKE IN A BATHTUB OF COOL WATER, the air-conditioning vent blowing cold air down on her wet hair and body, and chills running down her arms at a breakneck speed. She quickly pulled the plug and crawled out of the tub, wrapped a big white towel around her head, and another one around her body.

She pulled on a pair of pajama bottoms and an over-sized knit shirt and headed for the recliner. It was too early for Mason to show up in her room. He would be tucking the girls in and making sure they were sound asleep before he rapped on her door. Moses was sleeping soundly in the throw on the sofa. She started to wake him and carry him over to her chair, but something her mother said about never waking a sleeping baby kept her from doing so.

It was when she started back across the floor that she noticed another one of the girls' booklets on the coffee table. A smile covered her face as she bent to pick it up. The title of the newest one was *How to Marry a Cowboy*.

She smiled at all the stickers on the outside of the new book: cowboy boots, hats, bull riders, ropers, horse-shoes, and lassos.

The smile widened when she opened the first page and realized the booklet had been written by Mason and not the girls.

My dearest darling, Annie Rose,

It appears that the three books that Lily and Gabby wrote for you worked very well, so I'm going to make you one from me and hope that it works as well as theirs did.

All my love,
Mason

He'd signed his name in red and drawn a loopy heart around it.

Like his daughters, Mason wrote in the same style. The normal rule program was all lined out for her, but evidently this was more important than learning how to remember, how to be a mama, and how to be a rancher, since there were more rules than in the other books.

Number 1: *You've got to run slow enough that the cowboy can catch you.*

Number 2: *You have to go buy a new wedding dress, because the one you got is all dirty and torn up.*

Number 3: *You have to get married in the church or the cowboy's twin daughters won't believe that it's legal.*

Number 4: *You will have to kiss him in front of everyone in the church, including aforementioned daughters after the preacher says that you are married.*

Number 5: *You have to say "I do" when the preacher tells you to or else Damian's mama*

might call you a slut, and it's not proper to get ticked off when you are the bride at a wedding.
Number 6: *After you marry the cowboy, you have to move upstairs and sleep with him. He snores but not too loud.*

She read through it four more times and had laid it back on the coffee table when her phone rang. She hurriedly picked it up, expecting it to be one of the girls calling from upstairs to tell her that they couldn't sleep and needed something important, like a drink of water or warm milk.

"Hello," she said.

"Annie Rose," Lorraine said.

"Yes."

"I called to apologize for being such a bitch. I talked to Mason for almost an hour, and I was never more wrong in my whole life. I'd like it if we could start all over and be friends, and when the wedding happens, if you'd let us attend."

"Thank you," Annie Rose said. "But if and when we do take that step, you will definitely be invited. Nash said that he'd walk me down the aisle and even come to Sunday dinner if I married Mason."

"Nash offering to do that is a big thing, Annie Rose. He's one very fine judge of character. If he told Sam not to hire someone, then Sam didn't. And if the sorriest old cowboy in the county came up on the ranch lookin' for a job and Sam didn't want to hire him, there were times when Nash said he'd make a good hand. And he was always right. Let us know if it's anytime soon. We'll make arrangements to come home early. Just give us three days."

Annie Rose nodded then remembered to say, "I reckon we can manage at least a three-day notice, but like I said, he hasn't asked. It could be a year."

"I hope not. It seems to me that the girls won't be so afraid that you'll leave if you are really married to my son. I didn't realize how much not having a mother has affected them until we were there and I saw them with you. And what I misjudged as infatuation is love. I can hear it in Mason's voice. Good night now, and keep me in the loop. Oh, and we watched the goat DVD. It was a royal hoot."

"Thank you for calling," Annie Rose said. "Good night to you."

She checked on Moses one more time before she padded barefoot through the foyer and out to the front porch. She sat down in the swing, pushed it off into motion with her foot, and lay back on one of the two bright-colored throw pillows that had been left there when the girls had played outside that day. The moon hung in the sky like a queen, with the stars acting as her subjects. The one right below the moon was the one Mason had said was the fate star that had brought her to the ranch. As she stared at it, the steady movement of the swing and pure old exhaustion from the day put her to sleep.

<center>~~~</center>

Mason paced the floor in his bedroom. The girls were asleep. O'Malley had curled up on his pillow and he imagined that Moses was sleeping somewhere in Annie Rose's room. The little cobalt-blue velvet box on his dresser kept calling his name, and each time he passed it, he stopped long enough to open it and look at the sapphire-and-diamond ring inside.

Should he wait until the end of summer to ask her or pop the question at the rodeo the next night? He wanted Annie Rose to be his wife in every sense of the word, to be the mother to his girls, but he didn't want to rush her.

Finally, he picked up the box, crammed it in the pocket of his lounge pants, and carried it to her room. The door was open. Moses was sleeping on the sofa and the booklet with lots of cowboy stickers lay on the table. Mason smiled. She had obviously read it.

He checked the bedroom, but she wasn't there, so he padded out to the swing on the front porch. The story of Sleeping Beauty came to mind when he found her sleeping on the swing. This time the girls weren't dancing around, yelling about him getting them a mother for their birthday. This time she wasn't wearing a tattered wedding dress but a pair of cotton pajama bottoms and one of his T-shirts.

He'd known Annie Rose a little less than a month.

He'd known Holly her whole life.

He'd planned a romantic getaway and proposed to Holly on a riverboat dinner cruise in Savannah, Georgia, with violins playing in the background.

It wasn't fair to ask Annie Rose to marry him right there on the porch with crickets and tree frogs singing in the distance. But it felt right, as if fate had worked in a perfect circle and brought the moment to him.

What's not fair is that you are comparing two very different women and two very different times of your life, his inner voice said. *You've been blessed with a new love and a new start. Stop living in the past and get on with the future.*

He dropped down on one knee and carefully leaned toward Annie Rose until his lips brushed hers. Her eyelids opened slowly and she smiled, wrapped her arms around his neck, and pulled him closer for a longer kiss.

"I fell asleep looking at our fate star," she said when the kiss ended. "You must be my prince."

"No, I'm just your cowboy," he said.

"I like that better. I love the booklet you made for me."

Mason cleared his throat and said, "Annie Rose Boudreau, I believe with all my heart that we are meant to be together until death parts us. And I believe with all my heart that you are my soul mate."

She started to say something, but he put a finger over her lips. "Annie Rose Boudreau, I love you, and I'm in love with you. I've played out scenarios in my mind to do this, but this feels right, like it feels right to have you in my life, my heart, and my soul."

Her eyes popped wide open and she sat up.

"Will you marry me?" he asked as he popped the box open. "I chose a sapphire because of your gorgeous blue eyes. We can be engaged for a year, ten years, or we can go to the courthouse tomorrow."

"Yes!" she said without a second's hesitation and threw her arms around his neck. "Yes, yes, yes!"

He put the ring on her finger, picked her up, and carried her back into the house. "I love you," he murmured again.

"I love you," she whispered back as he gently shut the door into her quarters with his bare foot and laid her on the bed. "And I think two weeks is long enough for an engagement, Mason."

Chapter 27

A BOUQUET OF WILDFLOWERS THAT NASH HAD GATH-ered fresh that morning from the pasture lay on top of the *How to Marry a Cowboy* booklet. Fortunately, he had left out the red Indian blanket blossoms, so no one had to worry about chiggers. Bright blue ribbons, that matched the forget-me-nots in the bouquet, cascaded from the flowers to the floor when Annie Rose picked it up. A circlet of the same flowers and ribbons, with a pouf of illusion created by a short veil at the back, sat on her blond hair like a crown.

The girls said that she had to have a veil, because all brides had one, and she couldn't refuse them anything. This was their wedding as much as hers.

She wore a white eyelet dress with a hankie hem, and the traditional white satin high-heeled shoes. She expected to see Nash when someone rapped on the door of the bride's dressing room, but Gina Lou poked her head in the door.

"Hey, I hear there's a bride back here," she said.

"Gina Lou!" Annie Rose gasped.

Gina Lou crossed the room in a couple of long-legged, easy strides and hugged Annie Rose. "We got in from Africa last night and drove like hell to get here."

"I'm so glad to see you. If I'd known you could make it, you would have been part of the wedding party." Annie Rose grabbed a tissue to dab at her eyes.

"I know you would have, but hey, I didn't know until the last minute, and besides, I want to watch. I've never heard you as happy as you sounded on the phone. I'm so glad everything is working out."

Annie Rose tossed the tissue in the trash. "I can't tell you in words how I feel, Gina Lou. Having you here puts the icing on the cake."

"And are these your new daughters?" Gina Lou asked.

"I'm Lily and this is Gabby and you have to be Gina Lou. Mama told us all about you."

Gina Lou smiled. "Well, I bet she's told me more about you two. I'm so happy for all of you. We'll talk later. It's almost time for the ceremony to start, so I'm going to get seated."

Gina Lou winked at Annie Rose and slipped out of the room seconds before Nash peeked in and grinned. "You are a beautiful bride, Miz Annie Rose, and I'm glad you are coming to the ranch to be the mistress of it."

Mason stood at the front of the church with Colton, Lucas, and Greg beside him. He shifted his weight from one leg to the other and wished they would have gone to the courthouse the morning after he proposed. But Annie Rose said that the girls needed the wedding as much or more than she did. They needed to know that it had been done right so they wouldn't fear that she would leave anymore.

Laura was the first bridesmaid down the aisle. Emily followed her and then a very pregnant Natalie, serving as maid of honor, took her place next as the pianist played soft music. Mason thought that Gabby and Lily, in their blue lace dresses, would take forever getting to the front of the church. They smiled at him, held their heads high, and marched up on the stage like princesses to stand beside him.

Then the traditional bride's march began and all the people rose to their feet. From that moment, he didn't see another person. Just Annie Rose as she floated toward him on Nash's arm. Tears welled up in his eyes and he bit his lower lip to keep them at bay. A full-grown cowboy didn't cry.

"Who gives this bride to be married to this man?" Henry asked.

"Gabby, Lily, and I do," Nash said in a loud voice and handed her off to Mason. "We've waited a long time for this, Mason. You be good to her. And, Annie Rose, you be good to him. The ranch needs a family."

"Yes, sir," Mason said.

Nash kissed Annie Rose on the forehead and stepped back to the front pew of the packed church to join Lorraine, Sam, and Skip.

"You may be seated," Henry said. "We are gathered here today to join Annie Rose Boudreau and Mason Harper together. But we are also joining Gabby and Lily Harper to this couple and making a family as well as a new bride and groom."

〜〜〜

Annie Rose heard a sniffle behind her and caught a flutter of white as Lorraine dabbed at her eyes. She swallowed the lump in her throat in time to say her vows and then to say "I do," since those were very important words to the girls.

"And now Gabby and Lily have some vows," Henry said.

"I'll go first," Lily said.

Henry looked down at her and asked, "Do you, Lily Harper, take this woman, Annie Rose, to be your new mother. Will you treat her like a mother and not a nanny? Will you promise to love her forever, like you do your daddy?"

"I do," Lily said.

Annie Rose picked a small box from behind her bouquet of flowers, opened it, and fastened an open-heart necklace around Lily's neck. "I promise to be your mother, and I promise to love you forever too."

"Gabby Harper," Henry said, "Will you take this woman, Annie Rose, to be your new mother. Will you treat her like a mother and not a nanny? Do you promise to love her forever, like you do your daddy?"

"I do," Gabby said.

Annie repeated the process.

Lorraine sniffled again, louder this time.

"Okay, by the authority given to me by the state of Texas, I pronounce Annie Rose and Mason husband and wife as well as a new family. Now, Mason, you may kiss the bride," Henry said.

"That was beautiful," Mason whispered before his lips landed on hers.

When the applause quieted, Henry spoke up. "There's a reception out at Bois D'Arc Bend and everyone is invited. I hear that Nash and Skip have been smokin' beef for two days and that Lorraine made the cake, so if you don't attend, you're going to miss a good party."

"I love you doesn't begin to cover how I feel right now," Mason said when he and Annie Rose were alone in his truck.

"I know. Let's go home. Wait, where are our girls?"

"They are going with their grandparents. It was their idea." He chuckled. "I think they were serious about that new-sister idea."

"How do you feel about the new-sister idea?"

"I always wanted a whole yard full of kids. You decide how many it takes to make up a yard full and I'll be satisfied with your decision," he said.

They led the procession of vehicles from the church to the ranch. Mason hopped out of the car, shook the legs of his freshly starched jeans down over his boots, and removed his Western-cut jacket. He tossed it into the front seat of the truck, along with his string tie, and was on the way around the truck when the door flew open and Annie Rose stepped out.

"Look at that." She sighed.

The porch swing had been decorated with garlands of roses, wildflowers, and white ribbons, and O'Malley and Moses were curled up right in the middle of a long white satin pillow with lace edging.

"Do you like it?" Mason asked.

"I love it," she said.

"It's where I found you and I thought it would make a wonderful place for wedding pictures."

Her arms snaked around his neck and he carried her to the porch, pushed the cats to the floor, and set her down on the pillow. "Oh, Mason, this is perfect. Just absolutely perfect. Thank you."

He sat down beside her and pulled her close to his side. "It's where it all began, and when we are old and gray, it's where it will end. I'm glad we have a few minutes before they all get parked and out of their vehicles. I want to tell you that I love you and I'm glad you are my wife and that things still feel right and that we are going to make lots of happy memories right here on the ranch."

"I love you too and, Mason, we've already got a thousand memories. We'll add to our collection as the days and years go by." She laid her head on his shoulder.

―⁓―

After the reception, multiple toasts, and their first dance together as man and wife, Mason led her out of the house amidst a shower of birdseed and drove away from the ranch toward Savoy.

A quarter of a mile down the road he made a sharp right, opened a cattle gate, and headed across the pasture on a rutted lane with grass growing up between the ruts.

"Where are we going?" she asked.

"On a two-day honeymoon. Mother and Dad are taking care of the girls until Sunday morning. We'll meet them and Nash in church. Later, maybe in the fall, we'll go somewhere on a real honeymoon," he told her.

She squealed and clapped her hands when she realized that they were at the bend of the river, right where they'd gone that night to make love under the stars. And back under the willow tree was an RV. A wreath of wildflowers hung on the door with a bright blue ribbon. Written in gold letters across the ribbon were the words, "Just Hitched."

He carried her from truck to the door. "If you'll open it please, ma'am?"

She turned the knob and the scent of fresh roses wafted out to meet her. A path of petals led the way from the door to the king-sized bed at the back of the trailer.

"Oh, Mason, this is perfect. I don't need another honeymoon, but when we have a couple of days free, we can always come back here," she said.

"A perfect honeymoon for a perfect bride that I found sleeping on my porch swing a few weeks ago," he said.

She pulled him down on the bed beside her when he gently laid her down. "I love you so much."

He pushed a blond curl away from her face and kissed her with so much promise that it brought fresh tears to her eyes. They would grow old together. The fate star wouldn't have brought them together if it hadn't been willing to give them a long future together. She believed it with her whole heart.

"According to a famous author I know, there is only one thing left to do if I follow the directions in the new bestselling *How to Marry a Cowboy* book," she whispered as she unbuttoned his shirt.

"What's that?" He grinned.

"I have to sleep with the cowboy, even if he snores a little bit." She threw a leg over his body and straddled him, leaned forward and planted kisses all over his face as he reached around behind her and unzipped her dress.

"But it doesn't say that I have to go to sleep as soon as my head hits the pillow."

"No, it doesn't, and we will sleep, darlin'," he drawled. "But not until much, much later."

Dear Readers,

Writing the first line of a new book in a brand-new series is so exciting. Writing the last line of the last book in a series is bittersweet. The stories have been told, but it's not easy to leave behind the characters that have been friends for months and months.

What started out to be *The Cowboy's Runaway Bride* evolved into *How to Marry a Cowboy* somewhere along the way, and the title fits the story so much better, even if for a while there the folks on Bois D'Arc Ranch thought Annie Rose was a runaway bride.

It's the beginning of summertime, both in the story and in real Texas time, and as I write the last of *How to Marry a Cowboy*, I hope you are all enjoying long, lazy, relaxing days as daylight lasts longer. My tomcats, Boots and Chester, are still protecting the fenced-in backyard from grasshoppers, birds, and all kinds of varmints that might come calling. The roses and lilies are blooming and I spend a little time each day on the swing, thinking about the next four cowboys who have already arrived in my virtual world.

Two of them you met in *Cowboy Seeks Bride*—Finn and Sawyer O'Donnell—but the other two, Tanner Gallagher and Declan Brennan, are brand-new. There's a feud going on in Burnt Boot, Texas, between the

Gallagher and the Brennan families, and poor old Finn and Sawyer are thrown right in the middle of it. So keep your boots shined and your hats ready… there're more cowboys on the way in the Burnt Boot series.

Thanks again to the whole Sourcebooks staff, from Dominique Raccah, the brilliant publisher, to the art department, who does fabulous covers for my books, to the publicity department (bowing to Danielle at this time) and with a big hug to Deb Werksman, my truly awesome editor. Thank you to my agent, Erin Niumata, and the folks at Folio for all you do to make my life run smoother. But most of all, a big thanks to all my readers. Know that you are appreciated for your continuing support, for sharing my books with your neighbors and friends, or for telling them about them, for the reviews that you write, the notes that you send my way, and for reading my stories.

Have a wonderful summer!

Carolyn Brown

Read on for an excerpt from the first book in the brand-new Burnt Boot, Texas series from Carolyn Brown

Cowboy Boots for Christmas

THE THIRD TIME IS NOT ALWAYS THE CHARM.

Twice now, Finn O'Donnell had told the government he wasn't interested in anything that the FBI, CIA, or any of the other alphabet agencies dangled at him like a carrot on a long stick in front of a donkey. All Finn wanted to do was watch his cattle grow fat on Salt Draw Ranch and be left alone with his dog, Shotgun.

So that black SUV coming down his lane could turn around and go on back to wherever the hell it came from. They didn't have enough carrots in the world to make him leave his new home in Burnt Boot, Texas, and pick up his sniper rifle again. He leaned against the porch post, and with arms crossed over his broad chest, he waited.

The yellow hair on Shotgun's back stood up like a punk rocker's, and a low growl rumbled out of his throat. The dog took a step forward and Finn stuck a boot out to touch his leg. That's all it took for the dog to heel even when his body quivered in anticipation of attacking something, like the wheels of that fancy SUV.

"Easy, boy. We can tell them to go to hell a third time easy as we did the first two." He pushed mirrored sunglasses up a notch and tipped his black cowboy hat down to block the sun from his eyes.

Dead grass and gravel crunched under the wheels of

the black vehicle when it stopped in front of the low-slung, ranch-style house. Shotgun whined, but until Finn moved his boot, the dog wouldn't bail off the porch and go after the intruders.

"Not yet. We'll hear them out and then you can take a bite from the ass of their Italian suits as they get back in their van," Finn said softly.

An identical vehicle turned down the lane and parked right behind the first one. This was something new. Maybe since he'd moved to Burnt Boot on his own ranch and wasn't a part of his folks' operation in central Texas, they thought they'd best send out a whole committee to persuade him. Finn looked out over the tops of the sunglasses but the SUV windows were tinted and he couldn't see a damn thing.

"Looks like they've brought an extra van just for you, Shotgun. You want to join the Army, old boy? You'll have to do boot camp and learn to sniff out bombs and herd camels instead of cows. And boot camp involves more than chasing rabbits when I'm doing my evening run."

He removed his black felt cowboy hat with stains around the leather band, raked his dark hair back from his forehead, and resettled the hat on his head at an angle to shade his eyes better. Were they waiting for Christmas? If so, they were a little early because that was four weeks away.

He pulled his denim jacket tighter across his broad expanse of a chest and leaned on the porch post, his boot still touching Shotgun's front leg. The entire O'Donnell family had chipped in the day after Thanksgiving to help him move from Comfort, Texas, to Burnt Boot. His herd woke up in holding pens and by nightfall they were grazing on the grass growing on Salt Draw three hundred miles away. His sister, two brothers, and a dozen cousins would put him in a straitjacket if he let the brass out there in those vans talk him back into the Army after that move.

Then the door of the van flew open and a woman stepped out. He thought he was seeing things. Surely that couldn't be his Callie.

———

Callie Brewster had listened to the man in the front seat of the SUV tell her all the reasons why she and her brother should be in the Witness Protection Program. Now he was repeating himself and she didn't want to hear any more, so she threw open the door the minute the vehicle stopped moving.

He said something about not getting out of the SUV until they'd talked to Finn, but she'd made up her mind. She stomped the legs of her jeans down over her boots and started across the yard. She damn sure didn't need anyone to talk for her or before her either.

She didn't need anyone to protect her. She could take the eyes out of a rattlesnake with any weapon the Army slapped in her hands. She'd kept up her skills at the shooting range in Corpus Christi and kept in shape. But she did need someone to watch her back, and Finn O'Donnell had proven time and time again that he could damn sure do that.

From a distance he still looked the same. Broad shoulders, sculpted abs, biceps that stretched the sleeves of any shirt on the market, thighs that testified he was used to hard work, and hands that could be either soft or tough depending on what was needed. Yes, that was her Finn: the man she'd had a crush on for three years, though she'd never said a word about it. They were partners, sniper and spotter, and were closer than a husband and wife in lots of ways. But partners didn't act on crushes and they damn sure didn't get involved with each other, not when they had to do the jobs that Finn and Callie were called upon to do.

She threw back the hood of her jacket and put her sunglasses in her pocket. The moment he lowered his sunglasses and recognized her, he started her way, meeting her in the middle of the yard in a bear hug that brought her feet off the ground.

"God, I've missed you so much," he said.

Heart pounding, pulse racing, she was slow to let go when he set her firmly back on the ground.

"Lala?" she asked.

His wife damn sure wouldn't appreciate him showing so much affection to his old partner. Any minute now Callie expected her to come out of the house, maybe with a grenade in her hands.

He held her by her shoulders. "Lala isn't here, Callie. That's a story for another day. I can't believe you're right here in front of me. I've thought of you every day since I came home. What in the hell are you doing in Burnt Boot, Texas?"

Her aqua eyes locked with his crystal-clear blue ones and held for what seemed like eternity. There was no Lala and he was glad to see her. She had known this was the right decision.

"I need a place to stay." Her voice was an octave too

high but, hell on wheels, Finn O'Donnell had hugged her. She'd almost had a damn fan girl moment.

He stepped back and looked toward the two vans. Three doors opened as if they'd been synchronized. A kid, who reminded Finn of a young colt that hadn't quite grown into his spindly legs, jumped from the van. Shotgun ran out to the boy, put his paws on his shoulders and the two of them fell to the ground for a wrestling game.

"Remember me talking about my nephew, Martin?"

"He need a place to stay, too?" Finn asked.

She nodded and for the first time she had doubts about the whole thing.

"You brought government men. I guess this is serious?"

Another nod. "It is."

"Then I expect we'd best go in the house and talk about it." He draped an arm around her shoulders. "Okay if Martin stays outside with Shotgun? Old dog has missed kids since we've been in Burnt Boot. You haven't changed a bit in two years. You still as sassy as ever?"

"Callie?" the boy called out.

"You can stay outside if you stay in the yard."

"Yes, ma'am."

"Well? Are you still a pistol?" Finn asked as they took the three steps up to the porch.

"Damn straight, O'Donnell," she answered.

Callie's breath tightened in her chest. She could think it was fear of leaving Martin alone, but if she was totally honest with herself, it was the way Finn had hugged her and still yet kept an arm thrown loosely over her shoulders. Old feelings surfaced that she thought she'd buried long ago, and now there was no Lala in the picture. Sweet Jesus, could she trust herself to walk into a situation like this?

———◦◦◦———

Finn stood back to let Callie go inside first. "I've got a pot of coffee brewing and sweet tea in the refrigerator. Excuse the mess. I'm not even unpacked yet. I'd hoped that these men who brought you here wouldn't be able to ever find me again, but I guess Big Brother has his ways. Might as well come on in the kitchen."

Three men filed ahead of him and stopped inside an enormous great room housing a living room with a huge stone fireplace on the east end, a big dining room, and a country kitchen. Finn led the way to the kitchen area and motioned toward a round table flanked by six chairs. He hated to take his arm away from Callie for fear she would vanish into the cold winter air, and he had so much to tell her about what had happened since they'd said good-bye in Afghanistan two years ago. Lord, he'd fantasized about Callie right up until Lala came into his life, but he remembered how much he wanted to kiss her full lips and how his hands itched to brush her long, dark hair away from her face. He'd dreamed about waking up to those big aqua-colored eyes staring at him in the morning. And now she was right there in his kitchen.

"Have a seat," he said.

"Need some help?" Callie asked.

"I got it covered." He opened three cabinet doors before he located the coffee cups and then glanced back over his shoulder. "Coffee for everyone?"

Three men nodded.

"Black just like always, Callie?"

"I haven't changed a bit," she said.

He carried cups to the table then drew his chair close enough that his knee touched hers. "Okay, Callie, let's hear that story."

Otis picked up his coffee and said, "She needs to go into Witness Protection. She and the boy both. I'm Otis, by the way, and this is Special Agents Jones and Smith."

Finn shot a look across the table. "I know Jones and Smith. Pleased to make your acquaintance, Otis, but I asked her to tell me, not you."

Callie's hand shook as she picked up the coffee cup and took a sip. When she set it down, he covered her hand with his, squeezing gently. "Take your time. There's no hurry."

"My sister was killed in a car wreck a couple of weeks before I got out of the service two years ago. I came home to a six-year-old nephew in foster care. I convinced the authorities to let me have him. Last week he witnessed a murder in the alley behind our apartment complex. They want to put us in the wit-sec program but I refused."

"Go on," Finn said.

"Even though he's only eight, he got a good long look at the man who did the killing and they are going to let him testify when it comes time," Callie said.

"Are you willing to let this be a safe house for her?" Otis asked.

Finn turned to face Otis. "I owe this woman my life more times than I can count. If she wants to stay here, she damn sure can stay. We were more than partners and she was more than my spotter. She was my best friend, so does that answer your question?"

"Thank you, Finn," she said.

He cocked his head to one side. "Callie, this is a ranch. If I remember right, you joined the Army because you hated every damn thing there was about ranchin'. Are you sure you want to live here?"

"Guess I've found out there's worse things in the world than the cows, hay haulin', and calvin' season," she said. "I'm not askin' for a handout here, Finn. I'm willing to work. I'll work outside. I'll work inside cleaning and cocking or both if you'll give me and Martin room and board. And it doesn't matter if I like it, Finn. I'll do it until the trial is over, then we'll be out of your hair." She inhaled deeply. "I can ride a horse or a four-wheeler. I can pull a calf or drive anything that's got wheels and fix most anything that's got an engine. I'll work cheap and, in exchange, Martin and I get to live here without fear until the trial is over, probably in early February."

"That's putting a lot of faith in one man," Otis said.

"Not this man," Agent Smith said seriously. "I'd trust him with my life. Hell, I'd trust him with the life of the president of the United States. I've tried to hire him to do just that but he turned us down, twice."

Finn hated to unpack, do laundry, and most of all cook, and she'd offered to work inside or outside.

Finn O'Donnell, cats, dogs, and baby rabbits are one thing, but people are not strays. You don't train them. You don't get them well and turn them loose. Be careful, his inner voice warned.

"Have you gotten any better at frying a chicken? Is

your gravy still lumpy and your biscuits tough?" Finn grinned.

"Chicken will melt in your mouth and my biscuits and gravy are fine, thank you," she answered.

He hugged her close to his side, almost toppling her out of the chair. "Don't you lie to me, Brewster. I remember your burnt fried chicken and your biscuits could have been used as weapons of mass destruction."

She pushed away from him. "Don't you talk to me in that tone, O'Donnell. We were both drunk when we fried that chicken and we did it together and you were as much to blame for it as I was. I've learned to cook in the past two years. Raisin' a kid means making dinner every night whether I want to or not."

His heart kicked in an extra beat. He hadn't felt so alive since he left Afghanistan and surely not since he'd heard what a fool he'd been when he fell for Lala. "Okay, we'll try it until after the holidays. I wouldn't want to spoil Christmas for Shotgun and it looks like he's done took to that kid."

Callie laughed until she snorted, held her hand out, and said, "Shake on it. I understand it's all for your dog, not for me or my brother. Your crazy sense of humor hasn't changed a damn bit, Finn O'Donnell. Thank God for that."

"We were living in a furnished apartment." Callie shrugged when she caught Finn looking at the bags the federal boys unloaded on the porch before they left.

"What'd you do for a paycheck?" he asked.

"I worked as a trainer in a gym and taught women's

self-defense classes," she answered. "The Army didn't give me a lot of marketable skills for the outside world."

The muscles in his arms flexed against the knit of his long-sleeved Western shirt when he picked up one of the duffel bags and threw it over his shoulder like a bag of cattle feed. Then he stooped, grabbed the other one, and hefted it up on the other shoulder.

"You want to get the door for me and call the kid into the house? I'll show you where your rooms are," he said.

"Hey, Martin, a little help here," she yelled over her shoulder as she opened the door.

The boy came in a dead run with the dog right behind him. "Yes, ma'am. Wow, Callie! I bet Finn could pick you up."

Callie could feel the heat coming up the back of her neck, but she couldn't stop it. Soldiers didn't blush. They were mean and tough and could take out snakes, spiders, and even enemy combatants. But a visual of her hanging over Finn's back with her butt so close to his lips that he could kiss it—well, hell's bells, that would make the devil himself blush.

"I don't imagine she weighs as much as this bag," Finn said. "What'd you pack in here, Martin? Rocks?"

The boy picked up one of the smaller zippered bags and managed to hoist it up on his shoulder like Finn, but it came close to bowing his legs. "No, sir, but Callie put books in that one. This one is heavy, too."

"I bet it is, son. Just keep a tight hold on it and follow me. I'll show you where to unload it," Finn said.

The cold wind whipped around and came at them from the north, cooling Callie's scarlet cheeks considerably. "That wind feels like it's comin' off snow or ice.

Martin and I can share a room. Couldn't afford a two-bedroom place. Mostly I just slept on the sofa and let him have the bedroom anyway."

The dog shot into the house before the door shut behind her and flopped down on the rug in front of the cold fireplace, put a paw over his nose, and promptly went to sleep.

"No need for that. This is a big house. This wing has three bedrooms and a huge bathroom. Y'all can have your choice of rooms, but I bet Martin is going to like this one." He slid the bags off his shoulders at the doorway of one of the bedrooms.

"Which one is yours?" Callie dropped a bulging suitcase in the hallway.

He turned her shoulders toward the living room and pointed. "There's another wing off the living room. I chose a bedroom in that area because it has a fireplace. It shares a flue with the one in the living room. Actually Shotgun chose it when we first got here. We had a fireplace in my bedroom at the ranch in Comfort and he recognized it as a place to warm his bones after working all day out in the cold," Finn answered.

The deep Southern drawl in his voice still affected her the same way it had back when she first met him. She didn't know the story, but Lala was a complete idiot not to be living on the ranch with him.

Martin let go of the bag on his shoulder, and it fell to the hardwood floor with a loud thump. "Are you serious? Is this really my room? I'm afraid to shut my eyes because it might not be here when I open them again."

Callie peeked around Finn's shoulder to see Martin jump over all three bags and spin around in the bedroom, trying to see everything at once. "If I don't get nothin' else for Christmas, this will be the best one I ever had in my whole life. Can I invite friends over? There's two bunk beds, so I can have three friends, right?"

Callie heard him talking but her mind was on Finn's hand on her shoulder. She felt safe for the first time since the murder, but it went much deeper than that. Finn had always sent a wave of heat through her body. She'd just managed it better in Afghanistan.

"Callie!" Martin said loudly.

"Sorry, kiddo, I was gathering wool," she said.

"I asked if I can unpack my bag right now."

"Yes, you may," Callie said.

Finn leaned over and whispered, sending shivers up her spine. "I figured he'd like this room. We need to talk."

"He's begged for bunk beds since he was big enough to know what they were," she said softly.

Martin kicked off his shoes, climbed up to a top bunk, and sat cross-legged. "It's my dream room. Can I read them books? I bet there's some good stories in them. Can Shotgun come in here with me and sleep on one of the beds? Can I have friends spend the night?"

Before he could ask another million questions, Callie laid a hand on his shoulder. "Give Finn time to think and give yourself time to breathe. Yes, I'm sure you can read the books if you are careful with them. We'll talk about the dog and friends later on, but right now you get settled in while Finn and I have an adult conversation. Okay?"

Martin smiled. "Yes, ma'am."

Finn led the way into the living room and sat down on the sofa, patting the cushion beside him and motioning for her. "Callie, I mean it, I'm really glad to see you.

Not just to have a hand or a cook. I missed you. I tried to get in touch, but the phone number you gave me was disconnected."

"I tried to call you for a whole month after I got things straightened out with Martin. I figured you were married to Lala by then, but I wanted to know you'd made it home safe," she said. "How did you wind up here? And how long have you been here? The neat freak Finn I knew wouldn't still have unpacked boxes after even a week."

He reached over and ran the back of his hand down her cheek, sending another round of flutters to her heart. "I've been here two days, Callie. I know that's you sitting there, but I keep thinking you'll vanish if I don't keep touching you. We've got two years of catching up to do. Am I right in thinking there is no boyfriend, since you came here?"

"You are very right." She held his hand to her cheek a few seconds longer before letting go. "Now tell me how you ended up in this little place."

"The lady who owned this property, Verdie, sold it to me, lock, stock, and barrel. She wanted out of town before any more cold weather set in. I'm not sure what I bought in the house. I've spent two days in the barn and on the property counting cows," he said.

"But it's miles from Austin."

"Comfort. I lived in Comfort, Texas, not too far from Austin. I looked for a place there, but nothing fit. Crazy to think of a ranch fitting like a pair of cowboy boots, but this place did. When Verdie said she wanted to sell it as it stood, it seemed like a dream come true. And now you are here for a few weeks and it seems like old times, sitting here, almost like we were back in the tents after a mission."

"I missed that most of all," she said.

"Hey, Callie, when is supper? Do I have time to read a little while?" Martin yelled from his room.

"He's afraid to come out here for fear he'll wake up and this will be a dream," Callie said and then raised her voice, "Go ahead and read."

"Speaking of supper, we should probably go to the store and lay in staples. It's closed tomorrow," he said. "I make a pretty mean ham and cheese sandwich and I do know how to open a can of tomato soup to go with it, but I'm not even sure there's enough ham for three sandwiches."

"I'll make supper, Finn. I think I can do better than soup and sandwiches if you'll show me where things are located."

He chuckled. "Your guess is good as mine. I've been living on frozen pizza and sandwiches for two days."

He stood up and held out his hand. "Trust me, there's nothing in the refrigerator. The freezer is full but everything is frozen, and the pantry isn't too shabby but pickin's are slim on staples."

She put her hand in his. "Then I suppose we should go to the store."

How to Handle a Cowboy

The first book in the
Cowboys of Decker Ranch series

by Joanne Kennedy

—⁓—

His rodeo days may be over...

Sidelined by a career-ending injury, rodeo cowboy Ridge Cooper feels trapped at his family's remote Wyoming ranch. Desperate to find an outlet for the passion he used to put into competing, he takes on the challenge of teaching his roping skills to five troubled ten-year-olds in a last-chance home for foster kids, and finds it's their feisty supervisor who takes the most energy to wrangle.

But he'll still wrangle her heart

When social worker Sierra Dunn seeks an activity for the rebellious kids at Phoenix House, she soon learns she's not in Denver anymore. Sierra is eager to get back home to her inner-city work, and the plan doesn't include forming an attachment in Wyoming—especially not to a ruggedly handsome and surprisingly gentle local rodeo hero.

—⁓—

"Realistic and romantic... Kennedy's forte is in making relationships genuine and heartfelt as she exposes vulnerabilities with tenderness and good humor."—*Booklist* Starred Review

"The sex scenes are juicy...and the plot moves seamlessly."—*RT Book Reviews*, 4 Stars

For more Joanne Kennedy, visit:

www.sourcebooks.com

The Cowboy's Mail Order Bride

by Carolyn Brown

New York Times Bestselling Author

She's got sass...

Emily Cooper promised her dying grandfather that she'd deliver a long-lost letter to a woman he once planned to wed. Little does adventurous Emily know that this simple task will propel her to places she never could have imagined...with a cowboy who's straight out of her dreams...

He's got mail...

When sexy rancher Greg Adams discovers his grandmother Clarice has installed Emily on their ranch as her assistant, he decides to humor the two ladies. He figures Emily will move on soon enough. In the meantime, he intends to keep a close eye on her—he doesn't quite buy her story of his grandmother as a mail-order bride.

A lost letter meant a lost love for Clarice, but two generations later, maybe it's not too late for that letter to work its magic.

For more Carolyn Brown, visit:

www.sourcebooks.com

The Cowboy's Christmas Baby

by Carolyn Brown

New York Times Bestselling Author

'Tis the season for...

A pistol-totin' woman who's no angel

A tough rancher who doesn't believe in miracles

Love that warms the coldest night

After a year in Kuwait, Lucas Allen can't wait to get back to his ranch for Christmas and meet his gorgeous Internet pal in person.

When he pulls in, there's Natalie Clark right in his front yard with a pink pistol in her hand and a dead coyote at her feet.

Lucas is unfazed. But wait...is that a BABY in her arms?

Praise for Carolyn Brown's Christmas cowboy romances:

"Carolyn Brown creates some handsome, hunkified, HOT cowboys! A fun, enjoyable four-star-Christmas-to-remember novel." —*The Romance Reviews*

"Makes me believe in Christmas miracles and long, slow kisses under the mistletoe." —*The Romance Studio*

For more Carolyn Brown, visit:

www.sourcebooks.com

About the Author

Carolyn Brown is a *New York Times* and *USA Today* bestselling author with more than sixty books published, and credits her eclectic family for her humor and writing ideas. Her books include the Lucky trilogy *Lucky in Love*, *One Lucky Cowboy*, and *Getting Lucky*; the Honky Tonk series, *I Love This Bar*, *Hell Yeah*, *Honky Tonk Christmas*, and *My Give a Damn's Busted*; and her bestselling Spikes & Spurs series with *Love Drunk Cowboy*, *Red's Hot Cowboy*, *Darn Good Cowboy Christmas*, *One Hot Cowboy Wedding*, *Mistletoe Cowboy*, *Just a Cowboy and His Baby*, and *Cowboy Seeks Bride*. Carolyn has launched into women's fiction with *The Blue-Ribbon Jalapeño Society Jubilee* and *The Red-Hot Chili Cook-Off*. She's also having fun with her new Cowboys & Brides series, beginning with *Billion Dollar Cowboy* and *The Cowboy's Christmas Baby*. She was born in Texas but grew up in southern Oklahoma where she and her husband, Charles, a retired English teacher, make their home. They have three grown children and enough grandchildren to keep them young.